"... I see myself and the words, *'for murder of a police officer.'* And I almost collapse on the checkerboard tile floor... He died! That is a total shock to me. I remember him crumpling. That I remember. But die? Not that. It's unimaginable. Impossible. Not that the swing of that childhood Louisville Slugger couldn't have that effect. But that I was at the other end of the bat? That I was capable of this, of felling a man, of killing a man?"

Jeffrey Stevenson, a soft-spoken, apolitical college student and aspiring musician becomes a fugitive and one of America's "Most Wanted" after being cornered at an anti-Vietnam War rally he never planned to attend—and, in terror and desperation, murders a policeman.

After 25 years on the run, Jeffrey learns that his mother has died and his brother is now dying, and decides it's time to come home. With the help of his politically well-connected historian father, he cuts a deal with the Government, and returns to a world still wrestling with the passions unleashed by Vietnam, and to a family wrestling with its own passions: his dying brother, tormented not only by his illness but by the consequences of serious criminal and ethical acts... his father, grieving and angry over developments in both personal and public spheres... his brother's wife, embittered over the havoc wreaked by her husband, and reaching out to Jeffrey.

Blurred Images is the story of how Jeffrey confronts the realities of his new life, the conflicting perceptions and misperceptions of his previous life—and of the violent act that changed everything.

BLURRED IMAGES

First English Edition
2001

by Arthur Dimond

© 2001, ARTHUR DIMOND

Cover Design: Elinor C Thompson

No part of this book may be reproduced in any form without the express written permission of the Author.

Dry Bones Press, Inc.
P. O. Box 1437
Roseville, CA 95678

(415) 707–2129
http://www.drybones.com/

ISBN 1-931333-03-3

LCCN 2001094171

Publisher's Cataloging–in–Publication
    FICTION
    Arthur Dimond
    Blurred Images / by Arthur Dimond
    p.   cm.
    ISBN 1–93133-03-3
I. Author.   II. Title

BLURRED IMAGES

A Novel By

Arthur Dimond

DEDICATION

FOR MY MOTHER, GERTRUDE,

WHO INSPIRED MY LOVE OF

THE WRITTEN WORD AND THE MUSICAL SOUND

CHAPTER I

I can't break that habit so ingrained in me during all those years on the run. There is no room, large or small, no dim club, no seedy motel lobby, no roadside restaurant, no public place of any kind I can enter without instinctively scanning the faces, peering into corners and alcoves, ever probing. This is where they'll get me. This is where it will all end.

I remind myself, reassure myself, as I always do, that it's not me they see. Not my face. Not my name. No real part of me. All that changed long ago. What they see now is an artful creation.

Oh, Seth sounded good that night. Sooooo good. Hanging back in the shadows, holding my trusty bass, I plucked out my chords almost mechanically and listened to Seth with all the concentration I could muster, pretending I was off stage, an audience member, a critic, a devoted fan.

Silhouetted by the glare of the spot, enshrouded by cigarette smoke, Seth held that sax firmly and rocked slowly back and forth, playing *My Funny Valentine* more beautifully than he had ever played it, more mellowly, touchingly, than Desmond himself. I had heard him play it a hundred times or more. But never like this. Never better than this.

We were playing a club on the outskirts of Spokane, Washington.

ARTHUR DIMOND

Not a bad place. Decent location near a shopping mall. Nice-looking decor. Reasonably appointed bar, hovered over by pictures of some of the greats and not-so-greats who either had or hadn't played the joint, before or after it moved from downtown to the burbs. Didn't make much difference.

A bartender in a clean white denim shirt open at the collar, with a checkered bandanna around his neck. Nice cozy table area about half-full, not bad for a Tuesday night. A Western Yuppie crowd, you know, accountants and lawyers and insurance salesmen in clean designer jeans, sharply creased, red-checked shirts and kerchiefs, Lee belt buckles, high-shined alligator boots. And laid back, well-behaved, quietly appreciative; they knew when and about how much to applaud. No noisy drunks. No conspicuous yahoos— we'd had enough of those. They chatted just enough between applause points to let you know they were there.

The audience was now gently clapping for Seth. And Seth signaled for me to begin my solo. Suddenly the spot bathed me in bright white light, surprising me — ***startling*** me — almost as much as the audience; they might not have known I was there. With a minute movement of my neck, I nodded acknowledgment of the audience and launched into my solo.

With the bass, I've noticed, you go from one extreme to the other. First you're invisible. Then you're center stage. The other musicians step back and away and generously give you the stage to yourself. And you play so softly that you command attention. The chatting stops and the audience literally leans forward to hear. And except for the muted, dusky dusting of the drums, the other instruments go silent; yours is the only sound. And ironically, you make the most of it by pretending you're still in the shadows, producing that low, rumbly undercurrent of sound that is fully appreciated only when absent. Your face is blank, betraying nothing. You use an economy of motion, your fingers moving deftly, almost surreptitiously, across those thick strings; your elbows, your shoulders, your entire body barely moving.

BLURRED IMAGES

So for several minutes I had the stage to myself. Feeling loose and inspired by Seth's superlative performance, I played well, real well. I improvised some dynamics and some new ornaments, and despite myself, even put some body english into my playing. My instrument, almost as large as me, became my dance partner, and we strutted our stuff (albeit in a modest sort of way).

When I was finished, when the audience applauded, so did Seth and the other two band members. I bowed my head in humble gratitude and smiled diffidently. Then I found myself back in my customary shadow, as Jerry the piano player took over, launching into a high-pitched, syncopated melodic line.

And so the night passed, with me, much to my surprise, finding myself enjoying it more, much more, than usual. Why? I don't know exactly. Maybe it was the pleasant, casual setting. Maybe it was the program— a nice balance between classics, some Parker, some Mulligan, and others, and some pieces of more recent vintage, between Latin and New Wave and fusion and mellow stuff that didn't really fit anywhere. Maybe we were finally coming together like a real band; after a lot of early transiency, we were finally a unit. We had some continuity— the four of us had been together now for about five years and when we played, it was like four old friends having an animated, free-flowing conversation; it was spontaneous, but it also reflected some anticipation of style, some consensus of respective roles, and how they all worked together.

We extended the set because it felt so good and the crowd was warm and we reached a kind of tacit agreement — we and our audience — to knock off and drop the proverbial curtain only when it seemed right. And finally it did. Most of the remaining audience members filed out. And we sidled over to the bar for a drink or two before heading out ourselves. Back to a Super 8 along a service lane on the Interstate.

CHAPTER II

I sat quietly in the back seat of the van, and gazed out at the vast expanse of parched brushy land as we sped down the Interstate to Seattle. Hank and the others were jawing away about the previous night, about future gigs, about Seattle and a little action.

I smiled to myself. Four middle-aged guys in a van. Their hair thinning, graying. Waists expanding, pots overhanging the Levis. Flesh hanging a bit loosely around the jaws. Dark pockets forming under the eyes. Little dark hairs sprouting from the ears. Yet here they were, on the road, still excited with prospects.

Hank, at the wheel, suddenly noticed me.

"Hey, what's with Mr. Bassman?" he asked, half turning toward me.

"Nothing, just tired," I mumbled back.

"Sure all those solos aren't wearing you out? Too much action for you?"

"I don't think so."

"So, you want more?"

"Sure, more is good."

"Hey, gimme a break," Seth interjected. "The guy's exhausted the repertoire. There ain't no more."

And we all laughed. The joke was on me. but it was my joke, my punchline. So I lightened up a bit and laughed, too. But more on that later. For now, I quickly grew quiet again, receding back into my

BLURRED IMAGES

remote state, absorbing the monotonous scenery outside, the banter and the wisecracks inside.

I used these trips to reclaim myself, separate from the band. I enjoyed the camaraderie of the group, but I also craved privacy and protected it vigorously. I used to try reading in that backseat corner. But the purposeful interruptions cured me of that. As they did of my habit of plugging in earphones. When they caught me listening to Haydn or Boccherini or some other long-dead European, they wouldn't let it go. So, without props or other visible targets, I simply took refuge in my private thoughts. I transported myself across time and time zones. Sometimes I set the course. Other times I discarded the compass and succumbed to the currents of my mind and memory.

It's April. My father is raging. Sitting at his enormous walnut desk in his office off the living room. He's gripping a thin packet of papers and he's staring at it with unmistakable fury. Without asking — I don't dare — I know what the cause of his anger is. It's his tax returns. And they never fail to throw him into a rage. For days during the first half of April, we tiptoe around the house. Dinnertimes are tense affairs of carefully studied discretion. Any comment can set off our father. And the lack of conversation only compounds the stress. So my mother quietly and efficiently pops up and down, back and forth between the dining alcove and the kitchen counter. My older brother, Danny, systematically cuts his food and lifts it to his mouth, rarely raising his eyes to horizontal level; generally serious and reserved, taxtime tends to accentuate his demeanor. As for me, I am as devoted to survival as the next guy, in this case my brother; still, I at least raise my eyes and occasionally, every now and then, make an effort to lighten things up, to share the news of my day — trivial though it might be — with my family. Nobody's listening; for a moment or two I don't care, I yammer on and eventually stop when I get bored.

Through it all, my father sits bolt upright at the head of the table,

ARTHUR DIMOND

quietly and methodically cutting and chewing. When he is through, he pushes his chair back and rises and with an absolutely straight face and an exaggerated theatrical formality and politeness, says, "Now would you all please excuse me. I must finish getting raped." And he returns to his office.

This year, like every year, he waits till the last minute. He willfully forestalls, then compresses, the pain. And this year, as in previous years I can remember, he has a lot to do. Unlike most people of his circumstances, he insists on doing the returns himself. He says he doesn't trust anybody to do them. So he studies the tax laws thoroughly and painstakingly just as though he were conducting research for his lectures and his books and everything else in his professional life. Secondly, he refuses to pay anybody to do his taxes— "That's adding insult to injury," he says with a grunt and a nasty, dismissive look whenever anybody deigns to make the suggestion.

So tax season is intense and emotional. Fortunately, it doesn't last very long because of the compressed timeframe he assiduously creates for himself. The moment he starts, the deadline is upon him. Then before we know it, the season is suddenly over. It's April 15, and with the brightness of the tulips and the increasing warmth of the air — even in western Massachusetts — the month gets better.

The days grow longer and more relaxed. The semester at Dad's university moves into the home stretch, and we all look forward to our extended trips to yet another exotic destination where Dad mixes consulting and lecturing and gets what he hopes will be the last laugh on the Government in the form of a hefty tax break on the expedition.

And then there is his birthday. While he claims to be an unsentimental man, a stoic and a pragmatist to the core, somehow his birthday has evolved over the years into our family's most heralded and festive event. Family, friends — some from hundreds of miles away — plus dozens of associates from the university — descend on our house for an afternoon and evening of fun and revelry.

BLURRED IMAGES

In the early years, Mom did all the cooking and began her preparations weeks in advance. Then, as the crowd expanded over the years, and Dad's circumstances dramatically improved — from his fees and royalties and other sources — he authorized Mom (biting the proverbial bullet) to hire a caterer and serving people. And it became a great elegant (if boisterous) extravaganza. On those unseasonably warm late-April days, those wonderful harbingers of summer, the party would spill out on the expansive curved front porch of our corner Victorian, and onto the front lawn for badminton and croquet and touch football. Then in the early evening hours, with most of the adults loose and mellow with alcohol and good cheer, the roast would begin. And my father, his cheeks glowing red over his silver beard, always so neatly, almost militarily, trimmed, would laugh heartily at some of the most outrageous barbs thrown his way. And then it would be his turn and he would give as good — no, much better — than he got. He would deliver a rendition that was a combination stand-up comic monologue, pointed political commentary, and biting personal satire, laced with mimickry, occasionally crude, always on target. Nobody was immune from the onslaught, everybody was fair game. Especially the Democrats ("an ass is an appropriate symbol for them," he would often say, and vociferously deny any blood ties to Adlai), the Ripon Society and other liberal Republicans, the League of Women Voters, the NAACP, SANE, all the self-appointed do-gooders in our midst. If it was an election year, Dad would have a field day, an embarrassment of rhetorical riches, and the night would grow very long.

Later on, of course, I realized those birthday events were extravagant celebrations of my father's accomplishments and ego— an annual self-indulgence for setting up his soapbox, reminding his world who and what he was. But way back then, I didn't think of those things. And I didn't really care what he said, or what his motives were. I was just so glad to see our house filled with happy people, and my father so warm and funny and expansive and at the center of that wonderful, convivial assemblage. That's what really mattered.

ARTHUR DIMOND

And now, as we sped down the arrow-straight road toward the green of western Washington State, I realized that in a couple of days, Dad would be 80. I hadn't seen him for 24 years— 24 tax seasons, 24 birthdays. And I hadn't spoken to him since his 75th. Suddenly, unexpectedly, I wanted to call him, to wish the old man well on his 80th. But where do you begin?

A few years before, when we were doing a couple of gigs in some wintry college town — Ann Arbor? Madison? I forget — I dropped into a bookstore to browse around. I was wandering through the aisles, more or less aimlessly, when I found myself in the History/Political Science section. And before I even realized what I was doing, I was looking for signs of my father. And to my surprise, there he was. In fact, he had half a shelf all to himself. I randomly picked out one volume — *The Russian Revolution: A Doomed Experiment* — and leafed through it. I remembered that book. I remembered when it came out, back in the early 60's, when I was a junior or senior in high school, when we were in the depths of the Cold War. There was the Berlin Wall and the Cuban missile crisis, and this huge threatening force, destined to be with us forever, throughout our lives and the lives of our children, our grandchildren. And here was my father calling the Russian Revolution a phony event, an enormous aberration in Russian history— "antithetical to the Russian character, alien to the Russian experience," was the way he put it. He predicted that during our lifetimes, the Revolution would fail. He didn't say when. But he did say unequivocally that it would happen, that the Revolution would collapse of its own weight. Back then, when otherwise sane families were building bomb shelters, kids periodically, at the sound of sirens, were still diving under their school desks, backs to the tall, metal-meshed windows, heads safely tucked between their legs, back then my father was making that firm prediction. And he was being laughed at as some sort of crackpot by his fellow academics, by journalists, by most politicians. But it was he who

BLURRED IMAGES

had the last laugh.

So on that day, in Ann Arbor or Madison or wherever, as things were unraveling and his star was rising by the day, I leafed through that book, one of those pricey, "quality" paperbacks, and when I got to the back cover, there was a picture of the old man. It was the same picture that was used when the book first came out, when I was still a kid. He looked so young, so much more genial — **mild** would probably be a better word — and approachable than the text would suggest or that I could remember. He had his beard, sculpted, and darker of course. And he was wearing a bowtie. And he had an odd expression, odd for him, that is, a kind of bemused look that belied the harsh, scathing tone of the book, a look that suggested that this was all a bit of a joke and he knew the punchline, but you'd have to read the book to find it out.

On the inside rear flap was a biographical blurb. And when I flipped to the first few pages of the book, I found a dedication: *"To my sons, Daniel and Jeffrey, with the hope and the confidence that they will one day live in a brighter world."*

I was startled to see my name still in print like this, in this book. I flipped to another page and learned that this was the 19th printing. How many of these books are in circulation? Tens of thousands? hundreds of thousands? after all these years. And there was the new *Prologue,* which I read with particular interest. It was written recently with the hand of an old man I didn't know anymore. And it was confirmation of his predictions, vindication of his beliefs. **This** was the punchline. The old warhorse really did have the last laugh.

I dozed, awakening only when the van stopped.

"Are we there yet?" I asked.

"Yeah, in your dreams," Seth said. "This state should be challenging Montana for Big Sky. It never fucking ends."

We all chuckled, then got out, stretched, and slowly walked over to the Jack in the Box. Inside there was a little brown sign on a stainless steel stand that said: *Please Wait to be Seated.* We dutifully waited. After a long two or three minutes, just when we were about to take matters into our own hands, a pert, well-put-together forty-something lady with short chestnut hair and a straight, tight, checkered dress materialized. She gave us a very obvious once-over, something we were well used to, and led us to a booth at the far end of the front window. We slid in and immediately picked up our menus and perused them.

It was a weird hour to be eating a meal, about five or so. The place was practically empty— a family with young kids two booths down, and a couple of truckers at the counter, staring into their coffees, and that was about it. We hadn't eaten a decent meal all day and figured we'd load up here, hit the road, and make a straight shot to Seattle. We'd check into the Holiday Inn, our old standby, and head over to the club to check it out.

"What's that shit they got playing?" Seth suddenly blurted, more irritated than seemed appropriate.

"Sounds like one of those Fabian knock-offs," Hank said. "You know, bubble gum shit."

"I don't think I can take too much of it," Seth said. "I'm going to see if they have anything on the juke for people over 14... If the waitress comes, tell her I want the baconburger platter — medium — with a Sprite, OK?"

And he was up striding across the room, his snakeskin cowboy boots clip-clopping on the hard red-tile floor. A minute or two later, the waitress, a large fleshy woman, came over, looking like she'd been briefed by the hostess. She didn't bother with amenities. After her own, cursory once-over, she got right down to business.

She held up her order pad and looking down, asked without a hint of inflection, "What're you having?"

We met her on her own terms and crisply ordered Seth's baconburger platter, a BLT (with crisp bacon), a chicken salad (no extra mayo), and my breaded fried fish special (tartar on the side).

BLURRED IMAGES

We didn't indulge in our usual ragtime bullshit. First — our little joke — we didn't want to fulfill her expectations. Second, we knew we wouldn't get anything back. Third, God knew what she might do with our order.

She murmured, "Thanks," quickly gathered up our menus, and turned on her heel in the direction of the double kitchen doors.

Hank grinned, and said, "Is it something we said?"

"Maybe it's what we ***didn't*** say," Jerry, the piano player, offered.

"Whadaya mean?" Hank asked.

"Never mind," Jerry responded. "It's not worth it. She's just got a pickle up her ass."

Seth came back and slid in with us.

"How'd you do?" I asked.

"Not bad... We're next with Spyro Gyra."

"My boys! Way to go!"

In a minute or so, the waitress came back with the drinks and then, as promised, the high-energy Spyro Gyra sound filled the room. Seth relaxed, slouched, and leaned his head on the top of the cushioned booth bench.

"A cigarette is all I need to make me a happy man now," Seth said. "Don't they have a smoking area here?"

"Forget it, man," Hank said. "The only smoking area you're gonna find is the great outdoors."

"Fuck that," Seth said. "I'm comfortable here, I'm with you guys and Spyro... I think I'm just gonna have one right here."

"Hey, Seth, don't be an asshole," Hank said. Seth was a moody guy and he had a quick-flaring temper. Of the other three of us Hank had known him the longest by far — back to high school in Jersey — and he didn't mind confronting him when he thought he should.

"Yeah," Jerry said in support. "We're just gonna get in a fight with this bitch and she and her boss'll throw us out and we'll be out in that parking lot under that Big Sky hungrier than before...

or maybe in jail."

"Yeah, that could ruin the whole day... maybe a couple of 'em...And we'd miss the gig to boot," Hank said.

"Hey, at least if we're gonna get thrown out, let's wait until after we've eaten," I offered.

Seth, who had been absorbing the other comments, and seemingly ignoring them, turned on me.

"That's just like you, Mr. Bassman," he snapped.

"What're you talking about?" I asked, feeling the blood rising to my head.

"Just what I said... I'm talking about every time we're out to have some fun, to maybe get in a little trouble... an itsy, bitsy little bit of trouble" (and he held up his hand, the tips of his thumb and middle finger almost touching, and his eyes squinting at the formation) "you go wimpy on us... What the fuck are you so afraid of?"

"What the fuck are you talking about?" I blurted. "First of all, this whole thing is stupid, real stupid. I mean, what's the big deal, a lousy cigarette. First of all, can't you live without it for a half-hour? I mean, what's the big deal? And second, why are you always dumping on me?"

Seth stared at me. I stared back. And the others went silent, looking away.

Just then the waitress set her tray down on the fold-up stand and started picking up plates.

"OK, who's got the fish special?... Who's got the burger platter?"

And we each took our plates and turned our attention to the business at hand. We ate in silence and in a matter of eight or ten minutes were all done. Seth pushed his plate away, rose, and said he was going outside for that "famous cigarette." Hank and I got up to go to the Men's Room. Standing at adjacent urinals, I asked him, "What's with that guy? That fuse of his gets shorter by the day."

Looking down at his operation, Hank said, "He's getting a lot of

BLURRED IMAGES

shit from Jane lately... you know about being on the road so much, not calling enough... you know, the usual."

"So what's that got to do with me? He's on my case more than anybody else's."

"Nah... I think you're imagining things," he said. He shook himself off and moved toward the sink.

"Yeah, right," I said sarcastically, and followed him over. Without saying another word, we dried our hands and left the room just as one of the truckers was coming in. The guy, stringy and weatherbeaten and wearing a Denver Broncos cap, grunted as he passed.

Right outside was a vestibule area with a water fountain, a scale that told your horoscope as well as your weight, and a phone.

I stopped abruptly and stared at the phone. Hank stopped too, and looked at me curiously.

"What's the matter?" he asked.

"Nothing."

"Sure looks like it's something."

"Well, I thought of making a call."

"So go ahead... You got a few minutes."

"I think I'm gonna need more than a few minutes."

"Hey, it's up to you... If it's important, go ahead."

"Nah, it's OK... it can wait."

Jerry was waiting alone at the booth.

"You all set?" Hank asked him.

"Yep," he said. "Let's pay up and collect Joe Camel out there."

Then we piled into the van, with Jerry at the wheel, Seth riding shotgun and in a better frame of mind, and me and Hank dozing in the back seat as we drove into the sunset.

The last conversation is painful. Excruciating. I call in tears of anguish and anger in the middle of the night. And there's nothing that he or I can do.

My mother had died and I learned about her death in a two-

ARTHUR DIMOND

week-old New York Times *I found in an Econo Lodge lobby outside Houston. We had gotten back at one in the morning, still keyed up from an unexpectedly upbeat concert at Rice. We were sitting in the seedy lobby, drinking Cokes laced with rum and shooting the shit. And one by one, the others went to their rooms. I was in too much of a buzz to sleep, so I sat there absently leafing through issues of* Newsweek *and* People *and some wrinkled newspapers. Slouched in a vinyl armchair, I was flipping pages, just glancing at headlines and pictures, not really absorbing anything. And in my aimless travels, I somehow got to the Obituary page, a rare destination for me. As I was about to flip again, I saw the face, that strong angular face from a lightyear away that I knew so well. She was wearing a black dress and that favorite string of pearls, the ones her mother gave her when she graduated from college. She was looking off to the left, her head tilted slightly upward, her eyes focused on something, her chin protruding in that hopeful and confident way of hers. That was the picture that was taken when she was chief curator of the Berkshire Museum of Art. Her first major recognition. And oh, did she look beautiful. Then. Now. I stared at the picture for what might have been several minutes. Then I read the headline — ELIZABETH STEVENSON, MUSEUM DIRECTOR, DEAD AT 69 — and the lengthy article that followed.*

I grasped the newspaper with two tight fists and raced through the article. I felt faint. My breathing was tight and labored. And tears welled out of both eyes.

The night clerk looked anxiously at me. And rather than explain or apologize, I rose, folded the newspaper section neatly, and left the lobby for the privacy of my room. I dropped into the fake-rattan armchair and switched on the floor lamp. My eyes raced to the bottom. With relief, I saw my name, one of the sons, one of the small band of survivors; it had been so long, who knew? Then I read the entire article carefully, over and over, absorbing every detail. About her life. Her childhood spread over three continents. The daughter of

BLURRED IMAGES

a diplomat. Her prodigious academic career. Summa Cum Laude. Rhodes Scholar. Other academic honors. Her career. Her recognition as one of the world's leading experts on Italian Renaissance art. Her death— sudden, unexpected, from a cerebral hemorrhage. Her family— her husband, Simon, and her sons, and her grandson. And finally her funeral at Washington's National Cathedral on a Wednesday at 10 a.m.

And then it hit me. She was already buried. She was really gone. It was all over, and I had missed it all. I hadn't eulogized. I hadn't borne her casket. I hadn't said good-bye. I had been the missing man, the phantom son at my own mother's funeral.

I felt a powerful, almost physical force jolt my body. I threw the newspaper to the ground and shuttered and emitted a cry that alarmed even me, an involuntary wail from the core of my being. Then my heart started pounding, and my breath grew short, so short I couldn't even cry. The finality was overwhelming. My powerlessness in the face of her death, in the **aftermath** *of her death, saddened me like nothing I had ever experienced. I stumbled to the bed and dropped down on my stomach, my face buried in the pillow, the tears rushing out in a flood. I lay there for awhile until I truly grasped this stark new reality. Then I rolled over and lay on my back, my hands clasped loosely over my stomach, and stared at the ceiling. I continued to lay there, growing cold and stiff. I tried to force memories of her, but it was so long ago and specific memories were slow to come and take form; they appeared like dreams, transitory fragments, mental holograms, and then they vanished.*

Night noises intruded. Horns, sirens, screeching truck tires on the nearby interstate penetrated my reveries or broke the stream altogether. Then my father's image appeared. More dominant, more immediate. And that image grew stronger yet as the night wore on.

I look at the clock. Two-thirty-five. Five-thirty-five back east. Could be OK. He's a night owl **and** *an early riser. Or was.*

I find his number in my well-worn, though sparse telephone book, and dial it, quickly, before I can give myself the chance to change my mind. It rings about four or five times. Then it clicks, and I hear my father's voice, clearly and formally: "This is Professor Simon Stevenson..." and I say, "Dad... Dad?" and when he keeps talking, I realize that I'm talking to a machine. For a second, I actually chuckle— my father, of all people, entering the modern age. When the beep comes on, I say: "Dad, it's me... Jeff... I'll call you later." And I hang up quickly. Still concerned about taps and tracers after all these years. I figure if I'm going to get caught, at least it should be over a real conversation.

 I close my eyes, doze off, and awake to the phone ringing. I grab it. "Dad?... Dad?" There's a silence at the other end, and then a little laugh. "I'm afraid it's just the hotel operator. It's wake-up time. Good morning... and have a nice day." I rub my eyes and look around the room, lit by the lights I never turned off and softened by the early-morning sunshine trying to sneak through the cracks alongside the heavy lined curtains.

 I try my father again. And then again after breakfast. Each time, his recorded voice answers in the same stentorian, increasingly irritating tones. Through the day, driving across the bleak expanse of the Texas Panhandle up to Oklahoma, I grow progressively anxious. I'm depressed and desperate and can't share it with my fellow travelers. How can I explain not knowing, not going home for the funeral; for chrissake, I realize with a jolt, I had played a gig on her funeral day.

 I pretend to sleep so I don't have to talk. And then I try my father from a phone booth outside a roadside joint we stop at for lunch.

 Finally, in the evening, I reach him from a payphone at a diner down the street from our motel on the edge of Oklahoma City. He picks up on the fifth ring, right before the recording would have kicked in. Not the least bit out of breath, not like he's been running from the front door or the bathroom or something, but more like he's been sitting by the phone, trying to decide whether to pick it up. Maybe that's what

BLURRED IMAGES

he'd been doing on the previous tries. Sitting in a darkened room, staring at a phone. Who knows?

His voice bears little resemblance to his recorded voice or to the real one I knew so well. Gone is that timbre, that projective quality that resonated through lecture halls and dining rooms. What I hear instead is the low, hesitant voice of what sounds like a very old man. He actually sounds frail— a word never associated with my father. Is it my mother's death alone that has brought this on? Or is there something else— his health, some major setback? It could be anything or everything. After all, it's been five years since we last spoke.

"Dad?... Dad?"

"Yes?" he answers in that low, reedy-thin voice.

"It's me... Jeff."

"Yes, I know."

"Dad... I just found out."

He doesn't respond.

"I'm so sorry..."

Still no response.

"Dad, say something... Please."

He clears his throat.

"Jeffrey, what do you **want** me to say?"

The voice, still low, now has a tinge of its old bite. I warn myself to be careful.

"I don't know, Dad..."

My voice catches and tears start welling up again.

"Listen, Jeff," my father snaps, his voice rising, gaining strength. "You've been on the run for all these years, doing God knows what, living God knows where. And then — God knows how — you learn about your mother. And out of the blue you call me... Just what do you want me to say?"

My heart is pounding, my voice as dry as parchment.

"Well?"

"I don't know, Dad... I guess, something... I loved her too,

ARTHUR DIMOND

you know that..."

"Jeffrey, that's the **point**... You loved her. And she loved you... In a different way... in a deeper way... than she loved Danny... or even me. And she hadn't seen you for...for so long..."

"Yes," I say, nearly whispering, amazed I can utter anything.

Now there's a silence so long I think the line might have gone dead.

"Dad?... Dad?"

Finally he answers. "Yes?"

"Dad, it wasn't my fault, you know that."

"All I know is you've been gone... you've been an **outlaw**..."

"Dad, come on..."

"Jeffrey, you've been an outlaw... what other word describes it? Fugitive?... and we grew old without ever seeing you again... You really were the love of your mother's life and you were out of her life for all those years, right up to the end...I can't tell you how many times she broke down and started crying... something set her off... some reminder... and she just started crying... And now she's gone."

I'm speechless and trembling, using every ounce of my strength to suppress the sobs that are rising like a geyser.

"You wanted me to say something? Well, that's what I have to say."

I grip the phone and silently wait for more. For a minute, nothing comes. Then he says softly, barely audibly: "Jeffrey, come home."

"What?... What did you say?"

"I said, come home... Enough already... Stop running and come home."

I don't respond for a minute. Then I take a breath and force a steady voice.

"I can't, Dad... I'll go to jail. I don't **deserve** to go to jail. It wasn't my fault."

"Jeffrey.... Jeffrey, you killed a man... a policeman... They have the picture... A thousand newspapers ran the picture... Of course it's

BLURRED IMAGES

your fault. That's not the issue."
    Again I go silent.
    "Jeffrey, are you still there?" he asks after a long moment.
    "Yes, Dad, I am...And Dad?"
    "Yes?"
    "Dad, I'm not going to have this discussion again... And certainly not now."
    It's uncanny. What Dad is saying is word for word identical to his opening statement in a conversation we had had so many years before.
    *"Then **when**, Jeffrey?.... **When** will we have this discussion? This most important — most **seminal** — of discussions?"*
    "I don't know, Dad... But certainly not now."
    All I hear is his breathing.
    Then I suddenly say: "Dad, I have to go."
    "That's it?"
    "Yes, Dad, that's it... At least for now... I'm sorry... Take care of yourself."
    I hang up and then lean against the phone booth, breathing heavily and concentrating very hard to control myself.

CHAPTER III

We arrived in Seattle late at night and checked into a Travelodge on a treeless commercial strip just inside the city line. The next morning I got up very early, while it was still dark, quickly washed, dressed, and called a cab. Then I slipped a note under Hank's door, and waited outside in the dim, damp cool of the early morning. It was deadly quiet except for the distant foghorns from the harbor and the gentle spritzing of tires on asphalt from the occasional passing car.

The cab eventually arrived, driven by a Vietnamese or Cambodian with anxious eyes and a quick smile. I directed him to the ferry dock and sat back in the vinyl seat for the short ride down the near-empty avenues and streets.

A ferry had just arrived when we reached Colman Dock. It was disgorging a few dozen office workers, who silently cut through the light mist, toting their briefcases and bags towards the near-by office buildings.

I waited a few minutes, gazing at the departing figures, feeling profoundly and surprisingly sorry for them, leaving the islands and the harbor for their fluorescent-lit daytime habitats. Then, alone, I entered the cavernous granite ferry terminal, strode over to the one open window in a line of ticket windows and bought a round-trip ticket to Bainbridge Island from a groggy, disgruntled woman.

I sat down on one of the long, wooden benches shiny from varnish and God knows how many pants and shorts and skirts over

BLURRED IMAGES

the years. I was alone on the bench. Across and down the aisle, on the facing bench, were two young men in jeans and windbreakers. And over a few aisles was another young man asleep where he sat, his chin against his chest. Here and there were people stretched out sleeping—mostly men, a few women, most looking like they had real beds elsewhere, some looking like this was it, their matted hair pressed against greasy backpacks, leathery faces looking up, lost and forlorn even in slumber. At the far end, near the newsstands, just opening, was a stocky man with broad, blunt Eskimo features, methodically mopping the speckled, pitted stone floor. The big overhead clock said 5:41.

About five minutes later, a surprisingly bright, official-sounding voice announced that the 6:05 ferry was ready for boarding.

I and a handful of others slowly rose and moved toward the side door that led to the dock. Nobody spoke except for perfunctory "g'morning"s to the uniformed man who took our tickets before we stepped onto the gangplank and then up to the deck of the vessel.

I went directly to the snack bar where I bought a large steaming coffee in a cardboard container and a powdered jelly doughnut. Then I found the steel-grate stairs to the upper deck and once up there, unfolded a white-lacquered seat near the bow, and sat down. The seat was slightly damp, but I didn't really mind. I was pleased to be there, alone, with several uncluttered hours ahead.

Five or ten minutes later, the ferry sounded its horn. And with a great shudder and roar of the engines and vibration that went right through my bowels, the vessel moved away from the dock, out into Elliott Bay and soon into the Sound.

For an ungainly-looking steel craft, the ferry moved surprisingly swiftly through the mist, across the calm, gray waters toward the pine-covered island, brightening and sharpening in focus as we drew closer and the morning grew slightly older. I slowly sipped my coffee and absently munched on the doughnut. I had brought my Walkman and some tapes but chose to listen instead to the sounds of the vessel, the water, and the seagulls. My mind darted involuntarily from one part of my strange, anchorless life to another. To my music, my band, my loneliness. To this strange odyssey back and forth across the country, to a succession of tacky motel rooms, seedy dressing rooms, cluttered, bright-lit stages. To that day on the Oval, the day that changed everything. As we approached the harbor and the pier, and the ferry slowed down and turned and reversed its engines, my father emerged in my mind and as everything else vanished, he held his ground as he always did.

A long line of commuters stood on the pier. More animated than the earlier group. Standing in the low morning sunlight, chatting or reading their papers, khaki raincoats on or slung over their arms, briefcases stationed on the ground between their legs.

I rose from the chair, brushed some powdered sugar off my jacket, and tossed the cup and doughnut wrapper into a large metal trash can. Then I descended the steel-grate stairs and moved toward the disembarcation area.

As I walked down the pier, past the entire line of commuters, I felt myself being carefully studied. Years ago, I would have gone stiff, my hands and feet cold and clammy, terrified at the prospect of being recognized, chased, apprehended.

Now I just felt self-conscious, uncomfortable at being out-of-synch, coming when they're going, carrying nothing, alone, a stranger from someplace else or no place at all. Who the hell is this guy anyway? I mean, he doesn't look like a day laborer. Or a tradesman, walking and without tools. Or a tourist even; I mean where's his camera and his regulation red or green or yellow slicker? and besides it's too goddamned early for a tour.

I kept walking, past the line, off the pier, up the main commercial street and into the residential streets. The early-morning sunshine was quickly burning off the mist and fog, leaving the town glistening. Elegant, eccentric Victorians rose up into the firs and pines and birches. Fences of every description, each looking like it just had

BLURRED IMAGES

a fresh coat of paint, defined the borders and boundaries between houses, paths, driveways. Lush low foliage and ground cover softened the lines.

A few cars approached and passed me en route to the pier. A young boy, on a bike with a canvas newspaper bag over his shoulder, went by. A man in a black trench coat, carrying an overnight bag, burst from his house and practically sprinted to his car. An elderly woman in a flowered housedress moved gingerly down her broad wooden front steps, grasping the iron railing alongside, leaning stiffly on that railing the way old people do. I deduced her mission from the newspaper neatly encased in a clear plastic bag, lying on the ground at the junction of brick-lined walkway and sidewalk. I bent down, picked it up, walked up the pathway to the woman, now on the last step, and handed it to her. Her left hand tightly gripping the railing, she reached out with her other hand, its prominent blue veins protruding through spotted, nearly translucent skin, and grasped the newspaper before pulling it towards her. Then she looked up at me with clear and honest deep-blue eyes. There seemed to be a question in those eyes but she didn't ask it. She just smiled sweetly, and said, softly and with a slight tremor, "Thank you... That's very kind of you." Then she turned slowly and prepared for the ascent. As she gripped the railing and lifted one of her legs, I asked, "Can I help you?" And she answered, looking down at the stair and concentrating on the job of getting her leg up to it, "No thank you. I'm fine." "Are you sure?" I asked. "Yes, I don't want to hold you up." "It's no problem. I'm in no hurry... No hurry at all." "Well, if it really isn't any problem..." "It isn't." "Then fine. I gratefully accept."

So I grasped her thin left arm, its loose skin compressing under my firm hand, and wrapped my right arm around her tiny waist and slowly but surely helped her up those broad wooden steps to the porch, where she stopped for a moment and took several deep breaths. Then she turned towards me again and softly, with that sweet little smile, said, "Thank you." "No problem, ma'am. " (I never called anybody "ma'am"; it was silly. But she was one of those women for whom you instinctively used that designation; nothing else would do.) "I'm glad to help," I added. "You take care now."

As I turned to go down the stairs, she said, "Won't you have a cup of coffee or tea or something cool?" I faced her, and she was standing with her hands at her side, and an expression of expectancy.

I hesitated and she said, "It's the least I can do for an act of kindness." "It really wasn't anything, ma'am." "Oh yes, it was... and besides," she said with a light little laugh, "I could use the company."

So what could I do? I allowed myself to be ushered to a wicker chair with a needlepoint cushion featuring a portrait of a bluejay. She excused herself and went into the house, the aluminum storm door softly clicking in place after her.

I sat peacefully in that wicker chair and surveyed the view from the porch. It was lovely. An apple tree, cloaked in young-spring-green, stood on the lawn on either side of the walkway. A few robins perched on high branches chirping away. Daffodils sprouted randomly around the lawn. And tulips of red and blue and pink and purple lined the white picket fence and the walkway. The sidewalk, partially obscured by the fence and several burgeoning lilac bushes, was empty. And the only sounds I could hear were the low buzz of several lawn mowers, the sharper buzz of a near-by chain saw, and the resonant horn of a ferry, probably the one headed out of port back toward Seattle.

I heard the repeated clickings of the storm door and rose quickly to help the old lady who was inside, holding a small tray, and trying to open the door with her elbow. As I held open the door, she chuckled again. "You'd think by now I'd do something sensible like put a little table next to the door. One of these days..."

She placed the tray, bearing matching white ceramic milk pitcher and sugar dish, two cups of tea, and a plate of butter cookies, on a low wicker table between our chairs. Then she placed herself in front of the other wicker chair, looked back to check her position,

BLURRED IMAGES

grasped the two arms of the chair, and slowly and with some apparent effort dropped down.

"There," she said, with a satisfied smile and a few deep breaths. "At last..." Then, looking down at the tray, she said, "Now help yourself... I hope you're a tea drinker. I realized I don't have any coffee." "Tea's fine, ma'am... This is very nice of you." "Well, it's very nice of you to spend some time with an old lady." "So we're even." "Yes. I guess we are." And we both laughed, then went silent as we prepared our tea and took the first sips and munched a cookie.

Eventually she broke the silence.

"I don't mean to pry, but are you new on the island?"

"You're not prying... And no, I'm not new here. I'm just visiting."

"I kind of figured."

"How's that?"

"Oh, I don't know... Just guessed."

She sipped her tea, looked around the yard, and returned her benign gaze to me.

"So where are you from?"

"The Midwest," I said without hesitation. "Iowa... Dubuque, to be exact."

"I knew it... Not the Iowa part... But certainly the Midwest." She was more animated than at any point in our brief encounter, extremely pleased with her perceptiveness.

"How did you know?" I asked, enjoying her pleasure.

"Your manner.. and your good manners," she said. "People around here are... well, not exactly rude... but brusque, always in a hurry."

"That's too bad... I'd think on a beautiful island like this, they'd slow down, take the time..."

"You would, wouldn't you?... I don't know... Maybe they're too busy worrying about paying for all this beauty and peace and quiet..."

ARTHUR DIMOND

"That sounds about right," I offered.

After another few minutes, she said, "They're mainly from other places... California. Texas. New York... Not the Midwest, mind you." (And she laughed at her own little joke.) "Maybe they just bring their bad manners with them. Maybe that's it."

"You might have something there," I said with a smile.

We sipped and munched quietly for a few more minutes. To my surprise, I was enjoying myself.

"I have this strange feeling you're a native," I finally said.

She looked a bit confused so I explained, in a slightly louder voice.

"Of this island... you sound like you're a native of this island."

"Oh, no, I wish I were... But I came here a long time ago, as a very young woman... as a teacher, the fifth grade teacher..."

"That's nice..."

"It was nice, very nice... And I got to know two generations of children, watched them grow up, taught their children..."

"That's really nice."

"And I watched a lot of them move away... They coudn't afford to stay... That wasn't so nice."

She set her delicate jaw and looked straight ahead, out at the neatly trimmed lawn and the tranquil, shady street. I was surprised at her sudden change of tone and mood.

"But some stayed?" I offered.

"Yes, some stayed," she said. Her jaw remained set. But her eyes softened and grew vague and misty, and she seemed lost in thought. I started to rise and was about to excuse myself when the jaw unlocked, the eyes brightened and refocused, and she turned quickly to me.

"Oh, don't go," she said.

"I really have to... And I've probably overstayed anyway."

"Oh, please excuse me," she said. "I get all dreamy now and then. Here I was talking about bad manners... and look at me. I get in

BLURRED IMAGES

my little time machine and I abandon you."

"Oh no, it's not you... I really do have to go."

"What's the hurry?... I thought you had time."

"I'm sorry, I have do do something in town, then catch the ferry back..."

"Oh, I see," she said, visibly disappointed.

"Can I help you in with the tray?"

"No, no... I'll manage."

"You sure?"

"I'm sure... Now go on, do what you have to do and catch your ferry."

"Well, thanks for your hospitality," I said.

"It was my pleasure," she said, and extended her hand. I approached her and reached out to that veined, delicate, milky-skinned hand. As I grasped it, she looked at me directly in the eyes and seemed to study me more closely than before, more closely than I liked. I released my hand, but forced myself to maintain eye contact.

"My name is Eve Farrington. What's yours?" she asked in an oddly purposeful manner. "In case we ever meet again."

"Bill... Bill Porter."

"Well, Mr. Porter..."

"Bill, please."

"Well, Bill... You're a kind man... I've known many many boys and the men they grew into... And I have a feeling, a very strong feeling, that you're also an unusual man... Maybe some day you'll tell me your story..."

Her statement surprised me, left me slightly uneasy, on guard. I had an odd fleeting fantasy: I was in the presence of one of those mystical forest creatures you find in fairy tales. You stumble into their realm. You suddenly appear and they know who you are. Everything about you. Instantly.

The fantasy passed. I kept looking at her, doing my best to act casual and light.

ARTHUR DIMOND

"If I ever did, if I told you my story, I think you'd be bored... probably disappointed."

"I don't think so... I have this feeling it would be very interesting."

"And why do you think that?" I asked, almost tempted to extend the repartee, to make a little game of this.

"Just instinct," she said with that small, now-familiar smile. "I know boys and men and I have a vivid imagination."

I stood for a minute, mystified and increasingly uneasy, and then stepped back and turned toward the stairs.

"So long... Bill Porter... from Dubuque," she said with a lilt, as I descended the stairs and headed down the walkway.

When I reached the sidewalk, I half-turned and waved, then looped around several luxuriant, tree-shaded side streets, past more expansive and ornate Victorians set on grassy, hilly lots. Then I headed back toward the village. The streets were very quiet, emptied of school kids and commuting business types, and not quite ready for morning shoppers.

When I reached the village, I went directly to the pier to check the next departure. About 45 minutes to go. I decided to hang out in town, wander around, maybe get a cup of coffee. I stopped in a variety store to pick up a newspaper for the return trip, and on a whim, bought a few postcards of the island, the famous Needle, and the Seattle skyline from across the sound, Mt. Rainier in the distance. Without the slightest idea of whom to send them to, or whether, in the interests of prudence, to send them at all.

I went into the post office a few doors down to buy stamps. A few people — an older man in a plaid golf cap and a young woman with a shopping bag — were queued up at the open window and I got behind them.

While waiting, I absently took in the room. The light institutional-green semi-gloss walls. The postal rate sheets and mailing instructions. The first-cover stamps. The government employment listings. The

BLURRED IMAGES

"Most Wanted" poster. Of the dozen or so pictures, most were mugs, front and side. Several were blurry, blown-up snapshots confiscated from the wallets or albums or dresser tops or desk drawers of families and friends. With a visible lurch, I recognized one, my young self with my former name, my former face. And next to it was a computer-generated, age-progressed portrait that fast-forwarded my face to what it might have been had I not placed myself long ago in a secluded rural clinic and had my nose and cheekbones and jawbones broken and reset. My face remade so the only real similarity was the hairline depressingly receded to its current location. And my slightly outsized, protruding ears. And my eyes, my serious, questioning eyes.

I regained my composure and continued to stare at the pictures and the description and the explanation of why I was up there surrounded by the most dangerous criminals in America. A serial murderer. A brutal rapist. A convict who killed two guards while escaping from prison. A hate-murderer who bombed a synagogue. A father who murdered his children.

And there was I. An anomaly. The mistake in this picture. A long-faced, thoughtful-looking young man, really a boy, adjacent to his serious, jowly middle-aged self. A cop-killer. A fugitive since May 1968.

I had seen the boy gazing out from a poster like this long ago, barely three months after being on the run. That time, too, I had been in a post office, somewhere in Ohio, also trying to buy stamps for letters to my family and a few good friends, for a desperate attempt to explain myself, to clarify what really happened before fiction became indelible, immutable fact, and their minds became set and their attitudes hardened. And before whatever I did would be too late.

Waiting in that line, I see myself and the words, "for murder of a police officer." And I almost collapse on the checkerboard tile floor. Two large strong hands catch me under one armpit and grasp the elbow of my other arm, and the owner of those hands, a black man with a square jaw and silvery kinky hair, guides me to a plastic connected

ARTHUR DIMOND

chair under the posters. And he brings me a little cone-shaped cup of water. And he asks me if I'm OK, and I say yes. And he asks, "You sure?" And I nod and thank him and he gets back in line, looking at me every minute or so out of concern or curiosity or maybe suspicion, I can't tell. And when the lightness and mild nausea pass, and my breathing feels more or less normal, I get up abruptly and without saying anything to my black samaritan, move quickly toward the double glass doors and the street.

He died! That is a total shock to me. I remember him crumpling. That I remember. But *die*? Not that. It's unimaginable. Impossible. Not that the swing of that childhood Louisville Slugger couldn't have that effect. But that I was at the other end of the bat? That I was capable of this, of felling a man, of **killing** a man?

When I ran, I was thinking only of escape, of safety. Later, when it was quiet, when I had countless hours to review, to explore and examine every detail of that brief, terrifying encounter, I assumed the acceptable worst. That the slim, slight cop suffered a concussion, maybe was hospitalized, had a bit of recovery time, would be on his feet— was probably already on his feet, back on the job, no real harm done. When I mustered my courage and maybe found a lawyer, I would turn myself in and deal with the consequences. How bad could they be? I was a scared, confused, cornered kid. I had never been in trouble— never! This was all an enormous tragic accident. Everybody would understand. It was just a matter of time and everything would be OK.

That day in the post office I knew it would never be OK. I knew it when, out of the corner of my eye, I caught sight of posters and pictures in other post offices and public buildings on other days in other places. And now, in yet another post office, a half-continent and two-and-a-half decades away, on this day on this island, I knew it even better. That cop was still dead and they hadn't forgotten. And I still had the capacity to be shocked by the reality of it.

I left the post office and walked in a daze to the pier. I sat on

BLURRED IMAGES

a whisky-barrel seat near the boarding area, and gazed absently across the Sound, at the ferry, so small out there, slowly approaching from Seattle.

The vessel eventually arrived and its passengers disembarked. I boarded with a small, diverse group, a mix of shoppers, business types, and tourists. I headed up iron stairs and found a seat, already unfolded, more or less where I had been before. The sun was now shining brightly from a rare cloudless blue sky. I raised my head to the sun and closed my eyes and enjoyed its comforting warmth, thinking it might bring with it some sense of hope. It didn't but I took what I could get.

CHAPTER IV

The adagio movement in that Schubert trio is on continuous play in my head. And I am whistling in accompaniment as I walk toward the campus on a glorious spring day.

The cello is back in the room after another intensive rehearsal for the senior recital. Things are coming together. The kinks are coming out. The original pianist, that guy from Denver, has moved to a more compatible group and we have a new pianist, Sarah. She knows the trio and she is superb — **unbelievably** superb — at extracting every nuance out of that magnificent piece. And she is beautiful, even more so when she leans over the keyboard, real low, her long, deep-red hair practically touching the keys. She plays with absolute concentration, as her eyes dart from one hand to another, then up at the music. When she produces a bad note or — worse — derails in the course of a treacherous run, she grimaces; if she produces a second or third one in succession, she curses and glares at her hands and the keys and the notes on the pages as though they have betrayed her.

Working with her, I want to work harder. I don't want to disappoint her. I want her to pace us, to make us — me and the violinist, a Chinese-American from Hoboken — to do our very best, to perform the piece like the Beaux Arts. I want her to break into that stunning surprise grin when everything is coming together and working perfectly.

Now the cello is back in the apartment, resting in my room. And

BLURRED IMAGES

in its place, I carry a bat, a bruised and dented and now-anonymous implement I have had since high school, that has traveled with me to weekend outings, to camps, and now to college. Hanging from the bat is my equally historic, supple-as-silk Stan Musial-autograph outfielders glove.

Near the library I fall into step with an upstairs neighbor, a tall gangly pre-law student from Chicago whose name I don't know. He asks me if I'm headed for the rally.

"What rally?" I ask.

"You kidding me?" the guy asks. "There are posters all over the place."

"Oh, yeah," I reply lamely, with a weak little smile. "I haven't gotten out much lately... this big recital thing..."

"Right, I think I heard you practicing the other night."

"Yeah, that and every other night... I'm not keeping you up, I hope."

"Hey, with my study habits, you're doing me a favor."

We both laugh and walk for another half-block past the neat rowhouses with tidy, tulip-rimmed little gardens out front.

"So what's with the bat?" he suddenly asks with the hint of a smile.

"What do you mean?" I ask.

"I thought for sure you wanted to kick some ass at the rally."

"You serious?" I ask, genuinely surprised, and laugh. "I'm going to a softball game... It's the first real exercise I've gotten in weeks."

The guy absorbs that information with a wry, thoughtful expression, and we walk in silence for another minute or two until we pass through the ornate wrought iron gate and onto the campus.

"Where's the game?" the guy asks.

"Behind the fieldhouse... the meadow.."

"Great... the rally's in the Oval... right on your way."

So we walk and chat and as we do, dozens of students converge on *our path. And we all move in a single current through the campus.*

As we approach the Oval, a generous green expanse surrounded by the library, the administrative building, and the original liberal arts hall, we hear the sounds of the rally. The high-pitched didactic verbal bullets of the speaker. The responsive cheers and applause of the crowd.

As we pass between two of the buildings and enter the Oval, I can take in the entire scene. Hundreds of students spread out, sprawling on the lawn. Several hundred more streaming in. A makeshift platform all the way up front. A banner across the top: **'END THE WAR NOW!'**. *Speakers assembled on the platform, seated in a row of chairs.*

Then I notice the cops. Standing on the perimeter path, 25 or 30 feet apart, each with legs apart, hands grasping a billy club, face set stolidly.

I stop and so does my neighbor. Students circle around us like a stream around rocks, and move onto the lawn.

"What's the matter?" he asks.

"Nothing," I say. "I just don't want to fight my way through this. I think I'll cut back and around."

"You sure?"

"Yeah."

"OK... See you around."

"OK."

And I back away, retracing my steps across the rear of the Oval and the perimeter path and between the two buildings, going against the surging tide of the arriving students, averting collisions. Behind the liberal arts building, I pick up a path and make my way toward the playing fields, enjoying the sunshine and the solitude and the sense of freedom. In four or five minutes, I reach the fieldhouse, a huge-Quonset-like affair, and behind it, the fields, a couple of baseball diamonds at either end and, between them, a large area used for soccer, lacrosse, and other field-sport practices.

I stop and survey the expanse. It is extraordinarily, eerily, quiet

BLURRED IMAGES

that day. Absolutely pastoral. The robins and sparrows, usually terrorized by the clamor of activity, are there in force. Having reclaimed the field, they are skittering and chirping and flying about. A kid and a man, presumably his father, are running down the center, trying to get a kite aloft. And on the far diamond, a guy at homeplate is shagging balls to another guy in the outfield.

Whistling the Schubert adagio, a theme that has taken up permanent residence in my brain, I stride toward that other diamond. When I get there, I stand near homeplate and watch the batter attempt to hit several balls. The two guys have exchanged roles. And the new batter seems to be as out of practice as I probably am. Several times he tosses the ball upward, grasps the bat with both hands, swings the bat back over his shoulder, then swings it forward and airs it. He doesn't seem to mind — maybe it was that kind of day — and just picks up the ball each time and tries again until he makes contact. And when he does, he really does. That ball soars high over the infield and deep into center field. The other guy chases it and reaches it after it bounces several times, loses its kick, and is rolling slowly across the grassy ground. He casually picks up the ball, seems to study it for a minute and then throws it back to home, which it eventually, barely, reaches after several hops.

"What do you think of this world-class ball?" the batter asks with a grin. He's a chunky kid with prominent freckles and stringy light-brown hair slightly moist and matted from perspiration.

"Just about my speed," I respond, and grin back.

"You wanna take over for awhile? I'll get my glove and help Howie out there... He needs all the help he can get." And we both laugh.

He trots out to the outfield, and plants himself about 20 yards from the other guy. I pick up my trusty bat, take a few practice swings, and then try the real thing. I try to kill it and miss by a mile, that meaningless motion straining my shoulders and sending my body into a silly little pirouette. With less drama but equally paltry results, I take a few more swings; each time, I pick up the ball, pause for a minute, look out at the two guys in the outfield, plan my next moves, and try again. Then I gain a bit of rhythm and get a piece of one, and enjoy that sweet sound and sensation as the ball takes off, sailing high and far, sending the two guys scurrying for it.

After another five or ten minutes, I put down the bat and hustle out toward second base, signaling to my new companions to come in for a huddle.

When we converge, I say: "Could I ask you guys a dumb question... Where is everybody? Can they all be at that rally?"

It's supposed to be a pick-up game with a constantly rotating group of students. Every Saturday, same time, same place. Whoever shows, plays. Very low-keyed. Very informal.

They smile and one of them says, "Yup... The whole frigging campus's gotta be there."

"We're right in the mainstream, huh?" the other guy says with a grin.

And the first guy responds, without smiling, mock-serious, "Hey, we've got our priorities, right?"

The three of us stand there for a few minutes, out there at second base in the middle of a vast, virtually empty, sunsplashed space, feeling vaguely silly.

"Well, whadaya wanna do?" the first guy asks.

The other guy smiles and says, "I dunno...I'm getting more exercise than I'm used to."

"I guess we got two choices," the first guy offers. "We keep doing this or we call it quits."

I look around the expanse and then back at these two equally disoriented guys and say, "Let's hit a few more and then blow this soda pop stand..."

"Yeah, I guess we gotta accept reality."

So that's what we do. We each take turns shagging some more. Then I pitch a few in, and they bat. And then we pick up our stuff and

BLURRED IMAGES

trudge back across the field.

As we pass around the fieldhouse, rally sounds reach us. And with each step, the sounds grow stronger. I can't make out the words of a speech. But even so, I can sense the electricity, the connectivity between speaker and crowd. Phrases, sentences, paragraphs, are greeted with applause or roars.

When we reach the grassy passage between the administration building and the library, we slow down and then stop.

"What're you guys gonna do?" I ask.

"I dunno... What about you?"

"Oh, I think I'll mosey in and check it out... I mean the afternoon's already shot, so what the hell?"

And that's exactly how I feel. I need a break this afternoon and the rally's about the only game in town. One of my new companions shrugs and grins and says, "Yeah, what the hell... Even if it sucks, at least we'll catch some rays."

So the three of us drift onto the Oval green, wending our way for ten or twenty yards through the crowd, sprawled out on blankets, lawn chairs, open grass, most wearing faded jeans, cutoffs, T-shirts and jerseys of every description, some guys wearing no tops at all, exposing pale winter skin.

We find a place not far from the periphery and drop down. We're just close enough to make out the figures on the platform. The speaker is a compactly built young man with a swarthy complexion and a mass of curly dark-brown hair and a shirt in the image of the American flag. Seated beside him is a bearded guy with a leprechaunish grin. And on the other side is a clean-cut-looking young man, wearing a white T-shirt with what looks like a peace symbol; he looks familiar but I can't place him — as a quiet kid who sits near me in sociology — until later.

To my surprise, I find myself leaning forward, my head extended past my crossed legs, concentrating, trying to hear what that curly-haired guy with the nasal voice is saying.

ARTHUR DIMOND

"... So what do we have? Out in Nam, we have a war machine, a killing machine, that's relentless... And back here, we have a bunch of old men at the controls of the machine, sending kids out there to power that machine... And things ain't gonna change... unless we change them. You know why? Because this election is gonna be Tweedledee vs. Tweedledum."

Scattered laughter drifts through the crowd.

"On the one hand," he says, raising his right hand, "we've got you know who, still up to his old tricks... And on the other hand," he says, raising his other hand, "we've got... you guessed it... the Happy — goofy! — Warrior..."

"Now, Tricky Dick — let's call a spade a spade — he says he's got a 'secret plan' to end the war. But knowing him as we do, it's probably a secret weapon that'll also end Western and Eastern civilization as we know it..."

"And on the other side, we have the Humper. And he says he's his own guy, that he's independent from the Big Man... He says we're gonna see his true colors... Not brown after kissing the Big Man's butt for the past four years.

"But let's be honest... These two guys are gonna change nothing" (and he makes an 'O' with his thumb and index finger and holds it up and out)..."Nada... Zilch... And the killing will continue... And some of us are gonna be sent over... and be asked to kill.... and be killed.... to be **fodder! Fodder, for chrissake!**

"So enough already!... We're gonna say NO!... And we're gonna let these clowns know we're on to their tricks and we're gonna do whatever we can to stop them..."

"Now the GOPpers, that's a different kettle of fish— there's not much we can do to change them or their fearless leader... short of group lobotomies" (laughter from the crowd)... "But the Dems and the Humper? There's some history here... We go back a ways together... We can take a stand with them, put them on the spot, maybe shame them, embarrass them into coming to their senses... Maybe we can go

BLURRED IMAGES

to Chicago and make a stink at their convention... You know, crash their goddamned party..."

The applause is slow to build. But when it does, it's long and sustained and it's overlaid with hoots and whistles. And when it dies down, he begins to lay out the plan, the actual logistical details of the plan. Painstakingly. Almost lovingly.

After a few minutes, one of the policemen approaches the platform and, standing on the grass, directly below the lectern, says something to the speaker who stops in mid-sentence. The policeman produces a sheet of paper and shows it to the speaker who glances at it and shoves it back at the policeman, looking out at the crowd.

"Hey, guess what?" he yells. "The officer informs us that time's up... The permit he's got says we've got one hour on this hallowed ground and that's it. We're out of time, we've got to clear out and go home... Well, we never saw this paper... We never agreed to any one-hour limit, I can tell you that... So we've got a problem, I guess."

There's some rumbling in the crowd.

"But this is a democracy, right?"

There's some scattered laughter.

"And what do we do in a democracy, when we've got a problem, some issue we've got to resolve?"

Silence.

"Come on, you all know the answer."

The cop, now joined by several others, is raising the piece of paper and shoving it back toward the speaker. The speaker ignores it and the cop and continues to focus on the crowd.

"We **vote**! **That's** what we do! We **vote**!" Then, staring at the cop with the permit, "We don't throw paper at people with dictates they never agreed to just because they're saying things we don't agree **with**!"

"Yeah!" one student shouts.

"You said it!" yells another.

ARTHUR DIMOND

"Right on!" bellows a third.
"Fuckin' A!" shrieks yet another.
The crowd is alive again.
"OK, so do we vote to vote?" the speaker asks.
The crowd breaks into applause again.
"So here are the choices... very simple... Do we go, like the nice policeman says...?"

"NO!" the students bellow, practically in unison. "Or do we stay, stick up for our rights, and finish what we've got to say and do here?"

The answer is resounding. To my surprise, I'm caught up in the excitement. I'm cheering with the others. And laughing too. I mean, that speaker is great. He's funny. He has balls. I don't know how smart he is until later, much later, in the season, after his arrest and trial and exoneration and his often-merry crusade in a grim environment. But that day, without knowing anything about him and certainly anything that follows, he's impressive, inspiring us all to be fiercer and bolder than we are.

Me? I'm excited. But I'm also scared. Here I am, just looking for a break, an afternoon at play in the spring sunshine. And where do I find myself? In the middle of something that seems on the verge of going out of control. I'm enjoying the excitement, no doubt about that. But I'm also growing increasingly anxious that the mood is changing rapidly. The speaker is locked in struggle with first one, now several cops. There's no turning back. And we, the supporting cast, are being inexorably carried along. The speaker, I later learn, knows the script cold. We — or most of us at least — are playing it by ear.

More cops have massed in front of the platform and the crowd is shouting and the speaker is trying to speak but can't be heard any longer because the mike is dead.

At this point, I definitely want out. I turn slowly, looking for the exits. There are none. In fact, I'm stunned to see that the cops have multiplied. And they're now about ten feet apart and they are uniformly

BLURRED IMAGES

stiff, poised, and gripping either end of their wooden billy sticks across their blue-clad, brass-buttoned abdomens.

My attention turns back to the platform. The cops are up on the stand now. I can see them all arguing. But without the mike, without the projected words — the power — the event has deteriorated. It has lost its meaning, its aura. Now it's just a couple of grungy, long-haired guys in funny clothes in a squabble with a bunch of cops. Fingers are pointing and jabbing, bodies in defensive and combative poses. I really want out, but it's too late.

Even from a distance, I see the glint of metal in the sunshine and the next thing I know, they're handcuffing the speakers, even the cleancut guy from my sociology class. They're encircling them in a protected core and slowly moving down and away from the platform.

The students are up on their feet. But they clearly don't know what to do. Not a clue. It's early in the season and this is all new to them. Cops are still in the driver's seat. And they're still kids, really, and feel powerless to do anything but protest, hurl — lob? — ineffectual phrases at the cops and watch the drama wind down as the stars are marched away.

Then, just as the phalanx reaches the periphery path, a raw egg lands on the shoulder of one of the cops. He stops for a second and looks down in surprise, then disgust, at the yellow and white mess beginning to slide down his pristine blue arm. Then a second egg hits him dead center in his chest, adhering to some of the shiny brass buttons as it makes its descent. And then comes a third. Being so close to the periphery, I can see his pasty-white complexion redden and his mouth twist into an expression of rage. Before he has a chance to act, a battery of eggs rains down on the contingent. A few of them land on the speakers who stand calmly in the nucleus, two of them — the curly-haired guy and his elfin lieutenant — displaying small bemused smiles.

The cops have now stopped and are holding their arms up to protect themselves. And we students are now all standing out on the *grass, slowly, cautiously, inching closer. And there is growing laughter, too, because this is now sport, theatre, unexpected entertainment.*

As the egg onslaught fades out and appears to be almost over, the cops and their captives resume their march to the passage between two of the buildings. About ten steps later, just when the cops probably think they're home free, another object is launched from the crowd. This one isn't an egg. It's a rock and it hits one of the cops squarely on the temple. His cap flies off his head and he's down on his knees, his left hand up against his temple, thin rivulets of blood trickling through the fingers, creating parallel crimson streams down the cheek. Another rock descends into the group, now confused and a bit frantic. The rock drops harmlessly to the ground. But a third one immediately follows and strikes another cop on the leg. And then there's another... And another... And the cops now have their billy clubs out and poised. While several cops try to hustle the speakers out of the area, the bulk of them start to charge the crowd. This is no longer a police action. This is retaliation. These cops are pissed. Enraged. Their uniforms a mess of congealed egg, their caps awry at every which angle, some bloodied from rocks, these cops are out to get this unruly, defiant bunch of kids. So they charge and swing those clubs with swift strong motions, leaving dozens of kids lying on the ground, writhing and moaning, and handcuffing others.

I'm terrified. How did I get into this? And how do I get out? I pick up my bat and glove and begin to move slowly but purposefully away from the mayhem, toward the passage back to the path leading to the ballfields. Then suddenly, I hear, "There's a kid with a bat. Let's get him!" I turn quickly and see three cops — two big, beefy guys and one slim, medium-sized guy — charging me, their clubs up and ready.

That image remains. All these years. Three cops, all in blue, fury in their eyes, malice in their mouths, breath coming hard, sticks high and threatening. Coming down hard on a scared kid standing stock-still in a lovely glen, his childhood bat limply hanging down from

BLURRED IMAGES

a cold and clammy hand, wondering what would happen next.
   It happens in a flash. They're upon me and the first blow strikes. It hits my upper arm, my left arm, and the pain shoots through my neck and my entire upper body. Then another blow crashes down on my head. I had never taken a major blow to the head. And it's just like in the cartoons. I see stars — a whole galaxy of stars — and flashing lights. Then I'm in a pitch-black cave or chamber. I go unconscious for a moment, maybe longer. Then I'm back in the bright glow of the day. And I'm on my knees, looking up at the cops, their images blurry. And one of them says something to the other two, something about praying, and then they all laugh. And during that second that they relax and enjoy the joke, I muster all my strength and jump to my feet and start running. One of them bellows: "Why, that little fucker... Let's get him!" With the advantage of surprise, I gain an early lead. But they're rapidly closing the distance. Now they're right behind me. But I keep on running. I'm feeling woozy and disoriented and slowed down from the head blow, the fall. But fear — terror! — drives me on. I force myself to pick up my pace, but they're still with me; I can't believe how three guys, two of them twice my age and maybe twice my weight, can keep up. Yet there they are, breathing hard, within tackling range.
   Suddenly, without thinking, without planning, I turn. And in that split second, the only one I have, I swing my bat high and wide at one of the big guys and miss. The guy quickly recovers and says with a guffaw, "A regular fucking Ted Williams!" And while they are laughing, while they're distracted for that tiny moment, I act. Without really thinking, driven by terror and desperation, I swing again. I catch another of them — the slight guy — just over the left eye. And he's down. Just like that. More in surprise than in real shock, we all stare down at him, lying on the ground. And then I bolt and run for the fields, faster than I ever have, my head throbbing, my left arm aching, my heart beating wildly. When I reach the outfield of one of the diamonds, I throw the bat side-arm and it flies in a succession of

ARTHUR DIMOND

gyrating circles into the taller grass beyond. I watch where it lands and then sprint into the surrounding woods. Somewhere along a narrow path, next to a huge boulder, I bury the glove, digging purposefully with a sharp stick and my bare trembling hands.

CHAPTER V

I alternated between dozing and gazing, and before long we were back at the Seattle pier. In the terminal building, I strode directly to the payphones near the restrooms. Using one of the phones was an intense young man in a dark suit, beaten-up black attaché at his feet, receiver jammed between jaw and shoulder, hands flipping jerkily through a small spiral-bound notebook. He was telling somebody about an exasperating meeting he had just come from, and he was clearly upset, agitated, his briefing punctuated by the heel of his palm cracking the metal counter, by obscenities and barks followed by tight, scathing laughs.

I hesitated, but only for a moment before moving down the row, stationing myself at one of the phones, my back to the young man and the terminal. I quickly picked up the receiver and punched in my father's number scratched out on a folded Travelodge note sheet. When the operator came on, I said I was calling collect. Then the phone rang once, twice, a third time, a fourth, and just when I thought that formal, resonant voice would emerge, the ringing stopped, and I heard the click of a connection and then a thin, frail voice.

"Hello?"

"We have a collect call for Professor Stevenson from Jeff... Will you accept the charges?"

"Charges? From whom?"

"Jeff."

There was silence for a few seconds as my heart beat furiously, my entire body seemed to grow damp, and my mouth went dry. Then he said, softly, almost inaudibly, "Yes."

The operator clicked off and then it was just us. And for what seemed a very long and awkward time, we said nothing. Then I spoke.

"Dad?"

"Yes?"

"Happy birthday... A big one, huh?"

"Thank you," he said. Then nothing. Then:

"You're a day late."

"I tried to get you yesterday."

"I was partying."

"Oh, yeah, that's great. With who... Danny and Sylvia?"

There was a pause, a long pause.

"Dad, you still there? You OK?"

"Yes... but I'm not OK... And I was with Daniel and Sylvia... but we weren't partying, not even close... We were at the hospital."

"Hospital? What's wrong? Something happen to you?"

Again he paused.

"Dad?" I asked, now anxiously.

"It's not me... It's Daniel."

I thought I heard a catch in his voice as he pronounced his older son's name. I had rarely heard his voice as anything but strong or, if soft and subdued, then certainly clear and steady. This was new. Something had to be very wrong.

"What's the matter? Did he have an accident or something?"

There was another long and agonizing silence. I waited.

"He has cancer... lymphoma...He'll be dead in six months."

I felt a physical jolt. I lurched forward. It was like I was hit by a club, a blast, a huge black locomotive surging down the track. I grabbed the perforated aluminum phone partitition and held it for support. I couldn't speak.

"Jeff?... Jeff? Are you still there?"

BLURRED IMAGES

He sounded more irritated than concerned.

He asked again and I uttered a barely audible, "Yes." And then I asked, "How long have you known?"

"Just a week... We knew he was sick for awhile, but we didn't know how sick... or with what... They did their tests... all their terrible tests... and then we knew."

I didn't say anything. I *couldn't* say anything. Instead I began to cry, soft, muffled sobs, perhaps too low for my father to pick up with his declining hearing, more pronounced to me given the long gaps between our conversations. Or maybe he had no idea how to handle my distress, what with who he was, and where I was, and why we were speaking over this chasm of years and miles.

"I'm coming home," I said in the lowest of tones.

"What's that, Jeff? Speak up... please."

"I'm coming home," I said more loudly and clearly.

Now it was his turn to go silent. Finally he spoke.

"How?" he asked.

"I don't know how... I can't think of anything now... Anything but... this."

Again there was silence and again he broke it.

"Maybe I can help."

I was stunned.

"What do you mean?"

"I don't know what I mean... I'm not thinking too clearly these days."

"Yeah, I know... I understand. I'm not either."

After a pause, he said, "I still have some friends in high places... Not in this administration, heaven knows... But here and there... Maybe they can help."

"Really?"

"You never know."

There was another long pause. Then I said, "I'll call."

"When?"

ARTHUR DIMOND

"When I'm ready... When I've absorbed all this and can think straight."

"You've got to give me some idea."

"OK, in five days. How's that?"

"Its short, but that's OK... Pressure's good." And he meant it, sounding brighter than at any point in our brief somber exchange.

We said good-bye, quickly, with no ceremony, then hung up.

I briefly looked at the receiver now back on its cradle. Then I glanced at my watch. Nearly 12 noon. A full two hours to go before rehearsal. Relieved, I made my way up the aisle, past row after row of dull-shiny, lacquered wooden benches, dotted with a diversity of people reading, gazing, sleeping, then out the other end onto the sidewalk and across the broad avenue and up the steep street into Seattle's business district. And for an hour or more, I wandered, truly aimlessly, the Mozart through my Walkman forming the soundtrack. Images of people, signs, buildings, stores, restaurants, coffee shops, all materialized and vanished, providing an amorphous, silent backdrop for the drama of a few faraway people whose features and affects were still sharp and enduring.

At about 1:30, I dropped wearily into the back seat of a cab for the short ride back to the Travelodge. Rehearsing, playing that day and night and the night after night to follow were about the last things I wanted to do. What I wanted to do was to magically transport myself across the country, soar smoothly and effortlessly over batallions of police and judges and curiosity-seekers, to Danny's hospital bed. To be there. To be *allowed* to be there.

For now, I played. The music, the band, the audience, they were all there but seemed remote. I played my notes, alternating between mechanical and inspired, in the grip of my emotions, not knowing when each emotion would emerge, resulting in music that surged or simmered, that thrilled or went unnoticed.

I was more grateful than ever to be the bassman. Nobody, not Seth, or Jerry, or Hank, and certainly not the audiences, seemed to

BLURRED IMAGES

notice that I was playing the musical accompaniment to a dream. They thought it was just me, motoring along on cruise control, diverging little in speed or tone or direction.

But everything — *everything* — had changed. For the first time in 25 years, there was an urgency, a need to act, and a deadline; that word had real meaning now. And I didn't have a clue about a plan. Just the slim hope that an 80-year-old man with mixed emotions would save the day. And if that didn't happen, I would simply show up.

* * * * *

Sylvia picked up the phone on the first ring.

"Yes?" she asked, quickly, sharply, as though being interrupted by an underling on the intercom.

"Sylvie?"

"Yes?" she asked again, now with a tinge of irritation.

"Sylvie, it's me," I said. "Jeff."

"Jeff?" she asked, either not quite recognizing the name, or trying to decide *which* Jeff. Or maybe not believing it was me. I had to be a phantom-like figure in her mind; the last time we saw each other was at her wedding where I was my brother's best man.

She paused, then said, "You know?"

"Yes," I said, and suddenly, reflexively, my voice caught and I fought back tears.

"Your father?"

"Yes."

"He's devastated, you know."

"I know. So am I."

I expected her to add something. But she didn't, and there was an uncomfortable silence.

Finally I asked, "How you holding up?"

"Oh, OK... You know."

"And your son?"

He was an abstraction to me. A name, when I could remember it.

ARTHUR DIMOND

I had never met him and had never seen his picture.

"Michael? Well... I'll tell you about that saga sometime."

After a pause, I said, "I want to talk to Danny."

"I thought you might."

"Where is he?"

"Baskin Park Hospital."

"Where?"

"Baskin Park. It's a private hospital out in Bethesda, near the DC line."

"Do you have a number there?"

"Hold on. It's right here."

After she gave it to me, I asked, "Anything I can do?"

"From there? Wherever you are... Out of curiosity, where are you, anyway?"

"I can't tell you."

"I figured."

"So we'll talk?"

"Yes."

"Sylvie?"

"Yes?"

"I'm really sorry."

No response.

"Sylvie, did you hear me?"

"Yes."

"Well, I'm really sorry."

"Yes, I know," she said flatly. "Probably you most of all."

And then the phone clicked off.

I stared at the phone and immediately dialed the hospital number I had scratched out on the corner of the phone directory. I heard a few rings and then a switching sound on the third. Then a recording: "We're sorry but the patient you are trying to reach is unable to answer at this time. Please try later— but no later than 9 p.m. Thank you."

BLURRED IMAGES

* * * * *

At their wedding, I have to ham it up with my brother to dance with Sylvia. As the band plays Moon River, I march across the parquet dance floor to the sole couple, making its slow romantic progress, ostentatiously tap Danny on the shoulder and request the honor of a dance with Sylvia. Danny hams it up, too. He feigns surprise and offense at the intrusion, and after some initial resistance, relinquishes his new bride to the delighted applause of the hundred or so assembled guests.

Sylvia grins as Danny moves away and then gracefully slides into my arms. Petite and slim, she is a full head shorter than me. Her body nestles close to mine, and my chin practically rests on her head. To the continued lovely strains of Moon River, we make our slightly awkward way around the floor, feeling the concentrated collective gaze of everybody in the hall.

"My big little brother," she says, and smiles with obvious pride and pleasure. She pulls me a bit closer, close enough to feel the warmth of her body even through her ornate silk gown and to smell nothing but her perfume.

Then it is abruptly over. I feel a tap on my shoulder. I turn to see the mischievously smiling face of my father and to hear his less than welcome words: "May I dance with the bride?" Reluctantly, even grudgingly, I release Sylvia. As I do so, to my surprise, I feel mild resistance, her lingering grasp of my wrist. But the crowd is already applauding, enjoying the pantomime, this bit of famly sitcom. And I, always the shy one in the family, uncomfortably recede to the sidelines and watch the tall, erect figure of my father elegantly usher his lovely new daughter-in-law around the floor. Gradually other couples rise from their tables and fill the floor, engulfing my father and Sylvia until they become lost in the crowd.

I met Sylvia first. Like me, she was part of the university

community; her father was an economics professor. And also like me, she attended a prep school affiliated with the university. Since she was three grades ahead of me, we didn't share any classes. However, we were both on the coed field hockey team. That's where we met, if you call it that. That's where we formed some modicum of a relationship. A modicum because of the chasm in ages and ranks; it was unimaginable that a senior girl would treat a freshman boy with anything approaching esteem. And the fact that we all — the girls and the minority of us boys — wore the same feminine uniform, short skirts and jerseys, I and my male teammates were the targets of constant teasing (not always good-natured) by our female teammates. Now and then I defended myself with the lame statement that I had some Scottish roots and therefore men in skirts was in my tradition. That line was usually greeted with derision by the girls on the team, including Sylvia.

Sylvia, however, was different. To begin with, she *looked* different, strikingly different. Surrounded by large, beefy girls with long blonde hair and fair, often freckled complexions, Sylvia, in contrast, was small with dark-brown, nearly black, hair, and skin that was clear and olive-tinted. Her last name was Cameron, ethnically non-descript, and she looked nothing like her parents, so everybody assumed she was adopted and had roots somewhere in Eastern Europe or along the Mediterranean. She consistently deflected any questions on this subject.

Sylvia was also different in manner and style. She could be outgoing, even irrepressibly boisterous, when the occasion called for it— say, screaming from the sidelines for a goal or a toughened defense. But fundamentally, she was reserved and soft-spoken, an elusive, sometimes mysterious personality in the midst of her brash, noisy, in-your-face classmates and teammates.

And there was something else that caught my attention: her intensity. The first time I saw her, she was playing forward at a scrimmage. Even from the sidelines, it was clear that she was fully engaged, totally focused on what she had to do next. Get that ball,

BLURRED IMAGES

drive, and score. And when she received that pass, she dribbled skillfully with her stick, used her small, agile body to weave her way down the field, elude her opponents, and get within shooting range of the goal. She attempted the shot, with a fierce short swing, but it was blocked by a fleet-footed goalie. And a loud bellowing, *"Shit!"* rose high above the throng of players, and hung there as disapproving stares locked onto Sylvia from observers on and off the field. The action froze momentarily and when it resumed, Sylvia's coach promptly pulled her from the game and replaced her with another player: me. She wasn't sent back onto the field for the rest of the game, and each time I caught sight of her, she was sitting alone, cross-legged on the ground, sulking, angrily pulling grass clumps out of the soil. And when she caught sight of me, she glarely coldly as though I was solely and personally the instrument of her humiliation.

So our relationship began inauspiciously in an atmosphere of resentment (hers) and trepidation (mine). She wouldn't speak to me or acknowledge me for weeks. And I, in return, avoided contact.

Then several things happened that thawed the frosty atmosphere. She became the team's top scorer, actually breaking a school record, thus arming her with an aura that was unassailable by teammates, coach, and faculty alike. She was accepted at the college of her choice, Wesleyan, and won a generous four-year athletic scholarship. And Danny came home from college.

Danny came to our last game, to cheer me on, he said, but I suspected more to both tease me ("cute legs") and to check out the girls on the team. Sitting in the first row of the low stands, he did all three. At halftime, obliging kid brother that I was, I introduced him to a number of my teammates. He put on his coolest Joe College demeanor, smiling broadly at each girl he met, looking directly into her eyes, causing her to look away and giggle, out of either embarrassment or the obvious silliness of it all. When it was Sylvia's turn, she looked directly back at Danny, a small, bemused smile on her lips. He looked puzzled, glanced quickly at me for assistance (which I had no idea how to give). Then he recovered nicely by complimenting her on her game. She thanked him and said she had played better at other times, explaining that maybe she was nervous— it was the last game of the season, of her entire high school career. He said (mustering every ounce of unctuous college coolness) that maybe she was nervous because she knew he was in the stands. That small smile grew slightly larger and she said simply and evenly, "I don't think so." Then she said she had to huddle with her teammates and quickly excused herself. I ignored Danny's questioning expression and immediately turned and trotted off behind her over to the home bench. Later, back at our house, right before dinner, he asked me for her full name, her age, and other particulars.

When school ended just two weeks later, I went off to a camp in Maine for the summer. Danny stayed at home and worked as a lifeguard and swimming instructor at a day camp on the college campus. And at the last minute, Sylvia got a job at the camp as a junior counselor.

During one of my infrequent calls home, I spoke briefly to Danny, and — I forget if it was unsolicited or in answer to a question of mine — he made a passing but crystal-clear reference to Sylvia and how they were doing. "Moving right along," he said. "And thank you, little brother." "For what?" I asked. "Why, for making it possible. For introducing me to Sylvie."

When I returned home at the end of the summer, they seemed incapable of sitting in a room together without touching, and holding hands, and sharing giggly private jokes, until I and others were eventually driven from the room. Danny and Sylvia were inseparable and remained that way for most weekends and holidays throughout their college years and beyond, and into a marriage that seemed at the time so promising and so enviable, with me feeling more than a bit of that envy myself.

* * * * *

BLURRED IMAGES

Now I was in the Travelodge room, lying flat on my back on the queen-sized bed, staring at the ceiling. We had rehearsed for just a few hours, but I was exhausted, inert, seriously concerned that I would be unable to survive two sets lasting till midnight or beyond. Especially if I couldn't reach Danny before showtime. So I lay there, my eyes wide open, my breathing quick and short, my body tense and tenser yet as I systematically cracked my toes, my knuckles, every small joint in my body, and a couple of big ones. At one point, I lurched upward when the phone rang; it was the hotel operator waking me up at 5:45 p.m. in response to an earlier request I had forgotten about.

Phone in hand, fully alert, and aware of the scarce remaining time (given the time difference), I called that hospital number again. To my surprise Danny picked up and I was suddenly terrified and speechless.

"Hello?" he said, and after clearing his throat, sounding surprisingly like himself.

"Hello, who's there?" he asked again.

"It's me, Danny... Jeff."

"Jeff?"

"Yeah, Danny, it's me."

"Oh my God, this is great. Really great."

"I'm glad, real glad... Hey, Danny..."

"What?"

"You sound good."

"Better than you expected, huh?"

"Yeah, really."

"That's what everybody says... at least the people who call."

That stopped us short and kept us stopped for a long moment. Then he cleared his throat again, and spoke in a voice now lower, softer, more somber.

"You should see me though," he said.

I didn't say anything back.

ARTHUR DIMOND

"I look like shit. Like a fucking corpse with no hair. Not one."

Danny had always prided himself on his appearance. Not a strikingly handsome guy, he made the absolute most of what he had. Nice regular features, even white teeth, clear skin, a natural build for clothes. And that hair, that terrific mane of curly, dark-brown hair. While I always had a cowlick or a wave that jutted out and refused to cooperate, Danny always looked like he had just walked out of a $40-a-sitting styling salon. And now I pictured him in that hospital bed three thousand miles away, right outside the nation's capital, lying on his back, clad in a hospital gown, sallow back exposed, skinny calves sticking out like stalks, bald as an eagle. I fought back tears and tried to muster something to say.

"I'm sorry," I said. That was the best I could do.

"I know you are."

For a moment, neither of us could think of anything else to say. Then Danny said: "Jeff, I really miss you... I *always* missed you. But I really miss you now."

"Well, guess what?"

"What?"

"The feeling's mutual," I said, and then my voice caught.

After a moment, when I cleared my throat and took a deep breath, I said, "And guess what else?"

"What?"

"I'm coming home."

"You're *what*?" he asked, genuinely excited.

"I'm coming home."

"How the hell are you going to do that? After all these years?"

"I can't tell you. I don't exactly know how, or when. But it's going to happen, and soon."

I thought I heard sobs, but no words came over the phone. Then he said: "Jeff, you know what? You really made my day... Fuck the day— the *year*! It's been the worst fucking year, *couple* of years, of my life."

BLURRED IMAGES

"What do you mean?"

"I mean there's more."

"More? More of what?"

"More shit... a *lot* of shit... a *ton* of shit... I can't tell you now. It's too involved..."

"Come on... Are you going to leave me hanging with a statement like that?"

"Yeah, I am, for now... I don't have the energy... anyway..."

"Anyway, what?"

"It doesn't make any difference anymore."

I decided not to press it and changed the subject.

"Danny, you should know that Dad said he would try to help me... to help get me home."

He didn't say anything.

"Did you hear me?"

"Yeah, I heard you."

"Well, what do you think of that?"

"I don't know. I mean, if you had heard him all these years..."

"I can imagine."

"No, you can't imagine... And you don't want to."

I went silent again.

Jeff broke it.

"There's only one reason he's being Mr. Helpful, Mr. Loving Father now, and it's kind of obvious what that is..."

"Maybe you're right. Maybe..."

"Hey, Jeffy, there aren't any maybe's here. That's the reason."

His voice was rising, the words quickening.

"OK, OK, come on, take it easy."

Danny got quiet.

"Danny?" I asked.

"Yeah?"

"Look, I'm sorry about all this... So sorry."

"Hey, Jeff," he shot back sharply. "Do me one favor. Try not to

63

use those words too often... Please."

"OK, anything you say..."

"So I'll see you soon?" he asked, suddenly softening, slightly plaintive.

"Yeah, as soon as I can, as soon as we can swing it... I wish I could just hop on a plane and be there in the morning. I wish it could be that simple."

"Me, too, but nothing's simple. Absolutely fucking nothing."

"I know."

"Just be careful."

CHAPTER VI

Dad delivered with dispatch and efficiency. When I called him five days later, he was ready; he said he had been ready on day three, and had just been sitting on his hands for the last two, waiting for my call, confiding that he was not sure I really would.

He told me to call a lawyer, a man named Jesse Savage who had been an assistant attorney general in the first Reagan Administration.

"The *Reagan* Adminstration?" I blurted. "I don't get it. Why a guy like that? I mean of all the lawyers out there..."

Dad paused for a moment, then said in measured tones, "Because he'll be more believable, more effective. Please trust me on this... And another thing— he's very, very good."

"Hold on. What about *him*? Why would *he* want to take this on? take *me* on? I mean, I'm not exactly his sort of client."

"Let's just say, he's a friend, a good friend. We go back a ways, and he wants to help."

I mulled that over for a few seconds and didn't pursue it. I didn't want to offend my father. And I was genuinely grateful for his help. So I just said, "OK, Dad, OK, let's do it. Thank you. Thanks for all your help."

After some brief logistical calls with Savage's secretary, I was able to arrange my first meeting with the lawyer several days later. We met at his hotel, a nondescript business establishment in downtown Seattle. I called him on the house phone and he directed me up to a modest suite on an upper floor.

ARTHUR DIMOND

His door was slightly ajar. When I knocked, a deep, pleasant voice called out, telling me to come in. When I did, and shut the door behind me, there was Savage, in a crisp white shirt but tieless, sitting in an armchair, a full vista of Puget Sound behind him. He had several manila file folders on his lap and, through half glasses, was looking down at the contents of one of them; they appeared to be newspaper articles. He didn't raise his head for what felt like a full minute. When he finally did, he looked at me — *studied* me is more like it — over the flat tops of the reading glasses.

"So you're the famous Jeffrey Stevenson," he said. "I see you brought company," he added, nodding at the bass case I was holding propped up, and smiling.

He didn't get up to shake my hand. Instead he said, "Have a seat," and he gestured in the direction of a matching armchair four or five feet from his. Then he quickly resumed his reading.

I did as I was told. I made an effort to get settled in the low-backed, not particularly comfortable chair, and gazed out at the Sound, picking out and following the course of one of the ferries I had been on so recently.

"Please excuse me for another minute," he said. "I need to finish this."

I took advantage of the opportunity to study Savage. He was a compact, fit-looking man with smooth, taut skin, dark hair (hardly a trace of gray) combed straight back, large dark eyes set close together, and a small, currently tight-lipped mouth. I guessed that he was in his early 60's.

After a few more minutes, Savage closed the file, and put it and the others on a side table. He crossed his legs, clasped his hands, and now, with his glasses off, considered me, a thoughtful, slightly bemused expression on his face.

"You know, you don't look anything like your dad," he abruptly said. "You're just about the age he was when I first met him, but funny, you don't look anything like him."

BLURRED IMAGES

I was momentarily taken aback by what sounded like a critical observation, right out of the gate.

"Well, I had some changes, you know, to my face."

"Yes, yes, I know. But still..."

"Yeah, still..." I muttered, feeling a bit off balance.

"Well, enough of this banter, let's get down to business, OK?"

"OK."

"Your dad tells me we have a mission."

I nodded. "That's right," I said softly.

He maintained his gaze for another minute or so, adding to my discomfort.

Finally he asked, "How do you see this mission, Jeffrey? I.e., what's your goal?"

"I thought my father had already explained it all to you," I said.

"He did, but I want to hear it from you. Directly from you. How do you want this to play out? to end?"

"Isn't that obvious?"

"No, it isn't obvious. It really isn't. And your answer is critically important."

"OK," I said after a moment. "This is what I want. I want to be able to go home, to see my brother, my father. As soon as possible... And I don't want to go to jail. I absolutely don't want to go to jail."

"Understandably," Savage said, the bemused expression back on his face. "How do you expect to accomplish that?"

"I thought that was your job."

"It is. But I need some help from you."

I must have looked puzzled.

Before I had a chance to phrase a question, he said, "I need you to think about the magnitude of your crime and to think — logically, not legalistically, that *is* my job — to think logically and *realistically* how the authorities will view all this..."

I nodded, but didn't say anything. So he continued.

"I'll be brutally honest. They'll see a cop-killer who's been on the run for all these years, now trying to get off the hook, scot free, without any penalty whatsoever. Or at most, the infamous 'slap on the wrist.'"

"It sounds like that's what *you* think," I said, a tinge of defensiveness creeping into my voice.

"Jeffrey, it doesn't *matter* what I think. It's my job to be a devil's advocate, to make you see the opposing point of view. *That's* what matters. When you understand that..."

"I understand it..."

"You're sure?"

"Yes."

"And you understand how you're perceived, how that perception creates a major hurdle?"

"Yes, I do," I said, my voice going a bit higher with impatience. "So what do we do?"

"We try to convince them that you're not the premeditated murderer they think you are. We try to make them see, to understand, to *accept* that you were this terrified kid, cornered and threatened, that you had no choice, that there was absolutely no premeditation involved... How does this sound? Do you agree with all this?"

I nodded.

"So let's be Devil's advocates again. They're going to think all this is unmitigated horseshit— pardon the vernacular. They're going to think that not only were you a coldblooded killer — of a cop, no less — but also politically radical, part of the violent fringe of the anti-war movement..."

"You know that's bullshit!" I exploded.

"Hey, Jeffrey, remember, for the umpteenth time, what I know is irrelevant. I'm trying — *earnestly* trying — to make you see what they see, so that we can come up with a realistic, effective, and ultimately successful strategy. That's what this is all about, right?"

BLURRED IMAGES

* * * * *

Savage had already checked me into a room. So after a couple of hours of often-heated discussion, he said, "Class dismissed," gave me my key card, and suggested we meet in his suite at about six o'clock for another session, over dinner.

I stopped by my room and cursorily inspected it, judging it to be comfortable and functional (at least a notch or two above most of my accommodations during my years on the road), placed the bass in the closet, leaning it against a corner, left the hotel, and started walking briskly with no destination in mind.

My entire body was tense from the protracted, often emotional initial exchange with Savage. And my head was spinning; I was delirious with the knowledge that this was actually happening, that I had already begun the long flight home, but at the same time, I was daunted by the magnitude of the mission and by the fear of failing. Could we really pull it off?

And what about this man, this savior, on whom I was now so totally dependent? Politics aside, Savage was an intimidating, provocative individual. I had hoped for sympathy. I was getting anything but. He played his devil's advocate role too well. And in the back of my mind, I was still troubled by the question: with his make-up, his background, his world-view, why the hell was he doing this in the first place?

Eventually, maybe a half-hour later, my body relaxed a bit, and my head cleared. I oriented myself and made my way to the bus station, where I retrieved my battered suitcase from a key locker. I lugged it back to my hotel, and across the lobby to the elevators. Up in my room, I lay down on the bed and immediately fell into a deep sleep. The next thing I knew, the phone was ringing. On the second or third ring, I picked it up, and heard Savage saying, "Didn't we have an appointment?"

ARTHUR DIMOND

When I knocked on his door minutes later, he yelled out, "Come on in, it's open."

He was sitting on the same chair as at our first meeting. This time there was a magazine on his lap instead of a manila folder, and his feet rested on a hassock he had pulled over. All in all, he looked much more relaxed.

I apologized for being late, for needing to be called.

"It's OK, no big deal," he said with a wave of his hand. Then he said, "I'm having a Scotch. Would you like to join me?"

"Sure," I said. I wasn't much of a hard-alcohol drinker, but I didn't want to do anything to offend, to alter this expansive atmosphere. He told me to sit down. Then he quickly rose from his chair, grabbed his nearly empty glass, and walked over to a little kitchenette; for the first time, I noticed that he had a slight limp. He poured a generous portion of Scotch into a glass.

"Ice or straight up?"

"Ice... please."

He lifted the top of an ice bucket on the counter, stuck his hand in, grabbed a few cubes, and dropped them into my glass. Then he poured an inch or two of the amber fluid into his own glass and diluted it with a squirt of tap water.

He walked back across the room, this time more carefully due to the precious cargo, and presented me with the drink. Then he returned to his chair, placed his drink on the sidetable, and with a sigh, dropped down again into the cushions. He lifted up his glass, extended it toward me, and said, "Cheers." Then he took a substantial sip, and momentarily gazed out the window at the Sound, the sun descending towards it. I took in the same view. No doubt about it, it was a captivating sight.

Savage cleared his throat.

"So, Jeffrey, did you think much about our little conversation today? That is when you weren't sleeping— unless you dreamed about it, of course."

BLURRED IMAGES

He smiled, to make sure I knew he was kidding. He seemed to be doing his best now to ingratiate himself, to assure me that he had a cordial side, to avoid intimidating me. Who knows, maybe, political animal that he was, he was just playing me, making sure I didn't tell my dad that I thought his old friend, my new lawyer, was an asshole. Maybe, on the other hand, this was his technique, to relax me, get me to talk more easily and openly, to facilitate our task.

"Yes. I thought about it. A lot."

"Good. Any insights? Conclusions?... Questions?"

He took a sip of Scotch and looked at me thoughtfully, patiently.

"Yes. A question. Just one question."

"OK... Shoot!"

"Is this really going to happen? Are you really going to bring this off?"

"Why do you ask? Do you doubt my ability to make it happen?" he asked, amused rather than annoyed.

"No, no, nothing like that. It's really because it's just... just mind-boggling that after all this time, that we can do it, that we can get from here to there— and get there so quickly."

Looking thoughtful, Savage jiggled the cubes in his glass. After a moment, he said, "Jeffrey, do you know what the key is? Do you know what will get us from here to there, as you say?"

"No, I don't."

"Sympathy. We need to get people — the people who are critical in this process, critical to your fate — to see you as a person, a more complete person, outside of what you did, outside of their stereotype of you — all the stuff we talked about earlier today."

I didn't say anything.

"I'll bet you're wondering how we're going to do that, to actually do it, right?"

"Well..." I said, but he continued before I had a chance to say anything, to express a concern, state a few conditions. He charged ahead.

"Jeffrey, what we absolutely need to do is explain to them the main reason you want to come out, to go home. It's Danny."

I tried to interrupt but he ignored me and continued, rapidly and passionately. The first Scotch had relaxed him, the second one had seemingly energized him.

"Jeffrey, it's as simple as this. You need to humanize yourself, to make sure people understand you— because only through that understanding will they *sympathize* with you, and be prepared to rationalize the seeming leniency of your terms of surrender... Listen, Jeffrey, there are people out there who will say, 'Skin the cop-killer, hang him up by his nuts.' But I'm telling you, many of those very same people would understand family. Loyalty. Love. And they might even forgive you— just a little. They might even excuse you— after all those years... 'Hey, the guy's done his time,' they could say. 'Twenty-five years on the run, alone, lonely... He couldn't see his family. Hell, he couldn't attend his own mother's funeral. Now his brother's dying and his father could be right behind. Enough's enough, forgive and forget, let him come home.' I'm telling you, Jeffrey, the sympathy vote will win the day for you."

I just sat in that chair, gripping my glass, staring at Savage, emotionally drained by his speech. He stared right back.

"This has nothing to do with them," I eventually said, quietly but firmly.

"This has *everything* to do with them!" he said, maintaining his stare and clearly exasperated. Then he turned away and looked out at the Sound, now growing dark, demarcated by lights on its shores, and punctuated by lights on the ferries. When he turned back to me, he had somewhat regained his composure.

"Well, it's obvious we're not going to solve this one tonight," he said. "Let's revisit it later on. Right now, let's order dinner. I'm hungry."

BLURRED IMAGES

* * * * *

Over dinner of salmon and salad, washed down by a nice crisp white wine, we chatted about a variety of subjects — films, music, baseball, travel. Politics? He avoided it except occasionally to tell an anecdote or drop a name or two. Savage was a worldly man. Whatever the subject, he spoke comfortably and authoritatively. My world and worldview had been narrowly delineated for so long, so limited to me, my needs and wants and fears, that I was clearly and painfully ignorant of many larger things. I faked it for awhile, until our conversation essentially became a monologue by Savage punctuated by "Hmmmm's," monosyllabic comments, or supporting questions from me.

Now and then, Savage would interrupt himself to ask me a question, for example: "In your travels across this great country of ours, Jeffrey, what was your favorite region? favorite city?" Or something more general, such as: "What did you do with all that spare time, Jeffrey?" He would ask in an easy, chatty manner and I tried to respond in the same manner. But something in the abruptness of the question, something perhaps in his tone or expression set me off, told me that he was probing, searching for something.

Savage, sophisticated lawyer that he was, picked up on my reaction immediately. But initially, rather than pursuing the question, or challenging my reticence, or getting defensive, he shifted conversational gears. He returned to safe neutral subjects. And then when he shifted gears yet again, to continue the metaphor, he upshifted to more personal topics, and prefaced them with the disclaimer, "If I'm not being too personal, Jeff..."

In subsequent conversations, over numerous meals in that hotel suite —always in that suite! we were never seen in public together — he interspersed many personal questions with his anecdotes and observations. He saved the lawyerly questions designed to build a case for the lengthy working sessions we had between meals, sitting across from each other on those not-so-easy chairs. And Savage filled up a dozen or more legal pads and miniature audiotapes with a record of those exchanges.

But at meals, and we did share at least two of them a day, Savage would relax and expand, and try to get me to do the same. And after awhile, he would get into some of those personal areas. He would lower his voice to a more intimate level, lean forward ever so slightly, and ask, for example: "Jeffrey, did you ever have a girlfriend during those years on the road?" "Did you have any close relationships on the road?" "How did you deal with your loneliness?"

I gave him as little as I could. After all my years on the run, discretion was instinctive. The key to self-protection and survival. I was reticent to begin with; my situation made me chronically insular. Truth be told, too, there wasn't much to tell him. My life on the road was like a long, lonely march across an emotional desert. Linear and two-dimensional, with music my only real pleasure. I didn't form relationships — intimate or otherwise — because of the intrinsic transience of my life and because of my fears, my very genuine fears of being exposed and identified and apprehended. Virtually all my personal contacts were with my fellow band members. And only once did a real friendship form. That was with a piano player who wanted to seek fame and fortune in Australia, and have some fun along the way. He urged me to join him on this whimsical odyssey. And I was really tempted to do it. But, with no passport and great risks in obtaining and using one, I ultimately and reluctantly had to decline. A decision that highlighted and compounded my loneliness.

Women? Yes, there were women. I mean, we were musicians, for God's sake. And even though we were not exactly world-class musicians, there were women, often married women living humdrum lives in humdrum towns and cities who gravitated to second-tier suburban clubs, to that exotic breed of musical nomads who played those clubs. They were easy and fun, and some were even good-

BLURRED IMAGES

looking. They were out for a good-time, one-night-stand as much — no, more! — as we were. So after hours, we partied briefly in the clubs and then migrated to motel rooms. Many a morning I would wake up alone in bed with nothing to show for the previous night but a messy bed, some full ashtrays, and sometimes a mushy note written in lipstick with a phone number; once or twice the note was written on floral-scented lace panties. These kinds of nights got old and depressing. Sometimes I passed on them. But most of the time I didn't. I joined in because they passed for fun and helped me release pent-up tension. There was something else, too. My fellow band members thought I was weird enough as it was, without them thinking I was weird in the sexual orientation department. Lastly, the nighttimes were the worst times during these years, without something to fill them up, and replace — eclipse! — the loneliness with something that satisfied my physical needs and, more importantly, occasionally passed for intimacy.

I didn't tell Savage all this, or even close to all this. As I said before, I gave him terse guarded answers and he, seeing through this approach, apparently chose to ignore my answers and move on. But somewhere in the second week — I forget which question it regarded — he blew up.

"Jeffrey, why don't you tell me something about yourself? Why are you so afraid of opening up?"

"I'm not afraid..."

"Then what's your problem?"

"I don't have a problem."

"You're full of shit! You have a truckload of problems. And I can't help you until I know you — *really* know you — as a person, not some one-dimensional stick figure with a three-dimensional problem."

I looked at him, then down at my plate, at the remains of my hamburger. And then a few minutes later, I excused myself and went down to my room, to bed.

ARTHUR DIMOND

* * * * *

Early in the third week, Savage told me he was preparing to wrap up his case and move to Phase II — approaching the FBI with a proposal — and announced: "It's time to revisit that issue."

"What issue?" I asked.

"The sympathy issue," he said. "Remember, I told you from the get-go that this would be the key."

"And the key to the key is Danny— why I want to go back. Right?"

"Right. Exactly right."

"Well, I'm sorry. I just can't do it. I *won't* do it. It's too private. For Danny more than me. And I'm just not going to do it."

"What if I told you you could lose this whole bloody thing without the Danny issue?"

"The 'Danny issue'? Now it's an 'issue'"?

"Whatever you want to call it. To repeat: It's the key."

He paused, then continued.

"What if the authorities say, to guess at a likely quote, and please pardon the language, it's theirs not mine: 'Why the fuck should we cut a sweet deal for a cop-killing cocksucker like that?' And I say, 'Because he was a kid, and a good kid at that, and he didn't mean to do it. And what's more, he's suffered enough.' This supported by reams of legalisms and the details of what happened that day and a profile of your sweet, non-violent, apolitical self, your passion for fine music, et cetera et cetera. And they say, 'Who gives a shit? He killed a cop, he wants to come in from the cold, and we're not going to let him in. And that's that.'"

I stared at Savage for a moment, and then said: "You want my answer? OK, here it is. I'll take my chances. And that's that," I said, enjoying the effect of my mimickry.

Now Savage glowered at me, redfaced, exasperated.

BLURRED IMAGES

"You know what I think, Jeffrey?"

"I can guess."

"I'll be polite about it. I don't know why, but I'll be polite. I think you're terminally naive. And I think your high-mindedness is totally misplaced. If you're doing all this for Danny, I can tell you, unequivocally, you're not helping him or your case with this idiocy. You want to keep being a loser? You're writing the perfect script."

He stared at me for a moment, and then said with a sigh and a resigned gesture with his hands, "Well, I'm going to bed now. I'm all talked out, and I'm bone tired... Let me know if you come to your senses by morning."

I looked at him silently.

"You can show yourself out, OK?"

* * * * *

During the next two weeks, I saw relatively little of Savage. He went off during the day to meet initially with FBI agents, and then with a Federal judge. He gave me strict orders to stay in my room. He told me not to answer the phone, but to listen to messages as soon as they were left and the red light on the phone started blinking.

"This is a critical period, Jeff. We're out in the open."

"They don't know I'm in Seattle though, right?"

"They don't know, but they can guess. So stay out of circulation."

"But they don't even know what I look like."

"Jeffrey, I don't want to argue with you about this. In fact, I'm through arguing with you about anything. Just do what I'm telling you, OK? It's for your own good."

I nodded. And then he went off on our mission.

Our dinners together were less regular now— maybe every two or three nights, and they were brief, *pro forma* affairs. Between mouthfuls, while cutting his food, Savage gave me abbreviated, even cryptic, reports of his day's contacts. He gave terse replies to my questions, clearly telling me as little as possible. His cumulative annoyance with me — marked by occasional flashes of intense irritation, even anger — was palpable and consistent. Once, after several encounters like that, during a lengthy period of silence broken only by the sounds of utensils against china, I couldn't contain myself.

"Why are you acting like this?"
"Like what, Jeffrey?"
"Like you hate me."
"I don't hate you, Jeffrey."
"Then what is it?"
"I hate this case."
"You mean it's not your kind of case?"
"It's *not* my kind of case. You know that. It's old news."
"Then?"
"It's that you've forced me to run this case with one arm tied behind my back. Which means I can't be nearly as effective as I should be. Which means I — and you — can lose. And in case you didn't know — or haven't noticed — I hate to lose. That's what I really hate."

* * * * *

At the end of one of those sessions, I asked Savage, in deadly earnest, why he was doing this, handling this case, if he felt the way he did.

He looked directly at me and said, "I'm doing it for your father. He asked me, and I said yes."
"Just like that?"
"Just like that. He's never really asked me for anything."
"But this was no small favor."

BLURRED IMAGES

For the first time in quite awhile, he smiled, albeit ruefully.

"You're right," he said. "It was no small favor. I had to drop a few things to come out here to the beautiful Pacific Northwest and camp out with you."

Then he went silent again.

After awhile I asked the question I had wanted to ask many times before.

"How do you and my father know each other?"

He considered me as he finished chewing.

"That's a long story, and this has been a long day in a very long month. So I don't really have the energy to tell you the story."

"Can you tell me the short version?"

"You don't give up," he said and sighed. "OK, here's the shortest version. It's all I have the time or energy or patience for right now... It's actually a dedication in one of your dad's books. Maybe you've seen it."

I shook my head.

"OK, it goes something like this: *'To Jesse Savage, my dear friend and my stalwart comrade in arms on all fields of battle.'*"

* * * * *

A few afternoons later, earlier than he usually called, Savage summoned me to his suite, saying he had news for me. I hurriedly neatened up, threw some water on my face, ran down the hall to the elevators, and ascended to Savage's floor.

When I arrived, it was like the first time. The door was ajar. I knocked, Savage's now-familiar voice said, "Come in." And I entered.

This time, however, Savage was not nearly as crisp and commanding as he had been at our initial encounter. He was seated in that easy chair, his tie loosened but his suit jacket still on. He looked tired, sitting there massaging that bad leg of his, but he made an effort to smile.

"I did it," he said. "We have a deal. We can be on a plane tomorrow night. You'll see your family by Thursday morning."

The statement that it was he, not we, who won was not lost on me; I assumed it wasn't meant to be. Nor was Savage's lack of elation over the victory; it wasn't his kind of fight — he had established that repeatedly — and he clearly didn't win it the way he wanted to. But we won, we clearly won, and I was going home. That's the only thing that mattered.

CHAPTER VII

The nearly empty 727 descended into the blackness of northern Virginia, heading for the brightly lit runway of Dulles Airport. I sat between two men near the front of the coach section. On my left, next to the window, was Savage. On my right was an FBI agent from the Seattle office, assigned to escort me to the capital. Savage and I looked out the window. The FBI agent looked straight ahead. None of us spoke.

The plane touched down gently, cruised down the runway, and came to a gradual stop. When the signal was given, we got up and moved forward to the exit door; the captain and flight attendants were there, but rather than exchanging the usual banter — "Thanks for flying with us," "Have a good night" — they stood there stiffly, unsmiling, and nodded as we passed. Though there were no handcuffs — that was part of the deal, as stipulated by my father and executed by Savage — the crew had doubtless reviewed the flight roster and clearly knew who I was.

We arrived late at night— the last flight in. That was also part of the deal. And our destination was Washington, the seat of a now-more-tolerant government and the home of my father and my brother, and not western Massachusetts, the locale of my crime and the starting point of my odyssey. Indeed, after lengthy phone conversations during those last two weeks in Seattle, Savage had arranged a videoconference from Seattle with a Berkshire County prosecutor and judge in lieu of a court appearance, to resolve the federal-state issues and to

ARTHUR DIMOND

consummate the deal.

Now the FBI agent, a solemn, taciturn man with a narrow face, small eyes, and taut, shiny skin, gently grasped my elbow and ushered me through the exit door directly onto the special bus shuttle. Savage quietly followed.

There were plenty of seats but we all chose to stand and hold the stainless steel poles. In a few minutes, the bus doors softly closed and the vehicle moved quietly away from the plane. Though grasping the same pole, we looked past each other, through the large spotless windows, at the bright runway lights that punctuated the opaque northern Virginia countryside. As we approached the terminal, gracefully topped by a roof reminiscent of a ski-jump, Savage caught my eye and to my surprise, because he had never done it before, he winked and flashed a small, encouraging smile. Then, equally abruptly, he returned to his typically more serious expression.

The bus anchored itself sideways to the terminal gate. Green lights over the doors flashed and then the doors opened as quietly as they had closed. When they did, we were abruptly greeted by the force and noise and blinding, flashing incandescence of a small army of reporters, TV and radio crews, suddenly awakened to the climax of their mission. I turned, alarmed, questioning, back to Savage; he looked unsurprised, unfazed. Before I had a chance to ask the agent the same silent question, he was instinctively shielding me. And his right hand was out of his pants pocket and seemed poised.

An odd choreography ensued. The mass of reporters — maybe 25 — and cameras and lights and cables and recorders and paraphernalia, formed a dense, immovable, semi-circular wall. Microphones were shoved in my face and Savage injected himself between the mikes and me. So there I was, the star attraction, partially hidden by the agent and the lawyer. In the shadows. Familiar environment for the bassman. But I was no longer the bassman.

Savage, for his part, was like a man transformed. Over those five compressed weeks of talking and planning and periodic wrangling

BLURRED IMAGES

in that hotel suite, I had seen him in many modes, in many moods— thoughtful and sardonic, subdued and aggressive, charming and blunt. And also visibly tired, slumped in a chair, massaging that bad leg of his, as on that evening when he announced the deal.

No fatigue was detectable now. Nor, miraculously, any trace of that limp. He was out front now, at center stage, in the lights, effectively eclipsing me and our agent escort. Standing there in his expensive, well-tailored, blue suit with a polka-dotted kerchief bursting from his breast pocket like a summer flower in full bloom. Savage was clearly in charge.

Maybe it was the wink, maybe the smile. Maybe the stance, straight, shoulders squared, feet apart, hands free. Maybe the ultra-confident manner of this short, compact, physically fit lawyer. Whatever it was, I had the sense that he was going to go off whatever script he and I had ultimately more or less agreed to.

In one of our few exchanges on the long flight, I had asked Savage whether my father was going to be at Dulles. He had responded by subtly jerking his head up an inch or two in the Arab manner, I think, and saying "Nyet." A glib little joke and mixing of metaphors that had the instant effect of irritating me. I must have looked at him curiously, questioningly, because he said something like, "It'll be a bit late for him... Past his bedtime, you know." That flip remark surprised me — since whenever he spoke of my father, it was always with respect and affection — and irritated me further. I didn't pursue the matter. But as he stood at the Dulles gate, in the glare of lights and the presence of mikes in a corner of an otherwise deserted terminal, I understood things better. I understood that Savage had his own agenda, a distinct variation on the primary one, the discreet, low-keyed one we had discussed in our final sessions, after he had completed the deal, as we prepared for re-entry. That he had a separate speech, all memorized. That he had thought a lot about this scene. That he had probably planned it out meticulously and then kept his own counsel. That this, perhaps, was the reward he gave himself for having to wage an unwanted fight and to win his victory under a handicap. He clearly didn't want my father to witness — let alone participate in — any of it.

Savage held up his hands, palms out, and flipped them down a few times. In moments, the horde went silent except for the click and whir of automatic 35 mm cameras, camcorders, and audiotape recorders, the shuffling of notepad paper, a muffled comment or titter.

"Thanks for meeting us out here... especially at this hour... You know, it's really a bummer getting off a plane to a lonely airport, nobody there to greet you," he said and flashed that wink and grin, and they all laughed. Then he paused, looked down, then up, and began speaking in serious and portentous tones. I held my breath and willed myself to look up, at Savage.

"I'm Jesse Savage, Jeffrey Stevenson's attorney. And I'm here with Mr. Stevenson and with Agent Connerton of the FBI. We've just arrived from Seattle where Mr. Stevenson surrendered to the authorities. In a round of discussions there over a period of a few weeks, we first reached agreement with federal prosecutors on the terms of the surrender— principally involving the charge of unlawful flight to avoid prosecution. We formalized the agreement in subsequent sessions with a U. S. Federal Court judge in Seattle. Then, in a series of long distance phone conversations, exchange of documents, and videoconference sessions, we dealt with and resolved the federal-state issues and the purely Massachusetts issues— the heart of the case.

"In brief, after an extensive review of the case, state and federal authorities have concluded that there were clearly extenuating circumstances involved. To cut to the chase— There was no premeditation. None whatsoever. Jeffrey Stevenson had never committed a violent act in his life and he had absolutely no intention of committing a violent act on that day 25 years ago. As a result, the original charge of first degree murder has been reduced to involuntary manslaughter; Mr. Stevenson has pleaded guilty to this charge. And the federal charge of unlawful flight to avoid prosecution has

BLURRED IMAGES

been dropped."

Savage paused dramatically and briefly surveyed the assemblage. Then he continued in the same methodical, lawyerly tone.

"Net-net?... Mr. Stevenson has received a sentence of ten years probation. He will not be required to go to prison. He will, however, be required to report regularly to the authorities, and to perform one thousand hours of community service. He's returned to Washington, D.C. to be with his family—a family from which he's been separated all these years. And arrangements have been made with the Massachusetts authorities for him to begin fulfilling his probationary and community service obligations here. That's it... Any questions?... Please direct them at me."

The floodgates opened and a cacophony of "Mr. Stevenson"'s flew at me from all directions. Savage shot both arms up, looking for a moment like a football ref calling a "touchdown."

"Wait a minute! I just told you that all questions have to be directed at me. Mr. Stevenson has been instructed not to speak..."

"Instructed by who?" someone shouted.

"By *me!*" Savage shot back. "I'm his *lawyer!*"

Then he softened, saying, "There will no doubt be opportunities later... For now, I'll take the questions."

Even in our final planning sessions, we weren't really planning. Savage was laying out *his* script, at least the one he would share with me, in a dispassionate, premeditated lawyerly manner. A crisp, directed, seamless delivery leaving no pauses, no air for alternate or contrary opinions— except that one concerning the "Danny issue," and that critical one I won. On everything else, I nodded not so much in agreement but in a kind of obligatory assent. An acquiescence I was not proud of then, and even less proud of now— Mr. Bassman still playing in the rhythm section. It was an acquiescence borne of numbing fatigue from those weeks of tension and anticipation. Of my gratitude for the deal, the victory, and of not really thinking much beyond it. And, also, of the relief of being freed from the effort of concentrating, of dealing with the potential responsibility of the limelight, after all those years in the shadows— Mr. Bassman being asked to play a surprise solo, a long, virtuoso, highly *improvised* solo requiring skill, elegance, and some daring. I abdicated to the band leader— but not without considerable ambivalence.

Here was the result. Here on this *ad hoc* airport stage, Savage was making me feel like the kid, not the grown-up client paying for the big problem created by a kid. Professor Stevenson's fucked-up son. The one who went off the deep end. He could handle me any way he wanted in public because he was my human shield, and my problem solver. He was the big guy who knew best, who knew the ways things worked and how to make them work for him. And he knew something else. He knew how much I needed him at this moment. Because he also knew how scared I was. More than scared. Terrified. With the shock of re-entry. Come in from a long, dark night, into this fierce, seething arena. Switch on 50 megawatts of power, and perform. Better him than me and I was relieved. I was ashamed to admit it, but I was truly relieved.

Now I braced myself for the first question.

Fire one.

"Why did Mr. Stevenson turn himself in now? After all these years?"

"It was time. He was on the run for 25 years — a quarter-century of isolation, of loneliness... And the climate was right.. A new administration... The other party... Hey, we have a president who could have been in his place."

There were a few laughs.

Fire two.

"Jeff Stevenson *murdered a police officer*. How did he get off so easy?"

"First of all, he didn't — technically — *'murder'* a police officer. The charge — once all the facts have been laid on the table — is involuntary manslaughter. And second, he didn't get off easy— he's

BLURRED IMAGES

already served a 25-year sentence. And unlike incarcerated prisoners, he didn't know what his sentence really was; it could have been life. Furthermore, he was denied communication with his family, he was denied parole, and he had to support himself under the most difficult of circumstances. And finally, he does have some stiff requirements under his sentence. His life still isn't entirely his own."

There were a few more laughs, and a peppering of sarcastic smirks. Savage, maintaining his authoritative demeanor, didn't acknowledge them.

Fire three.

"Is your client the last fugitive from the '60's antiwar era to turn himself in or be apprehended?"

"Well, I haven't been keeping count... but as far as I know, he's the last of the FBI's 'Most Wanted' list to come forward... There may be others who aren't as notorious as Jeff Stevenson." And he laid that last line on so thick I could no longer look up. The ludicrousness of it all.

Fire four.

"Do you view Jeff Stevenson as a *symbol* of that '60's antiwar era?"

Savage paused — dramatically — for a moment, then smiled gently, uncharacteristically.

"Gentlemen — ladies — symbols aren't my business. They're yours. You create symbols. Maybe to magnify the significance of what you do, what you cover. I just represent clients, human beings with problems. Jeff Stevenson was wanted for 25 years for the death — the *unintended* death — of a police officer... The incident happened at an antiwar demonstration at a college... Abby Hoffman and Jerry Rubin were the main speakers... Throw it all together and you have a powerful symbolic stew... But take the individual elements and you have a case of an innocent, apolitical young man — *barely* a man, more a boy than a man — being in the wrong place at the wrong time. End of story."

Savage scanned the room quickly, then spoke again.

"Now we've had a long day, a long few weeks, Mr. Stevenson, Agent Connerton, and myself... So let's call it a night after one more question." Amidst a chorus of "Mr. Savage"'s and a fluttering of raised hands, Savage pointed to a thirtyish woman in the back, a print reporter judging from her pad and pen and seeming absence of props and equipment and coterie.

"Mr. Savage, how does a man with a background like yours — *politics* like yours — come to represent a man like Jeffrey Stevenson?"

"How would you characterize 'politics like mine,' Miss....?"

"Palmer."

She paused for a moment, then said: "Slightly to the right of your ex-boss."

A few reporters laughed.

"I think you're being generous, Miss Palmer," he said, giving rise to even more laughter.

"To whom?"

"Whomever."

"OK, whomever... As you said, time is short here... So let's cut to the chase... How come you're representing Jeff Stevenson?"

"As I said a few minutes ago, I represent human beings with problems... and Jeff Stevenson clearly fits that description... Anything else, Miss Palmer?"

"No, I don't think so... I prefer to do my dancing in ballrooms, not airports."

Savage glared at her for a moment, then took in the whole crowd, and said, "Thank you all for coming."

The TV lights stayed on and followed us as Savage grasped my elbow and, with Connerton right behind, ushered me around the crowd of reporters, out of the lounge area, toward the escalators and then down to the lower level. A young, fresh-faced guy in a dark suit approached us, pushing a cart bearing our luggage — Savage's

BLURRED IMAGES

matched blue valise and suitbag, Connerton's black leather overnight bag, and my beat-up brown vinyl suitcase. I had actually wanted something more presentable for my re-entry, for my coming-out party, but Savage insisted that I use my old battered, weathered piece; he said he thought it would be "a nice touch" to help reinforce the image of a "deprived," road-weary fugitive ("You mean 'slightly pathetic?'" I asked. "As you like," he replied). I was ashamed to admit that I was more than a bit discomfited — embarrassed — by that image.

The young associate, still pushing the cart, led the way to the exits, through the automatic doors, and out to the curb where another young associate, a very serious black man, also in a dark business suit, plus white shirt and funereal tie, sat behind the wheel of a sleek silver BMW. When the first associate tapped on the passenger side window, the other guy turned quickly, flipped the trunk, and flung open his door— seemingly all in one fluid motion. The two associates moved Savage's various pieces of sporting equipment— his golf clubs, tennis racquets, balls, gloves, hats, and navy-blue leather bag with some club insignia on it. Then they carefully loaded our bags in the newly reclaimed space.

As we got into the car — the two young associates up front, Savage, Connerton, and I in the back, me wedged in the middle, just like on the plane — we were suddenly bathed in light. The TV crews had caught up with us. Through the window, Savage smiled and waved in a statesmanlike manner. Then he quickly turned to the driver and barked, "Get the fuck out of here!... but *don't gun it!*"

We slowly pulled away from the curb, the cameras and lights following us as we moved down the road along that graceful terminal toward the airport exit.

Soon we were cruising at a moderate speed down a dark and nearly empty highway toward the capital. One of the associates, the black guy, I think, asked how things went, and Savage grunted something like, "What you might expect." He didn't elaborate and the associate didn't pursue it. Savage just looked out the window or straight ahead at the dark, desolate road. I couldn't tell whether he was still irritated at that last question or was lost in thought or just plain tired. Or maybe he figured that now that the lights and mikes were gone, why bother? I felt a slight movement and noticed that he was gently massaging that leg again.

The brightness of Washington radiated into the black, moonless night from some distance away. And then suddenly, as we came around a long gradual curve, we were almost upon the city. We crossed the Arlington Memorial Bridge, over the Potomac, and headed toward the Lincoln Memorial, lit up like the crown jewel it was, directly ahead, with the Washington Monument and the Capitol lined up neatly in the distance.

We reached the other end of the bridge, skirted the majestic memorial, and then eased onto the road alongside the inky river, past the glittering Kennedy Center and the ill-starred Watergate, two buildings that I had never seen, that had not existed when I was last in Washington during one of my father's sabbaticals.

We proceeded into Rock Creek Park, on roads whose every twist and turn I got to know so well as an adventurous teenager on an Italian racing bike.

And then we exited onto tranquil, residential streets enshrouded by stately oaks and elms and bordered by expansive brick and wood-frame houses set comfortably apart from each other. And within minutes, we came to a halt in front of a lovely Victorian, a miniature variation of that childhood house of long, long ago. The porch light was on, as was a living room lamp and another in an upstairs room. The black associate said, "Happy landings!" and flipped open the trunk lock from his seat. I shook hands with Savage, and when I thanked him, he said, "Well, it's been interesting, Jeffrey. Give my best to your dad. We'll be in touch." Then Connerton opened his door, stepped out to let me out, and got back in without a word or a smile or a handshake. I hoisted out my battered bag and my bass and placed them on the asphalt of the street, then slammed the trunk shut. I looked at the

BLURRED IMAGES

backs of the two heads through the rear window, then walked slowly up the herringbone-pattern brick walk to the house.

I trudged up the five broad wooden porch steps. When I reached the top, I noticed that the main front door was open. I softly placed the suitcase down and peered through the screen door into the dim hallway, debating whether to ring the bell or try the screen door and simply walk in.

A sudden thump on the porch floor made me jump. I turned quickly and there, in the far corner of the porch, was my father, slumped in a straight-backed white wicker chair, his head down, chin resting on his chest, arms hanging over the sides, black-rimmed glasses dangling delicately from thumb and forefinger. A thick manuscript lay on the floor in front of him, having apparently just slid off his lap.

I was touched, genuinely touched, that he had waited up for me, tried to stay awake to greet me. I stood there for several long minutes, studying this old man who was my father. With his head down, I could see only the top of his head. He always had beautiful hair and it was still beautiful— white and silky and parted with decisiveness. Just less of it, with the pink scalp and blue protruding veins showing through, looking so exposed and vulnerable.

What struck me, though, was his presence, his *physical* presence. He was diminished; that was the only word I could think of. Once such a powerfully built, formidable — often intimidating — figure, he now seemed half the size, frail, small-boned, brown moles and liver spots dotting loose white skin. And he was sleeping, breathing deeply, noisily, through his mouth.

The one familiar, reassuring facet of his appearance was his clothing— crisp white shirt (though tieless and open at the collar), sharply creased grey suit pants, and high-shined oxfords — always high-shined — planted firmly on the wood planks, a foot or so apart, the manuscript splayed out between them.

I sat down across from him, just a few feet away, in a matching chair, and continued to observe and absorb, appreciating this rare opportunity. I don't see my father for 25 years and now I see him in this purest of forms. I sat like that for a half-hour, on that porch where I had never sat, at a nether hour reserved for bass players and other creatures of the night. I didn't make a sound and I didn't move except to alternate crossed legs. I didn't want to do anything to alter or disturb or abbreviate the moment.

Eventually he stirred. He moved his hands, stretched his arms down and then out like a big bird preparing for flight. He slowly lifted his head. He opened and blinked his eyes — those ice-blue eyes that had once so intimidated me — and stared at me. He didn't seem startled at my being there. And he didn't seem to doubt that it was I; after all, he was expecting me and I was there, more or less at the appointed hour. Yet he was clearly puzzled about something. His eyes wide open now, his back more upright, he sat up and seemed to focus all his energy on me, on each of my features. He ran his fingers through that lustrous white mane of hair, and his eyebrows arched, forming four or five deep parallel, zig-zag crevices across his forehead. And he continued to stare.

"Dad?"

He didn't answer.

"Dad... it's me... I'm home."

He nodded absently.

"Is something wrong?"

"No... No, nothing's wrong... It's just..."

"Just what... Do I look different than you expected?"

"Yes, very different...Age, I guess."

I was leaning forward in my chair now, my face a mere two or three feet from his.

"There's something else, Dad. Look even closer."

And he did. He leaned slightly forward himself and stared even harder. And when he finally moved his head back and again settled into his chair and relaxed, I felt he understood. I attempted

BLURRED IMAGES

to explain anyway.

"I had to survive, Dad... I had to do a lot of things to survive... That's just the most obvious... And I've changed in many, many ways— some ways I don't even know about..."

My father was now gazing more calmly at me, not saying a word, letting me talk, seemingly listening, hopefully listening.

"Dad, I've been on the run for half a lifetime... I have a different face... I've had a half-dozen different names... and even more different life stories... I don't even know who I am anymore."

Tears were welling up in my eyes and my voice was catching, and my shoulders were trembling, and I didn't know what to do or say next to this old man who was my father whom I hadn't seen for 25 years, who had often been a stranger then, more an icon than a complete man and father. I dropped my head between my knees and took deep breaths to control myself and suppress the tears and regain my voice and composure. To my surprise and relief, I felt a firm comforting hand on one shoulder and then his voice, an unfamiliar warm and soothing sound that nearly made me break down with gratitude.

"I know who you are... You're my son, Jeffrey Stevenson... And you have one life story... And you're home... And I'm only sorry — so terribly, terribly sorry, sorrier than you'll ever know — that it took so long and it took what it did to make it happen."

And now his voice was breaking, and his face was damp with tears and his frail upper body was trembling with emotion. And then we did something we had never in my memory done before. We reached out and, still seated, spontaneously embraced and sobbed on each other's shoulders, and stayed that way for what seemed like a very long time.

93

CHAPTER VIII

Once, twice, three times, maybe more, my sleep was interrupted by insistent ringing. A clock? A phone? I couldn't tell.

My body was still in Seattle and besides it knew only the nocturnal schedule and rhythms of the bassman. It felt the profound fatigue produced by chronic wariness and defensive thinking, the occupational hazard of the non-stop, real-life chess player.

So I slept. Fitfully maybe. But I slept nonetheless. When I finally opened my eyes and became conscious of the fact that I was awake and safely in bed in my father's house, I rolled partially over on my side, looking for a clock, and once finding it, saw it was one in the afternoon. I rolled completely over on my back, put my hands behind my head and lay there gazing up at the sun-brightened ceiling, its surface shimmering with the shadows of gently swaying branches. In another few moments, I hefted my head and neck higher up on the wonderfully soft pillows and took a good look around this new room in this unfamiliar house.

It was a cozy little room, like a little girl's hideaway, with sharply angled eaves and a gabled window on either side. The walls were lavender and the curtains were white and chiffony. If there were a doll's house on a shelf or dresser, I wouldn't have been at all surprised.

I got out of bed and placed my bare feet on a soft, colonial-style oval throw rug. I walked to the rear window and looked out over a generous and very pleasant and informal yard. There was a lovely

BLURRED IMAGES

brick patio with white chaise lounges and a neatly trimmed, very healthy-looking lawn punctuated by a few young dogwoods and bordered by azaleas and rhododendrons and a number of shrubs I didn't recognize and a splash of tulips here and there. In the far corner was an inviting hammock slung between two venerable maples.

Neighboring houses were a comfortable distance away, their yards and patios and decks protected by hedges and Rose of Sharons and evergreens of all kinds.

I gazed out at this view for some minutes and deeply breathed in this new air, this new *atmosphere*.

My father had left a plaid flannel robe over the arm of an easy chair in the room and a pair of slippers, side by side, in front of the chair on the floor. I was struck by both his thoughtfulness and his sense that these were not likely possessions of a man on the run.

I studied myself in the full-length closet-door mirror. I didn't *look* like a man on the run. Rather, I looked like an average, workaday guy on a Saturday morning, tired eyes, gray stubble, with an itinerary no more urgent than the dry cleaner, hardware store, and lawn.

I turned, left the room, and descended the stairs. I had no trouble finding my father. He was out on the porch, seated in that same wicker chair with the same manuscript back on his lap. He had changed his clothes and looked fresher and crisper in an open-necked white shirt and what appeared to be suit pants, these brown-checked, and shiny, light-brown wing-tipped shoes. He looked up, smiled, and closed the manuscript, carefully inserting an index card in his place.

For an 80-year-old man, he looked remarkably good. He had shaved his beard at some point, leaving just his mustache, and his features still looked prominent, his skin rosy and shiny and showing less jowl and slack than I would have expected, than I had remembered from the early morning hours of this new, strange day.

It was the eyes that captured my attention. All the years, the fatigue and the sadness, and the bouts of grief, seemed lodged in those large, ice-blue eyes. As the poets — or shrinks? — would say, they were truly the windows into the heart and soul of this often opaque man. I thought they revealed a softness, a tenderness — a vulnerability? — that had never been evident before.

"Good morning, Dad," I said.

"Good morning, Jeff... Or should I say afternoon?"

I smiled, then looked around and out at the green and tranquil suburban scene.

"This is a nice spot, Dad... real nice."

"Yes, I enjoy it. It's not quite like the old place..."

"The 'manor'?"

"Yes, the 'manor,'" he said, with a smile. "I'm glad I have it... especially now."

He didn't elaborate. He just followed my visual tour of the porch and frontyard and street.

Then, abruptly, he said, "You know, you're a hot story."

"Oh, yeah?"

"You sound surprised."

"I am... I guess I shouldn't be, especially after the airport scene...Have you spoken to Savage?"

"Yes. Briefly this morning."

"What'd he say?"

"He said everything went fine. A lot of excitement at the airport. But otherwise fine."

I was going to offer my strong suspicion that Savage engineered some of that excitement, but decided to restrain myself.

"You know, you're both all over the papers... The *Post* has a front page story."

"I don't think Savage is upset about that."

"No, I don't suppose so," my father said, and smiled.

"What's the headline?"

He reached out to the side table and pulled the newspaper — soft and limp from constant handling — from under his manuscript and handed it to me.

BLURRED IMAGES

'VIETNAM-ERA FUGITIVE SURFACES IN CAPITAL; Killer of Policeman Cuts Deal with Government, Turns Self In'

I stared at the headline and then at the pictures. Me and Savage at the airport, getting into the getaway car. My official college student-ID shot, taken at freshman registration, looking clean-cut, serious, mock-mature, so young and innocent just inches before the threshhold to a new, knowing era. Then that famous one, the "smoking gun," the one some student had shot and sold to the AP. There I was, in mid-swing with that childhood bat, a split-second away from ending one life and forever changing another.

I looked up. Dad was studying me, large eyes larger still, questioning, trying to detect my reaction. I shrugged, looked down, and read the entire story. It was surprisingly straight and factual; words like "middle-aged" and "stocky" and "fugitive" jumped up at me, but that was it— no major problems. More serious and steadily irritating as I thought about it was the reference to my silence throughout the airport event, to my "role of the passive participant in his own big drama." Then, on the jump page, next to the story's conclusion, was a black-boxed commentary:

'END OF AN ERA'

I was "the last Vietnam-era fugitive to return," "the central character in the last chapter," "a symbol," "a bellwether."

I looked up at my father, still studying me, and said, "This is incredible bullshit."

He nodded and attempted a small smile. "I would put it more elegantly, but nonetheless, you ain't seen nothing yet."

His eyes darted quickly to the street. I turned. A dark-blue American sedan — a Ford or a Dodge — had stopped in front of the house and two guys in windbreakers were looking up at us. I rose from my chair and one of them whipped out a camera and shot a picture. When I made a move for the porch stairs, they shot again and then jumped back into the car and drove off.

"Who are they?"

This time Dad shrugged.

"I have no idea... All I can say is there are a lot of people interested in you... As I said, you're a hot topic."

"The phone calls this morning?"

He nodded.

"Who were they?"

"A mix."

"A mix of what? Who? Media?"

"Some."

"Yeah, and who else?"

"Some people who think you're a hero... and some who think you're the devil incarnate."

"You've got to be kidding."

"I'm not. Trust me. I'm not... You have no idea what you've stirred up here... what *we've* stirred up."

"Why the hell did Savage hold that damned press conference? That circus?... We could have done this whole thing quietly."

"It wouldn't have made any difference. Somebody would've leaked it... if not here, then back in Massachusetts, and that would've been a lot worse... You know what the message would be?"

"I guess."

"Well, we're probably guessing the same thing— that you would look like you were ashamed, afraid, whatever."

I quietly absorbed that for a minute or so. Then I blurted, "But a damned *press conference*?"

"Listen, Jeff, that was part of the deal."

"With the FBI?... The Justice Department?"

"Are you serious? Do you think they'd want it known that they let a guy like you off with such a good deal? That they paved the way

BLURRED IMAGES

for an even better deal with the state authorities?"

"Savage?"

"Jeff, welcome to Washington," he said, and smiled in a bemused sort of way. I didn't smile back. And Dad got immediately serious again.

"Jeff, please, don't look so shocked. Listen, I hired Savage because only somebody like him could bring this off... Look at him. You know his credentials, his background, at this point. You know what kind of man he is. You spent the last five weeks locked in a hotel room with him. You don't have to be a Washington animal to know what he's like at this point."

I nodded.

"He's a tough — and brilliant — guy who can deal with the Feebies... and bulldoze the state-level people... And nobody can accuse him of being soft on anything. And he pulled it off— better and faster than I could have imagined."

"And the press conference — and God knows what else is going on — that's the payoff?"

He smiled sheepishly.

"If you want to put it that way... It's how the game is played. I'm not saying I approve of it— but it's how it's played... and if we don't play, you don't score any points and you certainly don't win... Anyway, the story would leak out slowly and randomly and perhaps far more hazardously."

The phone rang. I looked at it, sitting on the wicker table between us, and then questioningly at my father. At first, he made no move. Then, on the fifth ring, right before the message system would switch on, Dad picked it up.

"Hello?... Hello?... Yes... No, it's his father... Yes, **Professor** Stevenson... No, he's still sleeping... Sure, sure."

He took down a message and placed the receiver back on the hook.

"That was *The Today Show*... They want you on tomorrow from the Washington studio."

"Are you serious?"

"Quite."

I stared at him.

"Look, Dad, I'm not ready ... I just came out of a kind of cave... into these bright lights... Do you understand that?"

"Yes, I do understand... I really do."

"Do you understand that I came home to be with you... with Danny... to get some kind of life back. I don't have any messages for anybody. I was the wrong guy then — just unlucky — and I'm the wrong guy now. I don't have anything to say to anybody outside this family."

"So what's your answer? I've been taking calls like this all morning... and there'll be more, believe me."

"Is this Savage's PR work?"

"Probably... but I wish you'd understand it would have happened anyway. This is a *bona fide* news event... and you, my boy, for better or worse, are the undisputed star."

He smiled, oddly pleased with his neat rendition.

"So what would you suggest?"

"I'd suggest a compromise. Don't say no. Say yes, but not now. Tell them the truth. You just came here. You need time to adjust, to think... to..."

"No, not that one... I know what you're thinking. I will see Danny— in fact I want to see him soon. Today. But I'm not going to use him as a reason, an excuse, for anything. This part is totally, absolutely, personal. I made that absolutely clear to Savage from the start."

Dad turned suddenly serious, even somber.

"Jeff, I'm with you on that. Completely with you... But look, let's settle this media thing before it gets even bigger, more complicated, which we both know it will... I want to help but we have to be together."

BLURRED IMAGES

"You mean we need a 'unified policy position'?" I asked and smiled. That deflated things, relieved the tension.

"Yes, that's exactly what I mean," he said, and smiled back.

"OK, I accept your compromise. I'll do it, but give me time."

"Oh, that's great... Now they're going to ask, 'How much time?'"

"I don't know. I don't know how I'm going to feel..."

"Just give them something to work with... to get them off your back for awhile. Mine, too, by the way. They live and die by the calendar."

"OK... in a month."

He laughed.

"What's so funny?" I asked.

"Jeff, they'll never buy that... Next month is like the next millenium to these guys... That's when they like to talk to historians like me."

"OK, two weeks."

"How about one? Next week. Tell your story before people start telling it for you. And some of those people aren't necessarily your friends. You're not going to like their version."

"OK, Dad, OK, you've convinced me. Let's just do it. Next week. And get it over with."

Dad opened his mouth, about to say something— I had a pretty good idea what. But he stopped himself before uttering a word. For him, an extraordinary act of will power.

CHAPTER IX

Danny was sitting on the edge of his bed, clad in maroon paisley pajamas, a plastic IV tube snaking up his right sleeve.

He was just sitting there, looking down blankly, a queasy expression on his sallow face.

There was my brother Danny, my handsome, jaunty brother, sitting motionless on the edge of a hospital bed. Not a middle-aged man. But an *old* man. *Ancient.* Gaunt and bald, and profoundly sad-looking. He didn't see me, so I stood in the doorway for a few minutes. Silently absorbing the scene. Suppressing a geyser of tears.

I turned quickly and walked briskly down the fluorescent-lit corridor and took shelter in the bathroom near the nurses' station. It was a one-person room so I locked the door and leaned with both arms on the sink and let the tears well up and stream down my face and drip in the sink as I stared at myself in the mirror.

I heard the doorknob moving and then a polite knock on the door.

"Occupied," I said softly.

The knocking resumed.

"Occupied," I said more loudly. The knocking stopped. And I continued in that position, leaning straight-armed against the sink, staring at my own image, looking for answers, for solace, for something. Finally, when my arms grew tired, I stood up and breathed deeply in that small, antiseptic room, sealed in from the world by shiny floor-to-ceiling pink tile and the whirring of the

BLURRED IMAGES

ventilation fan.

There was another series of knocks, louder, more insistent. And then a slightly urgent female voice.

"You OK in there?"

And I realized I had been in the room for some time. Clearly, audibly, I said, "Yes. Thank you... I"ll be out in a minute."

I turned on the cold water and rinsed my face and dried it with paper towels. I stuck a hand in my shirt pocket, looking for a comb. No luck. I ran my fingers through my wavy hair and created some semblance of neatness. Then I stood back from the mirror to take a look. Satisfied that I didn't appear either ill or suicidal — a distinct possibility when a man locks himself into a one-person hospital bathroom for 20 or 30 minutes or more, who knew? — I turned the knob and briskly, purposefully, opened the door. Sure enough, two nurses and an orderly were waiting expectantly.

"You OK?" one of the nurses asked, genuine concern in her look and tone.

"Yes. Thank you. I'm fine," I said. "I just had some momentary faintness," I explained, feeling I owed them that.

"You want to lie down?"

"No, really, I'm OK now... But thank you."

"Are you here to see one of the patients?" the nurse asked, a little more of a defensive probe in her voice now that the potential emergency was passed.

"Yes," I said.

"May I ask who?"

"Sure... Daniel Stevenson."

And in that moment, everything came together for the nurse. With her apparently new understanding, she simply said, "I see... Do you know where he is?"

I said I did, thanked her, and walked slowly down the corridor, feeling the eyes of the nurses and orderly on my back, following me.

ARTHUR DIMOND

When I got to the room, Danny was up, on his feet, in his robe and slippers. His eyes, however, still harbored that vacant look, and his mouth that tight, uncomfortable set. The IV tube was attached to the clear plastic bag mounted on a spindly, stainless steel unit with wheels. A nurse was grasping his elbow.

The nurse noticed me first. She looked up and nodded and said, "Hello." Curtly, flatly. Then Danny turned his head a few degrees toward me, and a dim light went on in those eyes. The light grew brighter with gathering recognition. And in another few moments, he broke into an enormous grin. I grinned back just as broadly. With some apparent discomfort, the nurse looked at each of us and asked if Danny needed her any longer. He said no and she quickly excused herself and left.

Danny took a halting step forward and looked at me for a long minute. Just looked at me, studying every feature of my redesigned face, seemingly trying very hard to bridge the years, to make the connection between who we were so long ago and who we were and where we were today. At that moment.

Finally, with some considerable effort, he cleared his throat and in a low gravelly tone, said: "Jeff, I'm so happy you're here. So happy. You have no idea." And he lifted and extended his arms and I stepped forward into the berth formed by those arms, and wrapped my own arms around my brother, feeling his ribs through his pajamas, hugging him, he me, and sobbing softly. And in those few minutes, I felt so gratified to be there.

Eventually, we gently released each other and looked at each other again. I suddenly felt uncomfortable and tongue-tied. So much emotion and anticipation had been invested in this moment, I couldn't get beyond the climax. Or I needed to prolong it.

I looked down at the speckle-tiled floor and towards his portable IV unit, and said, "You were going for a walk?" And he said, "Yes," and smiled. "May I join you?" And he nodded and smiled more broadly this time, gave the unit pole a light nudge forward, and took

BLURRED IMAGES

his first tentative, shuffling steps toward the doorway.

    We turned right, away from the nurses' station, and moved slowly down the corridor, Danny gently pushing the unit, then catching up, me walking alongside, my arm around his waist, as tiny as a young child's.

    We didn't say anything for awhile. We just shuffled down the shiny, pristine avenue, slowly but evenly, and gazed at the multifarious images. Patients seen through partially open doors, lying on their backs at various angles, talking quietly to visitors or staring at the ceiling tiles or TV pictures or into space. Other patients moving jerkily down the corridor preceded by stainless steel walkers or cruising by on smooth rubber-wheeled electric-powered wheelchairs like sleek limousines on an open highway. Nurses checking charts on the walls next to room entries or peering in at patients. Doctors on their rounds, in stylish suits and blazers and trousers and tassled loafers, breezing by importantly, stethoscopes suspended from necks, clipboards under arms, pagers clasped to leather belts.

    I glanced over at Danny, to my left, looking dead-set ahead, concentrating on the clock on the far wall or the IV unit pole or on nothing at all.

    We reached the end of the corridor and made our left turn and continued at the same pace, still saying nothing.

    He finally did say something, with a purposefulness that suggested he'd been thinking about it for awhile. But I couldn't quite make out the words, they were so soft and abrupt.

    "What's that, Danny?"

    Without looking at me, his eyes still directed straight ahead, he cleared his throat, and slightly louder and more distinctly, said: "I always pictured a walk in the woods."

    I thought about that statement for a few minutes, wondering what he meant, wanting to understand, to understand *exactly* what he meant. I turned to him and he, taking my questioning look as a cue, cleared his throat again. That sour, queasy expression crossed his lips again. And when it passed, he continued.

"I always knew you'd be home... Someday... one way or another... you'd be home... And we'd take a walk... A walk in the woods... Not here... But back home... you know, our real home... you know where I mean, around the lake, towards the little falls..."

He half-turned toward me and I nodded and smiled. He smiled back and then turned away, looking straight ahead, charting our course between those walkers and wheelchairs and slow-motion visitors and serious, fast-forward professionals.

"I never pictured this," he said, encompassing the bright-white arcade, the traffic, his IV unit, all with a disdainful, dismissive wave of the free hand.

We crept along now in silence, making two more turns, and eventually arrived back at his room. Danny was breathing more rapidly from the exertion. "You OK?" I asked.

"OK?" he echoed, and smiled strangely.

"You know what I mean."

"Yeah," he said.

I helped him to a sitting position on the edge of the bed. He sat there for a few minutes, breathing deeply, staring ahead.

"You want to lie down?" I asked.

"Yeah, but I want to take a leak even more."

I helped him up and eased him and the unit through the doorway into the adjoining bathroom.

"You need any help?"

"Nah, I think I can manage," he said with a rueful smile. "Though my aim isn't that great sometimes... Shut the door, will you?"

I did as he asked and stood outside the bathroom, my hands in my pockets, vaguely listening to the rush of the very heavy stream inside, staring out the half-ajar main door into the corridor.

After a few minutes, the bathroom door opened and Danny and his wheeled companion emerged.

"Oh, that's better, much better," he said with a small smile. "Now

BLURRED IMAGES

I'll really be fun to be with."

He moved slowly toward the bed. I helped him down again, first to a sitting position on the edge and then, after a pause, to a supine position. Stretched out, seemingly elongated. Eyes closed. Lips tight.

"Do you want to sleep?" I asked.

"No, what I really want to do is stay awake... I want to talk. We've got a lot to catch up on..."

He drowsed off for just a few moments, then woke with a start, and blurted, "Don't go!"

"Don't worry... I'm not going anywhere."

He smiled and closed his eyes and kept them closed as he dropped off into sleep. I pulled the covers up over him and dragged over a tan vinyl armchair with a grease stain at the top of the seat cushion, and sat down and watched him sleep, his bony chest rise and fall with his quick, shallow breathing, his protruding Adam's apple bob regularly from reflexive swallowing, his lips purse tight, his eyelids occasionally twitch— from dark visions? recurring dreams?

Once, a nurse stuck her head in the doorway, saw me there, and went away. Ten or so minutes later, another nurse strode right in, marched directly over to the bed, took a quick look at Danny, checked the IV bag, gave me a practiced once-over, and left as abruptly as she came.

At one point I dozed off, slumped back in the slightly angled chair.

Time passed in this timeless place.

When I woke, I got up and stretched. Danny was still sleeping, on his back, mouth wide open, breathing in that way only very sick people breathe. I moved into unexplored territory, the other side of the bed. On the night table, a few get-well cards lay flat on a hardcovered book, surrounded by plastic cups and a little tissue box. I moved to the windows, their curtains closed as they had been since I arrived. I parted them slightly; behind them were Venetian blinds. I separated a few of them and looked out onto a lovely scene of rolling green pasture and a stand of big trees— oaks? maples? I couldn't tell. I made a small decision to suggest when Danny awoke that he open those curtains and blinds, bringing in this daylight, restoring some sense of time and place to this dim, dismal room.

    The afternoon passed. He slept. I dozed. Once I got up and used the bathroom. As I stood and pissed, I looked around, ignoring the hospital-standard bars and buzzer, briefly trying to imagine that this was not my brother's hospital room, but some Holiday Inn or Days Inn or Super 8 room, one of the hundreds out there I had stayed in or one of the hundreds of thousands I hadn't, each a bright alternative to this. I shook off, washed my hands with that pungent, creamy hospital soap, and the moment passed.

    I returned to the chair and eased down. The movement, the crinkle of the vinyl must have awakened him. He opened his eyes and immediately moved them toward me.

    "Where were you?" he asked with a slight urgency.

    "In the bathroom."

    "Oh... How long have I been sleeping?"

    "A couple of hours."

    "Sorry..."

    "Sorry?... For what?"

    "I don't see you for a quarter-century, and what do I do?... I fall asleep on you."

    "Hey... give me a break... I mean, you're entitled."

    "Yeah... entitled," he said, and smiled that sour little smile.

    "You know something?" I asked after a moment.

    "What?"

    "You have a great view here," I said with genuine enthusiasm.

    "I know."

    "Well, can I open the curtains, the blinds, so we can see it?"

    "Nah, don't bother," he said.

    "What?" I asked.

BLURRED IMAGES

"I like it better this way."

"You serious? It's like a cave in here." Then I immediately said, "Sorry. That didn't sound right."

"Don't be sorry. I really do like it better this way. I don't know what I'm missing... You know what I'm saying?"

Unfortunately I did and I nodded.

After a minute, I asked him, "Do you want to go for another walk?"

"No, not really. I'm good for about one a day, and that was it. I just get so tired... so tired."

And for a moment, he closed his eyes and I thought he would nod off again. But he opened them, and looked over in my direction, and said, "Why now, Jeffy?"

"Why *what*?"

"Why'd you choose now... to come out, come back?"

I paused and looked at him and debated how to respond.

"You want the official reason or the real reason?"

"What do you think?"

"To see you, to be with you," I said without hesitation.

It was the answer he wanted and tears welled up in his eyes and he dropped his head back on the pillow and stared up at the ceiling, trying to collect himself, to control the wellspring.

"Jeffy, I always loved you, you know that?"

"Well, it was tough to tell sometimes when you were beating the shit out of me... or ignoring me."

"Yeah, I guess," and he smiled weakly through the tears. Then he asked, "Was I that much of a cliche of a big brother?"

I returned the smile and nodded. "Sometimes," I said. "But I guess our family wasn't too big on cliches. That's one thing to be grateful for."

His smile appeared again, quickly, then passed.

"And then you were gone. Suddenly. It was so strange. You have no idea. Here you were, this kind of flaky, go-with-the-flow kind of kid... You go back to college after your break. I didn't even call to say good-bye to you, preoccupied newlywed, you know... Anyway, what the hell? I figured I'd see my kid brother in a couple of months, right?... Wrong."

That was the most he said since my arrival, and he said it in a rush of words punctuated by quick intakes of air. It was a real exertion for him and he rested for a few minutes. I sat and gazed at him and said nothing, waiting for him to continue. Not sure he would.

In a few minutes, he did.

"Jeffy, when we heard... when we saw... read... The news was everywhere. We were in shock. We said there's got to be some mistake. This can't be our Jeff... We called your number. And who do you think answered? Some asshole who said he was with the FBI... the fucking FBI."

He stopped again and stared at the ceiling, with that odd little smile.

"And then we knew... This was really happening... And this was serious. Serious, serious shit. And you, our Jeff, our Jeffy, were really in the middle of this... You were it... But..."

"But what?"

"But we still thought... said... over and over... There's got to be some mistake. I don't mean that it didn't happen, that that cop didn't die... That really happened. But Jeffrey Stevenson doing it?... We just couldn't believe *that*. It was totally out of the realm..."

I sat quietly and passively and considered my brother, catching his breath again, restoring his resources.

"So what happened, I mean after the news... after the first shock?"

He considered that for a moment and was about to speak when a nurse came in, scanned his chart, checked the IV bag, gave him a kind of disapproving look, then departed without a word.

"I think we all still thought it was a big mistake. Somebody else did it. Case of mistaken identity and all that. This would all be cleared

BLURRED IMAGES

up. You'd come home. We'd all live happily ever after."

And he momentarily grinned, maybe surprised he was capable of a quip.

"But you know, it didn't happen that way. You were *gone*, really gone. And we had no idea where you were, when we would see you. It was so weird... and so terrible..."

For a minute, I thought he would break into tears again. But he didn't. He just stared up at the ceiling, blinking occasionally, and finally said, "But here you are... And here I am."

As he said that, he surveyed his surroundings, his *domain*, with sad — profoundly sad — and impassive eyes. This time the tears came and he let them come and he lay in that bed, tears streaming down his shiny face, blank eyes fixed grimly on the ceiling, his fragile body gently shuddering under the covers.

I got up and went over to the bed, sat on the edge, and held his hand. Eventually, the hand went slack and when I turned to him his eyes were closed, his mouth partially open, fast asleep again.

I held his hand for awhile and then gently released it and placed it down on the bed. I slowly rose and moved toward the door and turned only when I was about to cross the threshhold and looked back at Danny. He was still sleeping in that position. I could imagine him looking like that dead. In a casket. As I knew he would be before long. And people would tentatively approach and look and say a few correct things in properly somber tones or say nothing at all, then move on.

I stared at him like that for another minute and then made my way back down the corridor to the bathroom and then to the elevators.

On the ground floor, I went into the gift shop replete with the usual supply of books and cards and games and chotchkas designed to cheer up the ill or injured. I bought a newspaper, paying the stout friendly lady with the 'VOLUNTEER' button on her pink pantsuit tunic, right next to the big poodle pin.

ARTHUR DIMOND

I folded the paper in half, left the shop, and found my way to the Visitors Cafeteria just a short distance down the corridor.

It being mid-afternoon, the cafeteria was practically empty and very quiet. Only a handful of tables were occupied with soft-speaking couples or lone people sipping coffee, reading papers, or just sitting glaze-eyed. This was no ordinary cafeteria. Everybody here was here for a reason. Everybody had a mission, a story.

I took my place behind a few people in the line and opened the newspaper for a quick scan while waiting. There, on the front page, beneath the fold, was a picture of my father's porch, the two of us sitting knee-to-knee on our wicker chairs. The picture was grainy, a factor of dim light, magnification, and the difficulties, no doubt, of taking a picture surreptitiously through a car window from a fixed position.

The caption read:

'**HEART TO HEART— Jeffrey Stevenson, the Vietnam War protester and killer of a police officer, who surrendered yesterday, has early-morning conversation with his father, Professor Simon Stevenson, on the porch of Prof. Stevenson's home in Chevy Chase, MD. The Stevensons have allegedly not seen each other for the entire quarter-century since the younger Stevenson's crime and disappearance.**'

I glanced at the picture credit. Associated Press. So I knew this photo was getting national distribution, gracing the breakfast nooks and living rooms and offices and park benches and public transport vehicles — and cafeterias — across the country.

"*You fucker!*"

The words assaulted my ears like the sudden gush of a fire hose. I literally jumped, then turned slowly to the source, a stocky, barrel-chested, middle-aged man in a brown-checked sport jacket. Thinning, combed-back yellow-gray hair atop an angry red face and a

BLURRED IMAGES

thick neck damp with perspiration. Eyes wide and boiling.

"What?" I asked, more startled than seriously alarmed.

He stared at me, unblinking, his face aflame.

"You heard me, fucker... You're the cop-killer. You're the fucking commie piece of shit in that picture you're admiring so much... Right?"

I stared at him, amazed at his fury, having no idea what to do about it. The thought occurred to me later — not then, at the moment — that he could have had a gun and if he did, he wouldn't have hesitated to pull it out and shoot me dead, on the spot.

"Right?" he demanded, again, turning his eyes toward the newspaper picture and jutting his index finger at it.

"Yes. Right... That's me."

"So like I said. You're a piece of shit..."

I started to ease away from this maniac.

"Yellow piece of shit. Take off! Get the fuck out of here for another 25 years... Maybe when you come back again we'll give you what you really deserve!"

I continued to move away, faster now, toward the exit. The few other people near-by were staring at both of us. When I reached the exit, I turned, and there, fifty feet back, across the shiny linoleum expanse, that barrel of a man stood staring, glaring at me. He wasn't yelling anymore but he might have been. He stood, feet apart, right fist aloft, silently threatening. I turned and entered the corridor and, heart pounding, breath coming quickly, I strode quickly toward the main lobby, the automatic doors, and the open air. Once out, I hurled the newspaper in the nearest trash can. I stared at the can for a moment and looked up only when a camera shutter clicked in rapid succession and a car engine suddenly started, and the car with two men in it pulled away from the curb. Both the car and its occupants were immediately familiar. I could predict tomorrow's front-page picture.

I stared at the departing car till it turned right out of the parking lot. Then I walked quickly on the sidewalk in front of the hospital.

ARTHUR DIMOND

It led into a small private park with grass as pristine as a golf green, and lovely little flower and shrub beds and a stand of dogwoods and a magnificent weeping willow. I sat on a bench beside a Japanese-style pond and stared at the graceful wooden bridge and at a man in a striped bathrobe, a patient with an aluminum cane, who was attempting to cross it. A large solid black woman in a powder-blue uniform — a nurse or a therapist — walked very slowly behind him, not holding or touching him, but focused on his progress, no doubt poised to leap and stop a fall.

When the man and the aide finally reached the other side and the safety of the pondside path, I leaned my head back and closed my eyes and felt the warmth of the sun on my face. I might have been in a half-doze when I heard a soft voice.

"Mr. Stevenson?"

I opened my eyes and turned toward a young woman, sitting on the bench a few feet from me. She had red hair, freckles, brown-plastic-rimmed glasses, no discernible make-up, and a serious, earnest demeanor. She was maybe 25 or so.

"Who are you?" I asked, cautiously, a definite edge in my voice. "And what do you want?"

She stiffened visibly and straightened up on the bench.

"I'm Molly Krasner... and I'm with Friends of a Sustainable Peace."

"What?"

"Well, we're not that well-known... We're kind of small... We..."

"Hey, look, Ms. Cranston..."

"Krasner..."

"Look... I don't know what you want... I don't care... I just want some peace and quiet."

"I know, I understand... But please, give me a minute..."

"Look, you don't understand. You really don't. So please, just leave me alone."

BLURRED IMAGES

"Please, understand..."

"No, *you* please understand... *Please.* I have absolutely nothing to say to you or your people."

I turned to her and stared directly at her, through the glasses and into her light-blue eyes, and didn't say another word.

She looked away, then down at her hands folded tightly in her lap. Then she looked up and softly but clearly said: "We think you're an important man... We think you stand for something and would have a lot to say... I'm sorry I bothered you... Maybe some other time."

She got up quickly and walked away, back in the direction of the hospital. I watched her till she disappeared. Then I leaned back again and closed my eyes and absorbed the warmth and tried in vain to transport myself to a different place.

CHAPTER X

At my father's house, I found a stack of mail, several dozen phone messages, and Savage waiting for me, sitting comfortably, legs crossed, on one of the wicker chairs. We shook hands.

"Where's my Dad?" I asked.

"On the phone... again."

I glanced at the phone next to Savage. He understood, saying, "He wanted privacy." Then: "Have a seat?"

I hesitated and he quickly said: "Jeffrey, this isn't a social call. We need to talk... But let's wait for your father."

"OK. fine. I'll be back in a minute. Excuse me."

He nodded and I went into the house and down the corridor to the bathroom. On the way, I saw my father, standing up, gripping a phone, pressing it to his ear, looking very serious, even grave, and tense, the way I remembered him at so many moments. He waved and held up two fingers. I nodded and when I passed on the way back, he was still on the phone, still listening, still serious. He held up two fingers again. I had no choice but to rejoin Savage.

Out on the porch, Savage was reading what looked like a document of some kind. He put it on his lap when I came out. I pulled over a love seat, leaving the matching wicker for my father, and sat down heavily.

"So how's it going?"

I shrugged.

"So so?"

BLURRED IMAGES

"Yeah, you could say that."

Before he had a chance to reply, my father appeared, looking every bit as grim as when he was on the phone. He seemed to brighten up, though, when he saw me. He paused for a minute and then asked, "How'd you find Danny?"

I looked up at him, suppressing reflexive tears, clenching and unclenching my jaw, not responding.

He waited and I finally said, "Dad, can't we talk about Danny later? Let's take care of Mr. Savage's business."

We turned to Savage. He was sitting back, legs crossed again, taking it all in.

"OK, Jesse," Dad said, as he slowly and with some apparent effort lowered himself into the matching wicker chair. "You gave me a little preview before... why don't you fill Jeffrey in?"

Savage turned to me.

"OK, Jeff, this is the deal. The authorities want you to nail down some community service. Quickly."

"Quickly? What's quickly?"

"Two weeks."

"Oh, c'mon, give me a break. I've been back for two days..."

"I know."

"And our deal was— give me two months. I mean I'll start doing the probation stuff immediately. I understand that. But the community service part? We agreed that could wait. Give me a chance to get oriented. Settled. Let me spend time with my father... my brother... that was the whole point."

"Jeff, you have to understand..."

"I understand all right... I thought a deal was a deal... But apparently it's not."

"Well, other factors have come into play."

"Other factors?" I asked, leerier by the moment. "*What* other factors?"

"Well, for lack of a better word, call them political."

117

ARTHUR DIMOND

"Oh, shit!" I exploded.

"Come on, Jeff, calm down..."

"Calm down? Why the hell should I calm down? We spend five weeks locked in a hotel room hammering out a deal. And now you tell me... *political* factors are going to change it."

"Hey, Jeff, it's not a big thing... It's a detail. Just a detail."

I turned to my father.

"Dad, what's going on here? You hired Mr. Savage to work out the details, and the politics, and look what's happening."

Dad was fidgety, visibly uncomfortable. He didn't say anything for a minute.

"Dad?" I asked.

"Jeffrey," he finally said, "I understand how you feel... I really do... but you have to understand this isn't happening in a vacuum. There's more here than meets the eye."

"There always is," I said sarcastically.

The two men exchanged looks of concern, of commiseration. Then Savage said: "Jeff, look, we knew your case was big and we knew it would set off all kinds of sparks... You knew that too, right?"

I nodded and said, "That press conference didn't help."

Savage considered me and my remark.

"I had a feeling that would be your reaction."

"Then why did you do it? Or do it that way?"

"Because it was necessary. Necessary to lay it all out, to frame the issues, right from the get-go. I told you that in Seattle. It's the only way to go— there's no middle way. I thought you agreed."

"I did, but I wasn't prepared..."

"... For that kind of attention?"

"Yeah, for that kind of attention."

"Well, it's big, bigger and hotter than we thought. I mean, look at the coverage... And look at the mail and the faxes and phone calls. They're pouring in."

"Pouring in to who?"

BLURRED IMAGES

"To *everybody*... the FBI...the Justice Department... the Massachusetts congressional delegation, for chrissake."

"Yeah? And what're they saying?"

"Well, it's not a write-in campaign for president," he said, attempting humor.

"OK... OK," I said, leading him, not smiling.

"Some of it's pretty ugly..."

"The 'cop-killer' stuff?"

"That... and worse... a lot worse."

I absorbed that, saying nothing, looking absently at Savage. Finally I said, "What do these people want from me? I've already spent 25 goddamned years — my best years — in a kind of jail. And the charges? I mean they've been reduced. Drastically reduced. That says something. That's the point of all this, right?"

"They don't see it that way," Savage said softly.

"How *do* they see it?"

"You want the truth?... The *blunt* truth?"

I nodded.

"OK... and I don't think there are any surprises here... They see a pinko cop-killer, who's been free as a bird for 25 years and now he's back and off the hook...A privileged kid who kicked the system in the balls and gave it the finger to boot, who hasn't played by the rules, who's home free... all the stuff I told you out in Seattle."

He waited and studied me while I absorbed that. Then he continued.

"And you know how the media's been playing it— and replaying it... They're reflecting — and fueling — the public view. All the pinko, cop-killer stuff— and something else, too..."

He waited again, watching for my curiosity to inevitably pique.

"They're creating a symbol: The last anti-war activist — fugitive — to come in, to come home. Very simple, very powerful. Nothing deep or metaphysical here. They..."

Savage suddenly stopped, paused, then said: "You know, some

119

of those letters are pretty brutal... violent. There are people, probably a lot of them, who would like to kill you. They would like nothing better."

I stared at him.

"You look skeptical, like I'm making this up or something. Do you want to see some of these letters?"

"I would, but not now..."

"Are you sure?"

"Yes."

"OK, then you'll take my word for it?"

"Yes."

"Good. So let's get down to business."

He paused, then said: "Shifting gears: The first thing is your personal safety. Word's going to get around pretty quickly where you are. They obviously know the phone number here. And if they know that, they probably know the address— or they can get it. Right?"

We both nodded.

Savage turned to me.

"You know, you don't have to stay here. You can move to another place in the D. C. area. Or you can move out of the area altogether."

I shook my head.

"You sure?"

"Yes," I said softly. Then, turning to my father, I asked, "How about you, Dad? How do *you* feel about it? I mean, what about *your* safety?"

"You should be here," he said without hesitation. "This is your home."

"Dad, this is no time to be a hero."

He smiled and said, simply, "Heroics have nothing to do with it."

"So it's settled?" Savage asked.

BLURRED IMAGES

"Settled."

"So how about guards?... Bodyguards."

I looked at Dad. I expected him to look as stunned as I felt. He didn't.

"Jeffrey, don't look so shocked," Savage said. "People are threatening your life. Most are blowing smoke. But all it takes is one who isn't...The Government couldn't take care of this... There's no real legal justification for it... I mean you're not a protected witness or anything like that..."

"It's OK, Mr. Savage," I said, smiling for the first time. "I'm not interested anyway... It's a good idea, but I'm not interested. Dad, you with me on this?"

He nodded.

"Are you sure the two of you are being smart here?"

"No... I just can't see living in an armed fortress."

"It wouldn't necessarily be like that."

"What *would* it be like?"

"More discreet."

I paused.

"Will you think about it... the two of you?"

We looked at each other and nodded.

"OK," I said.

After a minute, I asked, "So, is that it?"

"Well, no, there is that pesky matter I raised at the beginning... your community service?"

"Oh, yeah," I said, growing irritable again.

"Well?"

"Well, what?"

"Well, are you going to go along?"

"Mr. Savage, can I ask you a question?"

"Sure," he answered, a bit cagily.

"What's the big deal? Seriously, what difference does it make if I start in two weeks or two months?"

"A big difference."

I waited for an explanation.

"You know these whackos who say they want to kill you?"

I nodded.

"OK, they're a minority, fortunately a tiny, distinct minority."

I listened and waited for more.

"The mainstream, most of these people who are following your story, most of whom never heard of you before this story... These people need to see you pay *some* kind of a price... They need visual evidence that you didn't come home to lead the life of Riley... like nothing happened."

"The life of Riley? Are you kidding?"

"No— and hey, I don't make any difference in this. I've told you that at least a thousand times. *They* make the difference and they need — they absolutely *need* — to see you doing *something* to prove you did something seriously wrong. Probation's kind of ... abstract... for most people."

"Is all this what you meant by 'politics'? What you really meant was 'public relations.'"

"Same thing, Jeffrey, same thing."

"So the point is... " and I didn't finish because I couldn't quite capsulize it.

"The point is the Feds are under excruciating pressure to prove to the public — and to various members of Congress — and the courts — that they didn't give away the store. That's the point. And the same kind of dynamics are operating back in Massachusetts— in microcosm of course, but you can bet the heat and pressure are even more intense, and making things down here even worse..."

I said nothing, silently taking it all in.

"So you understand the situation a little better now?"

I nodded.

"So what do you say?"

"I'll think about it."

BLURRED IMAGES

"Good. I'm sure you'll come to the right decision... You're a smart guy, Jeffrey, even if you act a little obtuse sometimes," he said with a quick grin.

He put his document in his briefcase, shut the case with an authoritative click, and rotated the little lock rollers. Then he rose, slipped on his navy-blue suit jacket, shook hands with me and my father, and with that slight, now-familiar limp of his, he headed across the porch to the stairs. On the way, he said, "Call me at my office tomorrow afternoon, OK?"

CHAPTER XI

Danny and I were outside, making glacial progress around that lovely pond on the hospital grounds, his IV apparatus in tow. In the hazy sunshine, the pallor of his face, the fragility of his body, were accentuated. But he seemed pleased and relatively relaxed.

"This is the first time I've been out in weeks," he said with a wan smile. "Thank you, Jeff... This is great."

A moment later, he pointed to the top of his head and said, "I put on my wig for the occasion. You like?"

I smiled back, and said, "Yeah, it looks great, real great."

"You know, I always wanted to be a blonde... and now I am," he said, and grinned.

I grinned back, and then said, "To be frank, I kind of liked you better as a brunette."

He pretended extreme chagrin, and said, "I'm so disappointed... so disappointed."

I gave him a little hug around the waist and said, with mock remorse, "I'm sorry, really sorry. I take it back. If blonde makes you happy, be a blonde. You look great, better as a brunette— but hey, it's your head."

We continued walking around the pond. Once when I turned to Danny, he had a small smile, and when I looked again, he still had it. I put my arm around his waist again and this time I held it there. We kept walking at that slow, steady pace, saying nothing for at least a few laps. Eventually Danny said he was tired and we sat down on

BLURRED IMAGES

a bench. I think it was the very one I was on the day before. There wasn't a soul around. And we just sat there quietly, enjoying the peace and the sunshine and the physical closeness.

"Is this the 'walk in the woods' you were talking about?" I eventually asked.

"Yeah, this is it," he said, and extended that soft white hairless hand and covered and clasped the back of my hand and held it there, just like that.

We sat like that for quite awhile, not daring to move, to speak, to alter the moment, to mar it.

Then Danny's grip tightened. I turned. He looked different, staring at something, intently studying it. I followed his eyes to a bronze sculpture on the grassy strip between the path and the pond. It was composed of two figures, half-facing each other, arms lifted skyward.

"What do you see, Jeff... in that sculpture?"

The question surprised me— it was his first reference in two days to anything outside our closed, cloistered world. I knew my answer would be important.

I had seen this statue in my previous travels in the park, but hadn't given it much thought. Now I looked closely and fortunately found its message clear and straightforward.

"Well, I guess I see hope... maybe even triumph... you know, over adversity, illness or whatever..."

"Good message, especially here."

"Yeah," I said, wondering where he was headed.

"Trite delivery," he said tartly, with finality.

I sat there, doing my best to look thoughtful, introspective. I turned to Danny, expecting some sort of self-satisfied expression. Instead, I saw a distant one, a sudden, remote sadness. And at the same time, I felt his hand release mine.

"What's the matter?" I asked with a note of real urgency.

"Jeff, I've fucked up royally... in ways you couldn't imagine."

ARTHUR DIMOND

"What do you mean?" I asked.

"I can't tell you now... It's too long and I'm too tired."

"Jesus, Danny, you can't say something like that and then just leave me hanging..."

"It's just too much to go into now."

"For crissakes, that's what you said the last time, you know, over the phone from Seattle."

He looked at me blankly, like he had completely forgotten, then turned away.

"Oh, c'mon, give me a clue... **something**!"

He turned and, with moist eyes, looked directly at me. Then he said, "Let's just say I'm not exactly what you see... I've done things, too."

"Too?"

"Like you. I've done things. Different things than you... Very different. Nobody got killed, not that I know of... But people got hurt... and nobody... **nobody**... calls me a hero."

I was stunned. I looked away, back at that statue, wondering if the answers lay with it, those vertical arms, in that presumed kinship, or in something more subtle. I looked back at my brother and now he was really crying, his head hanging, his shoulders heaving.

I instinctively put my arm around those frail shoulders, and then I started crying, too. In the presence of that sculpture urging hope and the encouragement to prevail.

We sat there for some time, an hour at least. A patient and nurse passed slowly, staring, more curiously than sympathetically. A young boy, his mother not far behind, ran down to the pond's edge and plopped a toy boat in the water. A friendly Golden Retriever, no owner in sight, ambled into the park, right over to us, sniffed and licked first my hand, then Danny's, then ambled away. And eventually, we both regained our composure and rose with some effort and made our way along the pond and back to the hospital, my arm around his waist in that now-familiar, accustomed manner, his hand gently nudging the

BLURRED IMAGES

IV apparatus forward. We passed through the automatic glass doors, across the lobby, to the elevators and up to Danny's gloomy realm. As I helped him down onto his bed, I said quietly, as sensitively as I could, "You'll tell me those things when you're ready, won't you?"

And he said oh so softly as he closed his eyes, "When I'm ready."

In seconds, he was asleep and I slipped out of the room. Once in the corridor, I walked quickly toward the elevators and punched the "Down" button. The elevator arrived in seconds and lurched to a stop, its doors opening. As I entered, the sole passenger, a pretty, dark-haired woman, stepped out and stared at me as we passed. Given my recent experiences and current state of mind, I didn't return the stare or respond in any way. I just pressed the "G" button, watched the aluminum doors clank shut, and descended.

CHAPTER XII

Late that afternoon, Dad and I sat on his porch sipping Scotches. We didn't say much, we just sat there on those matching wicker chairs and looked out, watching the occasional passing car, or young child in a stroller pushed by a detached, Latin American-looking nanny, or dark-suited commuter returning early from downtown, walking briskly from the bus stop, swinging a briefcase.

Finally Dad spoke. He asked me a question as though we were in the middle of a conversation. Or maybe he was mulling over this question for some time and he had no sense of its abruptness.

"What do you talk about all day?"

"Who?"

He looked surprised.

"You and your brother. Who do you think?"

"Me and Danny?... Not much."

"Not much? In all that time?"

I looked closely at my father.

"Are you probing?" I asked, attempting a smile.

He averted his eyes slightly and said, "Not at all. Why would I have to do that?"

"I don't know. Maybe you think we talk about you."

"Oh, come on, Jeffrey. I'm not that self-centered."

I didn't respond.

Then he said, "Tell me. Please. I'm curious. It's as simple as that."

BLURRED IMAGES

I studied him for another moment and then, with a smile, said, "Dad, like I said. Not much."

"Really?"

"Really... There's so much to cover, we don't even know where to start... and besides, he's tired most of the time. Dog tired. It's tough for him to keep a conversation going..."

Dad didn't say anything.

"We spend most of the time getting used to each other. And walking and sitting. And holding hands."

"Holding hands?"

"Yes," I said firmly and turned to him with a slightly disapproving look. "It comforts him... It comforts me, too."

We were silent for a few minutes. We just sat there looking out at the street, jiggling the ice in our glasses. Finally I spoke.

"Dad, he's so lonely. And so scared, I think."

Dad didn't say anything. He didn't turn to me. He just kept staring out at the street.

"Dad, doesn't anybody visit him besides me? Do you? Does his wife... his son?"

He didn't answer.

"Come on, Dad, does anybody?"

"I don't know."

"You don't know?" I suddenly exploded, surprising myself. "Why the hell not? He's your..."

"Jeff!" he bellowed, startling me. "Don't talk to me like that! *I won't tolerate it!"*

A sudden torrential wave of the old Dad. That phrase. That look. That stern patriarchal look. I was stunned speechless. Eventually I said, "I'm sorry, Dad. Sorry for the outburst. I just feel so bad for Danny. He's so alone. I'm like this liferaft. This emotional liferaft. Do you know what I'm saying?"

"I do," he said, relaxing slightly.

"Why am I the only one who seems to care?"

ARTHUR DIMOND

He didn't say anything. He just set his jaw tightly and firmly and stared out at the street. With faintly moist eyes.

"Because..."

"Because what?"

"He'll have to tell you. I don't want to be the one to ruin your reunion... your little idyll..."

I stared at him for a moment.

"He said he would... when he's ready."

"Well, there you have it."

"Have what?"

"Your answer."

"I don't have anything."

"You have the beginning of an answer... a clue."

I paused and studied my father's face.

"What's he done that's so terrible?" I asked.

"Infidelities," he said without hesitation.

"Infidelities?" I asked, pondering the word, a large word that few people would feel comfortable using in normal conversation, but one which my father not only used but tapped for every bit of moral value.

He nodded.

"To his wife?"

"To his *family*. His **entire** family— you, me, his son, his mother, her memory... and also to his clients, and his profession... and the law itself."

His voice rose steadily as he progressed. He sounded like the Biblical prophet I had often envisioned when I was younger, like the stern, righteous guardian of truth and light I sometimes thought he fashioned himself after. When I turned toward him and stared at him, he seemed to become suddenly self-conscious. And to make a determined, physical effort to restore his composure.

Then he asked, "Did I shock you?"

BLURRED IMAGES

"Yes," I said softly and tensely. "You did... you really did."
He kind of snorted.
"Are you really that angry at him?" I asked.
"Yes, I am. I'm afraid I am," he responded.
"And you won't tell me why? *Specifically* why?"
"No, I can't. And I won't," he said. "I'm going to leave that to him. But you're going to have to ask him... That's the only way he's going to tell you."

CHAPTER XIII

The next morning I played the cello for Danny. We sat by the pond in clear view of the statue of hope and I played one of Bach's cello suites.

Danny had called me at home very early. Dad was out, on his morning constitutional, doctor's orders, and I took the call. I was in the kitchen, preparing a pot of coffee. I stopped, measuring spoon in mid-flight. I listened, letting the phone ring several times before approaching it and gingerly, very gingerly, picking up the receiver, half expecting one of those hate calls, those brutal obscene diatribes or those penetrating, unsettling silences. Or maybe a rush of words from a TV producer, upbeat, insistent verging on imperative. Either way, an unwelcome intrusion.

I raised the receiver to my head and said, tentatively, "Hello?"

"Jeff? Is that you?" asked a thin, breathless voice at the other end.

"Danny?"

"Yes, yes," he responded, clearly relieved it wasn't our father.

I paused for a brief moment, then said, "Hey, Danny, you really surprised me. What's up? Anything wrong?"

"No... Nothing more than the usual," he responded.

"Well?..."

"Jeff, could you bring your cello to the hospital?"

I was genuinely taken aback.

"Do you still have it?" he asked quickly.

BLURRED IMAGES

"Yeah, but..."

"But what?"

"You never had the slightest interest in my music..."

"Yeah?"

"In fact, you absolutely hated it."

"That's not true."

"Oh, yeah?... What was I supposed to make of your putting on the Grateful Dead — or the Doors, or whoever — full blast — whenever I practiced?"

"Well..."

"Or the time you hid my cello in your car trunk?... Or... what did you call Bach, you asshole?"

He didn't respond, and he didn't laugh, the way I might have expected him to. In fact, he didn't utter a sound for a minute or two. Then he simply said, "Times change." That's all he said for a whole minute. Then he said, "Jeff, please... It would mean a lot to me."

I thought about that. His sincerity — his sad, earnest sincerity — was overwhelming. But I threw out a caveat.

"Danny, I haven't played the cello — *really* played it — for all these years."

"I know. I know... I don't care."

"You're telling me you're the same undiscriminating cultural lowlife you were then?" I asked, trying to feed him the lines he couldn't or wouldn't feed himself.

"Yeah, I guess so," he said weakly, without a trace of humor.

So I relented. I opened the case which my father had thoughtfully put in my room, on the adjoining bed, like a roommate, or a possible lover. There was my prized instrument, resting on its fitted blue-velvet cushion, untouched, unharmed. I lifted it out and sat on a straight-backed oaken chair and placed the cello in front of me between my legs. First I faced it and studied its lovely shape, its graceful lines and contours, its finely aged wood, its strings, intact and surprisingly limber to the touch. Then I turned it 180 degrees around and placed my arms around it and ran my hands gently along its sides and almost embraced it.

I picked up the bow, comfortably nestled in its appointed slot in the case. And slowly, carefully, moved that bow across the strings. And that sound... that sound... was so rich, so deep, so mellow, it brought up a rush of old associations and the sensation of soft, warm tears in my eyes.

While the voice, the basic, inherent voice, and the timbre, were lovely, the instrument was clearly out of tune. So I spent many minutes tightening the strings, ever so slowly and carefully to avoid breaking them, bringing the pitch up by tiny increments, to a tolerable level. And when I did, I made an attempt at the suite. Not a sterling performance, I was the first to admit, but certainly acceptable given the passage of years.

Hours later, seated on the wooden bench across from the pond in the little park adjoining the hospital, I played that lovely piece for Danny. He sat at the other end of the bench, in his plaid bathrobe, attached to his IV unit, the sunshine reflecting off his pasty, pale-white forehead. Once or twice, as I made my way through the piece, haltingly, sometimes clumsily, most of the time (I'll flatter myself) lyrically, I glanced over at my brother. He was gazing out at the pond, at the statue of hope. He looked so engrossed in the music or the thoughts the music evoked. At times, he appeared absolutely awed and transfixed. I was gratified, certainly. And I was also intrigued; his reaction was not what I expected.

A few patients and an orderly stopped on the path to listen. Then a few more. And Danny got this irritable look; he wanted this concert all to himself. Then the audiences moved on and Danny relaxed and concentrated and assumed — well, an almost religious expression. At one point, I saw one of those dark-suited men materialize across the pond with a long-lensed camera. He triggered his automatic motor— I could actually hear it across that distance and over my music, like an out-of-synch metronome. Danny started to rise, glaring fiercely at the

BLURRED IMAGES

photographer. I played without pause and he soon sat down.

During that brief period, I was at peace, truly at peace. And I think Danny was as well. The music — the *rendition* of the music — wasn't great; that was for sure. But I felt it more profoundly than I ever had before. That was the point. That was the real point.

CHAPTER XIV

An uneventful lunch in the cafeteria. Then a call to Savage, per his request, from an open pay phone, the cello case lying safely at my feet. I dialed his direct number; I only had to get through one line of defense — his secretary — to get to him. She said it was no problem, he was expecting my call. Then, almost instantaneously, after a click, then another, Savage's pleasant, slightly nasal, professional voice came over the phone.

"Hello, Jeff, how are you?"

"Fine."

"Good. You can now be more fine."

"What do you mean?" I asked, instinctively on my guard now when Savage took on that upbeat, take-charge tone.

"Well, I did it... I got our original deal back," he said.

"What?"

"You heard me. The original deal. Two months. You've got two months to get on your feet. Spend time with your brother, your father. Pull yourself together. Whatever."

I was dumbstruck.

"You kidding me?" I asked.

"No. Of course not."

"Are you sure?"

"Of course I'm sure... Hey, Jeff, why are you so suspicious?"

"Why do you think?"

Savage didn't speak for a minute. Then he said, clearly,

BLURRED IMAGES

dispassionately: "Jeff, it sounds like we're back on the same track as yesterday. And I'm getting a little tired of this. I just called in some pretty big chips to protect your tender ass. That's on top of the chips I called in before. Not to mention what it took to cut your deal in the first place— the chips... and the smarts... and the *balls*. Do you understand?"

Savage's voice had risen, losing some of its practiced professional control. I didn't say anything.

"You still there?" he demanded.

"Yes," I said softly.

"OK, as I was getting to yesterday, are you going to share with me what's bugging you— about me, that is? It's been building for weeks."

I didn't reply. I just stood there, gripping the phone tightly, staring at the wall.

"Well, I'm waiting... I don't want to go through this bullshit every time I talk to you. I mean I go out to Seattle. Drop everything. *Everything.* Sit in a hotel suite for five weeks. *Five weeks!* Come up with a plan, get your agreement on the plan..."

"You wore me down..." I interrupted.

"With all due respect, Jeffrey, that's bullshit! You bought into the plan. Then I did my job. I executed it. Pulled out the stops. Contacted everybody I knew. Called in that first round of chips. Did everything I could to save your ass. And now I have to put up with this bullshit?"

I suddenly exploded with a barrage of my own.

"This... this speech of yours... *This* is bullshit! *This* is why you bug me, why you piss me off so much. It's so fucking sanctimonious I want to puke. From day one, you've reminded me of what a bad thing I did and how you rode in on your white stallion and saved the day, and how grateful I should be. Well, I've resented your attitude, your superior attitude, and — I'll put it on the table, counselor, now that you ask — I really *am* suspicious— of you, why you, of all people, have come to represent me. I didn't get it at the beginning and I don't get it now, and that really bothers me."

He didn't respond.

"Mr. Savage, did you hear me?"

"Yes, Jeffrey, how could I miss?"

"So?"

"So, what?"

"So I want to know— why you've done this, especially since it was apparently such an effort, such a sacrifice."

I waited and he finally spoke, slowly and in a deep, forbidding voice.

"Jeff, listen carefully to two things I have to say. First, as I told you out in Seattle when you asked — remember? — I did it as a favor to your father. To repeat, my only reason for doing it was to help an old friend, your father. You're right, absolutely right. This isn't my kind of case— and you're not my kind of client. If it wasn't for your father, I wouldn't have taken this on in a million years. It was all for and about your dad. Period. And second...

"What *about* you and my dad?" I interrupted sharply. "I mean when I asked how you know each other, you gave me some bullshit answer, the dedication of one of his books..."

"And second," he said, ignoring me, forging ahead.

"That's bullshit!" I interrupted again, my voice rising. "One more of your superior brush-offs..."

"Why you..."

"There you go again. This is our problem. This is what always happens between you and me. I'm trying to *communicate*. And you just dismiss me, what I have to say. I had — have — a legitimate question. A *relevant* question. How do you know my father? What did he do for you that was so important, so special, that you would do all this for him?"

"I've told you. And I rest my case."

I almost laughed into the phone, the cliche was so ridiculous.

BLURRED IMAGES

"My second point, Jeffrey, the one I tried to make about five minutes ago before you rudely interrupted me, is this: I would really like to say, to tell you, especially after this new exchange, and also while we're using the vernacular, 'Fuck it!... I quit!' But I won't. I'll stick it out. I'm a professional, and I'm committed to your dad. I'll see it through — we only have some loose ends to tie up, anyway — but I'll only do it on one condition."

He stopped, waited for me to ask the obvious follow-up question. I didn't. I waited.

"I won't deal with you," he said with conviction. "Only with your father. It's too much wear and tear dealing with you. So he'll be our intermediary."

"That's fine with me."

"Then that's that."

"Yeah, that's that."

"Tell your dad I'll be in touch with him."

"Tell him yourself!"

Then I heard the click. I held my receiver for a number of seconds and then hung up.

CHAPTER XV

I jogged through the pre-dawn residential streets, enjoying the stillness, the darkness, the cocoon-like quality they conspired to create.

Occasionally the mood was broken by the glare of headlights from a slow passing car or milk truck, or the softer glow in a driveway of back-up lights enshrouded in white exhaust clouds. Or a lone compatriot runner who shouted "Good morning" and expected an equally exuberant response.

The predictable repetitive motion felt good. But this was a middle-aged body, abused for many years by strange hours and bad meals and second-hand smoke, and generally unaccustomed to exercise. It could go only so far and so fast. So I took it easy, maintained a leisurely if steady pace, avoided hills where possible, slowed to a near-walk when I got really winded. I had a route and I followed it religiously and could anticipate how I would feel at each turn, at each landmark along the way.

After the first several outings and the routine was in place, my father asked me over breakfast if I felt nervous — "apprehensive" is the word he used — out there alone in the dark.

"You mean, that something could happen to me?"

"Exactly," he said.

"You're probably not going to believe me, Dad, but I really don't think about that... It doesn't really cross my mind..."

"Maybe it should."

BLURRED IMAGES

"Why?"

"Because you're pretty vulnerable... and not too popular in some quarters... But you know that."

"I do... but, believe it or not, I actually feel safer out there."

"I think you're into denial."

"Maybe so. Better that than paranoia."

"Jeffrey, get serious. It's not paranoia. It's prudence."

"It's a little late for that."

"What do you mean by that?"

I felt the tension rising rapidly, unintentionally, from a quiet breakfast conversation. My father nipped it. His expression suddenly changed. He looked at me in a pensive, puzzled sort of way and softly said, "Never mind." Then he rose from his chair, said he had some editing to do, and left the room.

To my surprise, I found myself smiling. Dad was mellowing. The self-proclaimed contrarian, enemy of the cliche, was doing what older people were expected to do: mellow. Years ago, he would have upped the ante, escalated the debate. Now he stated his case, engaged in a brief thrust-and-parry, then left the battlefield without ever coming close to a genuine skirmish.

After a few minutes, I stood up stiffly from my chair, cleared the dishes, arranged them in the dishwasher, left the kitchen, and went upstairs.

Out of the damp sweatsuit, showered and shaved, now dressed in jeans and a striped rugby shirt, I sat in my room and practiced the cello. Even after a few days of playing, after the command performance for Danny, the activity still felt strange, the position — the relationship of back and arms and hands — somehow disjointed. The bowing motion awkward. Once in awhile, I would imagine it was the bass, now safely ensconced up in the attic, and pluck and finger and strum those jazz progressions, and all that felt so familiar, so natural, though clearly incongruous in the bright morning light and the solitude of my suburban bedroom.

ARTHUR DIMOND

I practiced through the morning. I worked through my exercises, then the suites, the solo of the Boccherini concerto, the cello parts of favorite Brahms and Schubert and Haydn trios from so long ago. I practiced for me, sure, for my solace, my pleasure. But I mainly practiced for Danny, for my solo recitals for my audience of one.

CHAPTER XVI

Despite my initial resistance, Savage sent me a PR team. He did so with the support and collaboration of my father. Indeed, Dad, in his new role as intermediary, conveyed the news to me, in a reasonable yet insistent way. I asked, "Is this more for his benefit than mine?" "No," he answered. "And by the way, he's right, much as I'm sure you hate to admit it. I mean it's an axiom around here. If you don't present your case, define your position, others are going to do it for you—they already are. So, Jeffrey, you might as well have professionals help you do it right." I ultimately acquiesced, more with bemusement, to my surprise, than resentment.

The team was composed of a comfortably rotund man in his mid-, maybe late-, fifties, with a neatly trimmed snow-white beard, thinning silver hair combed back, and elegantly turned out in a navy-blue suit; and a slim, intense young woman with short light-brown hair and a self-conscious manner, wearing blue-framed glasses, and a business suit, navy blue, like his. They each had monogrammed leather briefcases. And she also had one of those leather, logo-embossed portfolios with the slot inside for the ubiquitous yellow pad.

The three of us sat on the front porch of Dad's house, sipping iced tea I had prepared from a can. I had suggested going down to their office but they said this would be better, at least for the first meeting. They would be right near my neighborhood anyway, passing by on the way back from Bethesda, so it was very convenient.

We sat while they attempted to make small talk for several

minutes. Then the man glanced at his watch and said, "OK, let's get into it." And simultaneously, they each had pens out and pads on their laps, hers the one in the portfolio.

He produced a half-inch-thin manila folder from his briefcase. He opened the folder, passed out copies of a memo from them to Savage and me, and suggested I take a few minutes to review it. The memo was neatly organized, as I would have expected. It opened with *Background* — beginning at the beginning, *The Incident*, as it was called, and taking it through *The Deal* and *The Return*. Then there were *Public Relations: Phase I: Activities to Date*— the airport press conference, phone interviews, and the like. Then there were *Interview Requests*, a long list — one item per line — running for nearly two pages, single-spaced, that covered the gamut from the local weeklies to *"Sixty Minutes."* The final section was *Public Relations: Phase II: Recommended Strategies and Tactics*. Its text was brief: "To be determined."

I looked up. They were studying me, but attempted smiles — practiced professional smiles — when our eyes met.

"What do you think?" the man asked.

"Well, it's a bit overwhelming," I said.

"What do you mean?" he asked.

"Well," I said, looking away slightly, "I don't know if I'm up to all this."

The man and woman looked at each other and exchanged small enigmatic smiles, sharing a private joke or some secret I didn't understand.

"That's what we're here for," he said. "We'll work with you and make sure you *are* up to it. That's what we do."

Now the woman piped in.

"Mr. Stevenson... Can I call you Jeffrey?"

"Jeff is fine."

"OK, Jeff. We think you have a fascinating story— and we're going to help you tell it in the most effective way possible... We're

BLURRED IMAGES

going to help you get your messages out!"

I gazed at her, vaguely considering her effusive statement. For her part, she looked a bit uncomfortable, not receiving the enthusiastic response she probably expected.

"Is something wrong?" she finally asked.

"No, not really," I answered.

"Then what is it?" she asked.

"Well..."

They were both looking at me intently, elbows on wicker arm rests. Her hands clasped, a pen protruding from clenched fingers. One of his hands supporting his chin, the other hand poised with pen.

"Yes?" he asked.

"I don't really have any messages," I finally said. "I just have a story."

"Yes, a fascinating one."

"Yeah, I know. But messages? Lessons? I don't think so. I'm just glad to be back. It's been such a long time."

"Maybe that's the message, the *real* message," she said, glancing at her companion. "Sense of place, of home — of *roots* — in a turbulent era. The lengths, the risks, a man on the run — a *fugitive* — will take to come home, to be with his family."

She was excited, on a roll, but the man was shaking his head, slowly and steadily. Off her stride now, she turned to him, the color rising to her cheeks, a look of consternation coming on quickly. Now it was my turn to be amused, but I suppressed my smile.

"Hal, what's wrong with that?"

"Sandy, there's nothing *wrong* with it. It's a good message. In fact, it's a *terrific* message..."

"So?"

"Well, it's not exactly fresh. I mean there are lots of people who come home from terrible ordeals every day. So let's say this is a nice sidebar. But what's the *real* story here? What's *really* unique? What are we trying to *say*?"

ARTHUR DIMOND

They were having a dialogue between themselves, ignoring me, or simply oblivious to me, the central figure in the drama, like two surgeons discussing a procedure across the supine body of a semi-conscious patient. But abruptly, just as I, despite myself, began to find the discussion interesting, they seemed to take notice of my presence.

"Jeff, would you please excuse us for a few minutes?" Hal asked.

"Sure," I said, momentarily flabbergasted. "Do you want me to go inside. Or vice versa?"

"Please, the former, if you don't mind. Just so we can, you know, sort this thing out."

"Sure, no problem. Give me a holler when you're ready."

I rose from the chair and walked across the porch and into the house. I went in the living room and did something totally out of character. I turned on the TV and sat down and, with the remote control unit, flipped stations until I found *'Oprah!'* And I sat back and watched without really paying attention. I turned up the volume just to underscore the point that I wasn't eavesdropping.

In about ten minutes, Hal appeared at the living room threshhold and asked me to join them again. I turned off the set and went out to the porch.

Once seated, Hal said, "Jeff, we must apologize. Usually we're a bit more organized, you know, have our act together, at a client meeting..."

The very fact that I was now a public relations client was a novel and vaguely amusing concept to me.

He continued: "You understand, and this was kind of a last-minute thing, that this is an unusual story — an unusual *evolving* story — and there are a lot of threads. We're just trying to grab on to the strongest one, the strongest substantive thread, *symbolic* thread, and weave a story, if you will, that has some symbolic value, symbolic *impact*... Do you understand what I'm saying, Jeff?"

BLURRED IMAGES

I nodded.

"And you know we're working under a bit of a handicap."

"What?"

"You know..."

"No, I don't. I don't know what you mean."

He hesitated for a moment, then said: "Some things — *thing* — we can't go into now."

I suddenly got it.

"My brother?"

"Yes."

He paused for a moment before asking: "And nothing's changed there — in your thinking?"

"No."

"That's too bad. That would be it. That would be our Barbara Walters story..."

I didn't respond, so he changed direction.

"Well, given all that, et cetera, et cetera, et cetera... Sandy and I had a little disagreement, a little 'creative difference,' as they say in the trade. But I think we're all together now, and we want to share our thinking with you... OK?"

"OK."

"So this is the story," and he looked down at his notes and then over at me to make sure he had my attention. He was clearly excited. "The last antiwar activist from the Vietnam era returns after a quarter-century on the run. It's a different era. The Cold War is over. There's a more tolerant atmosphere. There's an anti-Vietnam protester in the White House, for God's sake. The sidebar is he's returned to his family, his roots — OK, Sandy? — the family values thing?... But the main event... the *message*... is: It's time to close the Vietnam era and move on. It's time to take those negative feelings — opposition to an unpopular war — and convert them into something positive."

"Something positive?" I asked, genuinely puzzled.

"Yeah, you know, the community service thing. Doing good for the community. Giving back, you know."

"Sure, I know, but that's not going to happen for a couple of months. And besides, I'm only doing it because I have to... Talk to Savage, he knows all this better than I do."

"We know. We know."

"Then you have to know this is a joke. This whole thing is a big joke."

Hal studied me for a moment. He looked like he was about to say something, but before he got it out, I asked: "Hasn't Savage told you about the hate mail? The threatening phone calls?"

"Yes... So?"

"So doesn't that kind of say something about the 'tolerant atmosphere' you mentioned?"

"No, not really, that's just a crazy fringe..."

"I don't think so. I think there are a lot of people out there who hate my guts, really hate my guts. Some have come right out and said it to my face. And there are a lot more people who will see this as the big joke it is..."

"So, Jeff, do me — us — a favor."

"What?"

"Give me a *better* idea. Stand back from all this for a minute and give me an alternative. Your version of the story. Your take on it. A message with enough truth and light to satisfy you, and enough sizzle to satisfy us. And enough of a rationale to..."

"To what?"

"To keep your ass out of a sling, to be perfectly blunt."

"What are you talking about?" I asked, now on my guard.

"I'm talking about the point of this exercise."

"Which is?"

"Something important has happened here."

"OK..."

"As I understand it, major concessions have been made to allow this momentous event — your return — to take place... You

BLURRED IMAGES

with me?"

"Yeah... So?"

"So two things. One, every major event has a message. Or it's not major. Right?"

He didn't wait for an answer.

"And two, in the case of this event, messages — truth-and-light messages — need to underscore, to *justify* concessions. Concessions that were not entirely kosher, that involved some favors, some stretching of the rules, the procedures... you know what I mean?"

"So that's the point, right?"

"I'm not sure what you mean."

"Savage needs a little— what's the expression? Spin control?"

"Yeah, something like that. And it's not just Savage."

I raised my eyebrows in a question mark.

"It's the Government, too. This whole thing puts certain agencies, certain people in — how shall I say?— a potentially awkward position."

I thought about that for a minute or so.

"Then why, if this is so complicated, so awkward, did they all let this happen, *make* this happen?"

"That's a good question, Jeff, an excellent question. And I don't have the answer. Maybe we can just chalk it up to luck."

"*My* luck?" I asked incredulously.

He nodded and smiled at the joke.

"I can see you don't believe me. But I really don't have the answer. I can guess but I don't think I want to go into that now. First things first."

"That question *is* first... or should be," I said.

"Not for this mission," he quickly said.

He seemed to be waiting for a response, but I didn't say anything. Then he leaned forward and looked at me with a serious, surprisingly penetrating expression.

"Jeff, we need to know — Jess Savage needs to know — all

ARTHUR DIMOND

philosophy — all *bullshit* — aside... Are you on this mission? In other words, are you with the program — with *us* — or what?"

CHAPTER XVII

Danny's room was enshrouded in a faint fluorescent glow from the corridor and the sparse gray daylight seeping through the window coverings.

Earlier in the morning, he had had another chemo session and felt too weak and queasy to walk. So he lay in bed, on his back, on top of the covers, still in his plaid robe, seemingly swaddled in it. Staring at the ceiling, looking lost and forlorn. And I sat in that vinyl chair beside the bed, looking around but mostly at him. The cello case lay untouched, on its side against the far wall, unlikely to be opened.

I tried to make small talk, but there were few appropriate subjects. Family, work, the daily routine... aches and pains... were all sensitive or off limits unless he said otherwise. And he hadn't said otherwise yet.

So he lay there and stared upward, eyes wide open, forehead creased, licking parched lips, swallowing with difficulty. Once I asked him if I could rinse his face, his lips, with a moist washcloth. He nodded immediately, gratefully, and I was glad to be able to get up and do something constructive for him. Once the phone rang and since Danny made no move for it, I picked it up."Daniel?" a female voice asked with a note of urgency.

"No... I'll get him..."

"That's OK," she said. "I'll call later."

And she hung up.

"Who was that?" Danny asked. His first words in an hour.
"I think it was probably Sylvia."
"It probably was," he said with a quick, sour smile. Nothing more. Then he stared back at the ceiling.

Once a nurse came in, checked the IV bag and the chart, frowned, looked briefly at Danny. Then left. The usual.

A bit later, the phone rang again. I must have been dozing because I jumped. Danny's eyes were open but they looked blank and again he wasn't making a move. I stared at the phone for one more ring and then grabbed it.

"Daniel?"

The same female voice.

"Sylvia?"

A pause.

"Jeff?"

"Yes... Don't hang up."

"I need to talk to Daniel."

"He's... kind of sleeping."

"Could you wake him?"

"Well, I don't know."

"Please... wake him... I have to talk to him."

I looked at the phone, then at the inert form of my brother, then back at the phone.

"I'll see... I'll try."

"Thanks," she said tartly.

I buried the receiver in my chest, in the folds of my shirt, and leaned over to Danny.

"Danny," I said in a loud whisper.

No response.

"Danny," I whispered again, even more loudly.

His eyes, still blank, moved toward me.

"What?" he asked, sounding dull, disoriented.

"It's Sylvia again. She wants to talk to you. She sounds... kind

BLURRED IMAGES

of tense, upset..."
"Oh, yeah?" he asked. Definitely not connecting.
"Yeah. What should I tell her?"
"Tell her... I'm sleeping."
"You sure?"
"Of course I'm sure," he said, irritation tinging his rising voice.
"She sounds like it's urgent."
He didn't say anything at first. Then he said, "She always sounds like that ... Don't worry about it..."
"So..."
"So... again, tell her I'm sleeping," he snapped, showing real emotion for the first time. "You can handle it."
I held the phone against my chest for another few seconds, then took a deep breath, freed the receiver, and said: "Sylvia, he really is sleeping. I tried to wake him, but..."
"Right," she said sarcastically.
I felt the heat and color rise to my cheeks, and just stared at the phone, wondering what to say.
She broke the silence.
"When he wakes up, would you please give him a message?"
"Sure."
"Tell him that I want a divorce."
"What?"
"You heard me. Now please. Just pass that on to him. That'll get his attention."
I expected to hear a click and a dial tone. But I didn't. She kept the line open. She didn't say anything, but I could hear her quick, punctuated breathing. "You're shocked, right?"
"Yes."
"Nobody's told you anything. Right?"
"Well..."
"Your father, huh?..."

"Well, kind of..."

"Your father never 'kind of' does anything," she said with a short loud laugh. "What did he say?"

"Nothing specific... Just generalities."

"'Generalities'?"

"Yeah, you know..."

"Kind of..." and again she laughed, loudly, nervously.

"And Daniel?"

"Well..."

"An absolute sphinx on the subject, right?"

"What do you mean?"

"He hasn't said anything, I'll bet..."

"Well, his mind's been on other things... I'm sure you can understand."

She didn't reply for a moment. Then, slowly and pointedly, making sure every word registered, she said: "Jeffrey, I understand everything, but not the way you mean. And you, unfortunately, understand very little. It's not your fault. I'm not blaming you. I'm just saying you can't possibly understand the situation unless someone explains it to you or you ask the right questions."

After a moment, I said, "Sylvia, he's so sick." I said it very softly so that Danny wouldn't hear.

"What?"

Slightly louder, my mouth turned away from the bed, I repeated, "He's so sick... I can't... I *won't* ... ask him any questions like that."

"Then ask your father. He loves to talk..."

"I know..."

"Then ask him."

"I did."

"And?..."

"He told me to ask Danny."

"So we're back at square one."

"So?"

BLURRED IMAGES

"So ask him..."

"I will... maybe... at the right moment."

"There won't *be* any right moments... Except maybe when you pass on my message."

"I'm not sure I *am* going to pass it on..."

No answer. Just the sound of short, quick breaths.

"I think I should leave that to you," I said softly but firmly.

CHAPTER XVIII

Jerry Rubin died the day before I went on *'New Day.'* Forget the fact that the merry prankster of the '60s YIPPIE anti-war movement had long since evolved into a player, albeit minor, in one **YUPPIE** fad or another. Forget the fact that he had even worked for awhile on Wall Street, that canyon of greed, the scene of one of his more memorable stunts. Forget the fact that he died as the result of what *The New York Times* called "the mildest of rebellions": jaywalking. Forget all those inconvenient things and more. Just remember one thing: that it was a gift to the media and my PR people trying to find a new level of meaning in Jeffrey Stevenson's return.

* * * * *

I sat under bright studio lights and before the watchful red Cyclops eyes of three TV cameras. I sat stiffly on a comfortable, tweed-upholstered arm chair in front of a full bookcase, between two plastic philodendrons and across from a pleasant-looking youngish woman with curly reddish hair, a fresh peaches-and-cream complexion with the hint of freckles (artfully camouflaged under professionally applied make-up), dressed in a stylish blue business suit, adorned in the most discreet of jewelry.

On the other side of the cameras and lights was a studio audience of several hundred. But we were temporarily oblivious to them. As though in the intimacy of a home — hers? mine? — we sat for several

BLURRED IMAGES

minutes quietly watching a tape on a studio monitor. It was a cleverly edited production showing highlights of Jerry Rubin's very public life. Showering dollar bills on the trading floor of the New York Stock Exchange and gleefully laughing at the bedlam that ensued. Nominating a pig as a candidate for U. S. President. Promoting a networking party for young professionals. Hawking a powdered beverage called WOW. Then that grainy black-and-white photo of my defining moment, my most famous moment, my death swing on that college green so many years ago. Dissolve into color footage of my arrival at Dulles, my re-emergence. Cut away when Savage approaches the mikes. Cut to a medley of newspaper stills— on Dad's porch, in the hospital park, throwing the newspaper in the trash. Voice over. Closing message: "Jerry Rubin. Jeffrey Stevenson. Two very different men. Two lives galvanized by the same events a generation ago. One's gone. One's back. In an era that's very, very different."

The screen went momentarily blank and then filled with the image of the two of us in our little living room. Then a close-up of the woman, with a thoughtful, empathetic expression, still apparently looking at the monitor.

She turned to the middle camera. Its dim red eye suddenly brightened. She looked directly at the camera and said: "We're back live. I'm Betty St. John. And I'm here in the studio with Jeffrey Stevenson..."

Up to that point I had been calm. Almost detached, as though I were viewing all this as a third-party observer, maybe on my home TV, maybe from the safety of a seat out there in the studio. Certainly not as a central player, *the* central player. First, in the back seat of the cab, wedged between Hal and Sandy, the key members of my personal public relations team, making small talk, following our path through light suburban Washington traffic. Then in the make-up room as a nice, chatty lady with several bead necklaces and large hoop earrings, who looked like my high school history teacher, applied powders and creams to my face, before a wall-sized mirror surrounded by bright lights. Then, as we, my team and I and an assistant producer, an earnest young man in a blue-denim shirt and funky fish tie, strode briskly down a long, cinderblock-walled corridor and up a narrow, dimly lit stairwell. Even as we sat in a cramped but comfortable waiting room, as we alternated between chit-chat and a last-minute review of "messages"— even then, I remained calm and possessed.

At the mention of my name, however, on camera, before that watchful red eye, my detachment abruptly vanished. My heart beat furiously. My breath came short and labored. My sweat glands, system-wide, opened up and began pumping out what seemed like huge volumes of noxious juices that I was certain were seeping through my suit, that could be detected in the far reaches of the studio and maybe beyond.

Betty St. John turned to me and the bright-eyed camera's lens zoomed in.

"Mr. Stevenson, did you ever meet Jerry Rubin?"

I stared at her. I couldn't seem to find my voice. She looked at me questioningly and didn't appear to understand. She coaxed me with her eyes.

"No," I finally mustered, gutturally, barely audibly, like a low growl.

She pressed on.

"Did you ever think your lives would become intertwined?"

Again, I stared at her. This time, I didn't quite understand.

"Your return? His death?"

I kept staring at her.

"Is there a connection? Is there a... *message* here?"

I still stared. I couldn't find an answer. I had been intensively prepared for this line of questioning. We had discussed it. Rehearsed answers. I knew them. I knew the words. But I couldn't *utter* them. My body wouldn't cooperate. My heart still raced out of control, my breathing even more difficult. What's more, my bladder felt ready to

BLURRED IMAGES

explode and my voicebox locked tight.

Betty St. John waited for one more brief moment. Then she put on a big smile, turned to face the camera, and said: "We have to take a break now. When we return, Jeffrey Stevenson will have the answer to that question— a big question that I know has been on your minds since this very unusual story began unfolding."

The red eye went dim. The smile on Betty St. John's face vanished. Hal and Sandy were suddenly before me. St. John, clearly exasperated, asked: "What the *hell* is going on here? Is this stage fright— or what? Something I don't know about?"

"Stage fright," I muttered.

"Well," she said, "we have approximately one hundred seconds to get over it. Or we're going to have some pretty rough sledding here."

Hal put his hand on my shoulder.

"Jeff, you gonna be OK?"

"Yeah, I think so."

"Can we do anything for you?"

"No... thanks."

"Water?"

"No... Yeah... sure."

Hal smiled and moved away quickly.

Now St. John spoke. She was thoughtful, empathetic again.

"Look, Jeff, forget you're in a studio. Forget about the audience. Just think about us. Having a quiet conversation...in a corner of a nice cozy living room... maybe even yours."

I nodded.

"That's what this set is all about," she added, with a sweep of her hand and a surprising smile, as though she had just had a fresh revelation.

I nodded again and made an effort to smile back.

"OK," she said. "We just got the signal... In 30 seconds we're on again... You ready?... You OK?"

159

ARTHUR DIMOND

I nodded. Hal, back now, handed me a cup of water and gave me a shoulder squeeze. Sandy smiled tensely. And they both quickly left the set.

The stage lights brightened. The now-familiar red eye lit up. And we were off and running again.

Betty St. John faced the camera and said: "We're back live with Jeffrey Stevenson, a Vietnam-era fugitive who recently emerged after being on the run for 25 years...I was asking him before the break if he saw a connection between Jerry Rubin's death and his, Jeffrey Stevenson's, return... Mr. Stevenson?"

She looked at me hopefully, encouragingly. I focused on her. I made a conscious effort to ignore the camera, the audience, not to mention my full bladder. I opened my mouth. Miraculously, words — clear, intelligible words — emerged. Maybe I would be OK. Now all I had to worry about was the substance.

"Yes... I guess there was a kind of connection between my life and Rubin's. Not a *direct* connection... but *some* connection."

"What do you mean?" she asked, coaxing, clearly still anxious.

"Well, I didn't know him. Not even close..."

"Yes?..."

"But our lives were certainly affected by our times... the war..."

"Yes?..."

"Well, the war made him do the things he did... ***compelled*** him, I guess, to do the things he did... and..."

"Did he influence you?"

"Hardly," I said, actually smiling, and then suppressing it.

She didn't smile back.

"He was at that campus rally that day, right? He was one of the speakers?"

"I must have missed him. I got there late. I wasn't even planning to go to the rally. I just wound up there."

"Really?" she asked, pulling back, her eyebrows arched, looking directly at me.

BLURRED IMAGES

"Really," I said, softly but firmly, after a moment.
Then she took a breath and said.
"Let's fast forward. Mr. Stevenson, what did you do during your 25 years on the run... on the road?"
"I wandered."
"Where?"
"All over. Every region. Almost every state."
"And what did you do?"
"Do?"
She was staring at me, clearly unhappy again with my performance.
"For a living. To keep body and soul together..."
I paused too long.
"Was your family sending you money?"
I nearly jumped at this abrupt tack.
"My family had no idea — *ever* — where I was."
She smiled, satisfied that she had finally generated some emotion, sparked a definitive reaction from me. She kept it up.
"What about the Movement?"
"Movement?"
And then she gave me her here-we-go-again look.
"You know. The ***Anti-War Movement***. Jerry and Abby and company... Were *they* sending you money? Helping you in any other way?"
This time *I* stared at *her*. Genuinely shocked.
"That's ***ridiculous!***" I exclaimed. "I wasn't even *in* the 'Anti-War Movement'..."
Her eyebrows arched again, but she was smiling. She had something going here.
"***They*** thought you were. Your name, Jeffrey Stevenson, was a buzzword, a watchword. Your act that day — at that rally you 'wound up at' — entered the folklore of the Anti-War Movement. You were a hero to some... and you were also a devil to others..."

ARTHUR DIMOND

She was leaning forward now, fixing me with that meaningful expression of hers, momentarily, quietly, studying my reaction as her statement sank in.

"Did you ever think you would become an historic figure?... a *symbol*?"

"I don't really think I was... am."

"Well, you're in a distinct minority, Mr. Stevenson," she said, that reflexive eyebrow doing its thing again.

"I can't help that," I said softly, then immediately surprising myself and possibly her, saying: "It was all a mistake, an accident."

She studied me for a moment, conscious of the camera's eye on her. She formed a skeptical look and maintained it for the final moment. Then she turned away from me and directly toward the camera.

"Well, we've run out of time and have to cut to station identification. We've been here with Jeffrey Stevenson, the self-proclaimed accidental hero — or villain — of the Vietnam era... back from a quarter-century underground and on the run... back to mainstream society in a very different era... Stay tuned and we'll see you in a few minutes, with a very unusual senior citizen— a grandmother cum inventor, with a truly unique invention."

When the bright lights dimmed, she relaxed and sat back in her easy chair. I didn't move. I looked everywhere but in her direction.

"Well, that was inspiring," she said, her bell-like voice laced with sarcasm, then turned bright. "But we pulled it off... Glad you got over your 'stage fright'... Gave us a nice close, huh?... Thanks for being with us, Mr. Stevenson."

She extended her hand, shook mine once, quickly, from her chair, and promptly looked down at the notes on her lap. Then Hal and Sandy and the assistant producer escorted me off the set.

CHAPTER XIX

Danny was lying on his back, staring at the ceiling over his bed. His eyes were wide open and they were red, with the white dried salt of tears caked on swollen lids and slightly concave cheeks.

"Danny?" I asked softly.

He didn't answer.

"What's the matter? What happened?"

He didn't answer. He just nodded, almost imperceptibly, toward the stainless steel meal tray to his right, directly in front of me. On it, alone, were a jaggedly torn-open envelope, certified mail stub attached, and a document by its side. I didn't have to ask what it was. But I did.

"Look!... *Look!*" he said, like low, throaty, trembling barks.

I gingerly picked up the document and read the cover letter. Stark realities couched in clear, polite, business-like prose. Then the multi-paged attachment, laden with dense, abstruse legalese, spelling out procedures and timeframes and the like in minute detail.

I looked up, expecting Danny to be watching me, gauging my reaction. But he wasn't. He was still staring up at the ceiling.

I wasn't shocked, of course. But I was genuinely surprised by the speed with which this packet had reached my brother's bed. Maybe even that she went ahead and did it. I didn't have to act.

"Danny, I'm sorry, I'm so sorry... How could she do this to you? Here? Like this?"

He didn't say anything for a minute. I wasn't really expecting an answer. And I didn't press it.

He kept staring at the ceiling and I eventually clipped the letter and the document back together, placed them in the envelope, and put the whole packet on the side table behind the phone. As though hiding it would diminish its power.

The phone rang. Once, twice. He made no move for it. And when I did, his right hand suddenly shot up and violently, angrily, waved my hand away. The phone rang twice more before stopping, triggering the voice mail system.

I dropped down on the vinyl chair. I sat there looking gloomily at my brother, nervously kneading and pulling at my chin with one hand. Alternately cracking knuckles and wrists. Ill at ease for the first time in my brother's grim lair.

A nurse came in and did her routine checks. The chart. The IV bag. The patient's face. I could have sworn she gave me a disapproving look as she strode across my field of vision. Like I was responsible for the patient's dark spirits. Then she left without uttering a word.

Time passed. A half-hour. Maybe an hour. Maybe two. I might have dozed off and lost track.

The phone rang again. We both lurched upward. We went through the same drill again. I looked questioningly at him. But he was oblivious, again staring at the intimately familiar terrain of the off-white ceiling, his eyes slowly moving, closely following the halting course of a large brown spider.

"Let's walk," he abruptly said, his voice fuzzy with dry phlegm.

"Can I help you up?" I asked, a bit more upbeat, grateful for this break.

He nodded, and I rose. I asked him if I could raise the upper part of the bed, to make it easier for him. He nodded again. I lifted the hand-held control unit, studied it for a second, and pressed the right button. Accompanied by a pleasant humming sound, the bed responded and my brother's head and back rose slowly. I extended my arms and he stopped me with an index finger, first raised, then

BLURRED IMAGES

pointed at his throat. I stepped back and waited while he frowned and made that sour look and pursed his lips and forced his Adam's apple to move up and down. After a few minutes, he nodded and gestured with his hand for me to come closer and he made small efforts to pull himself up from the bed.

I pulled down the covers, exposing spindly, bare, hairless, sheet-white legs. I gently inserted my left arm between his lower back and the mattress, around ribs as lean and hard and brittle as kindling. And I placed my right arm behind his broad, bony shoulders and gently yet firmly hoisted him up. As I pulled, he slowly, steadily, and with some effort, slid his legs to the side. Finally, with me supporting his upper body, he sat on the edge of the bed, breathing quickly, gazing blankly at the speckled linoleum floor, collecting himself.

"You OK?" I asked after a minute or two. "You up for a walk?"

He nodded, then said, "Gotta take a leak first... You see my slippers anywhere?"

I was pleased. Those were the most words he had uttered since my arrival.

I bent down, grabbed his slippers, right there, side by side, and carefully put them on his feet. Then I looked up and asked, "Ready?"

He nodded and I helped him off the bed.

"Wait a minute," I said. "Can't forget your friend."

As I wheeled his IV unit around the bed, he gave it a rueful glance and then slid off the bed onto momentarily shaky legs. With my help, he shuffled over to the bathroom.

"I can handle it from here," he said.

"You sure?" I asked.

"Yeah."

And he closed the door, leaving me to wait outside for what seemed a very long time. Finally the door opened and he emerged, making an effort to smile. I helped him on with his blue plaid robe and, my hand grasping his elbow, gently ushered him to the corridor.

ARTHUR DIMOND

Slowly, agonizingly slowly, we made our way down the corridor. For one whole length, then two, he didn't say anything. I was used to his silences now. They were often comfortable, the ultimate indication of an intimacy. But today I was anxious, impatient. I needed to know vital truths. But I didn't know how to get to them.

Danny made it easier. He surprised me. On the second lap, with no prompting, he spoke.

"What do you think, Jeffy?"

"Think?"

"Of this fucking soap opera... My life."

To my amazement, he chuckled. And he actually grinned.

"Look at me," and he looked down at his body and over at his wheeled traveling companion. "Pathetic. Fucking pathetic."

I waited quietly, not knowing if he was rambling or going somewhere.

"Jeff... I'm dying," he said, almost matter-of-factly.

I turned to him and stared.

"Don't be shocked. It's happening. Every day is worse. It never gets better... Never!"

He kept walking that slow shuffling walk. And staring straight ahead. He didn't say anything for a few minutes. Then he took a breath and said: "That's not my point. That's just a fact. A shitty but inescapable fact... So you can understand things."

My eyes were welling up with tears and I was afraid to talk. To betray how I felt. He was several steps ahead of me in this discussion. I was still absorbing what was unknown and unthinkable such a short time ago.

Quickly, mercifully, before I might have uttered something maudlin, something heartfelt but potentially tainted by the smell of cliche, Danny continued.

"You think Sylvia's a heartless shit for doing what she did? ... Right?"

I nodded.

BLURRED IMAGES

"You're shocked. Appalled... right?"
Again I nodded.
"Well, she is a shit. And her timing always sucked."
I silently absorbed that.
"But you know what?"
"What?" I responded softly.
"It was going to happen anyway, maybe even sooner... That's a long story."
He was on a talking jag, but I didn't know which way he was going. I didn't know what to ask, and didn't have to. I just let it come, to gush to the surface like a newborn geyser.
"What gets me is the fact — and this is what I was getting at before — she doesn't have to do any of this. It's so unneccessary. It's such a waste... of everything! I mean I'll be gone soon, very soon! So what's the point?"
I stared at him.
"Hey! Don't look so shocked. I mean, face it! I'll be out of her life and she'll even get something — whatever's left — for her pain and suffering... Without the lawyers — the *fucking* lawyers! — getting their pound of flesh." And then he, the lawyer, laughed and snorted.
"And you know what this means?"
Again, I remained silent.
"It means that she is so angry at me — so fucking incredibly pissed — that she wants — *needs* — the satisfaction of shitcanning me."
I stared.
"She needs to make this happen, to have some control over it— even if it hurts her own interests... It's as simple as that."
I continued staring, unable to produce an intelligent response.
"She doesn't want the money. Not really. Or not as much as you might think. And God knows, she doesn't want sympathy for a widow, a victim of fate."

ARTHUR DIMOND

He chuckled quickly, mordantly. Then he suddenly went somber and mute and we proceeded down the corridor in silence. When we rounded the next corner, I started to say something. I wanted to take this conversation to the next level, to learn some of those vital truths. But I couldn't bring myself to. So we continued in silence and the privacy of our thoughts.

CHAPTER XX

Hal and Sandy, my public relations counselors, were not deterred by my '*New Day*' debacle (my word, not theirs— theirs was "debut"). They prepared a memo neatly organized into sections such as *Program Profile, Interview Theme, Client's Performance, Message Count & Analysis, Upcoming Interviews, Next Steps*. And they invited me to their K Street offices, where we spent a couple of hours secreted away in a small, windowless conference room reviewing the document.

When we entered the room, Hal removed his suit jacket and placed it carefully on the back of his chair. As he sat down, he said, "Well, Jeffrey, that was a helluva debut, a real baptism by fire, huh?"

I nodded and made an effort to smile.

"You were probably thinking dark thoughts about me and Sandy that day... you know, for setting it up."

"No, nothing like that... I just thought my performance..."

"Was disappointing?"

"Sucked. Totally sucked."

They chuckled.

"Well, our opinion, Jeffrey, is that you're being too hard on yourself. I mean, this was your first shot. Right out of the gate. If anything, we were disappointed in ourselves. We felt we hadn't prepared you adequately, you know, more dry-running, more rehearsing, and the like..."

"No, you were fine... When it came down to it, I just froze. I just couldn't find the words. I looked at her, and at that little red light on the camera, and I just went absolutely, totally blank."

"You were better, much better, after the break, you know that."

"I still sucked."

Hal chuckled again, and exchanged quick, meaningful glances with Sandy (who hadn't said a word yet beyond the amenities). Then he turned serious and leaned toward me, his hands clasped on the table.

"OK, let's say we all could do better. And that's what we're going to do. That's why we're here this afternoon."

We proceeded to walk through their memo, item by item, point by point. Things went smoothly until we got to *Message Count & Analysis*.

"Our problem, our *fundamental* problem," Hal said, "is that we haven't reached a consensus on this. That's what's hanging us up."

I stared across the table at them for a moment before speaking.

"Hal... Sandy. With all due respect, that's what's hanging *you* up, not me. I've told you from the beginning— I don't *have* any messages. I just have a story."

They stared back at me, clearly frustrated.

"So we're back to square one?" Hal eventually asked.

"I don't know what to say."

* * * * *

Hal and Sandy had a mission: to generate the widest possible coverage for me and my story. If they could imbue the story with messages, themes, or symbols, all the better. If they couldn't, they would forge ahead, albeit disappointedly, with what they had.

They booked a tight schedule of interviews for me with the leading media that had been knocking furiously at our doors. Accompanied by Hal or Sandy or both of them, I took a succession of cab rides around the capital, to studios and news bureaus. And at each,

BLURRED IMAGES

my performance steadily and miraculously improved.
 I was consistent; that in itself became my *modus operandi*. Without any real help in this department from Hal and Sandy, I trained myself to tell my story calmly and factually. I described who I was and what I was about in 1968. What that spring day looked like. How I ended up at that rally. What led me to take that desperate lethal bat swing. What I did in the subsequent years on the run.
 I was consistent, yes, but the story evolved around me. Every time an article appeared, or an interview was broadcast, it generated a wave of angry calls or letters. Studio audiences at talk shows were now peppered with vociferous individuals who heckled and jeered; at one show, one of them threw a hard object that came crashing down at our feet on the floor of the set; the object, appropriately enough, turned out to be a baseball. The pitcher was promptly escorted out of the studio by two security guards and, I learned, subsequently arrested.
 The noise level rose outside the studios as well, with appearances frequently greeted by street protests. Not massive affairs. But rather small groups of people, largely middle-aged, mainstream-looking men and women bearing placards reading *'JAIL TIME, NOT AIR TIME'* and similar, if not so clever, sentiments, and displaying fierce, resolute faces. Once one of them, a hefty woman, jumped out of line when she saw me, blocked my path to the studio's doors, and screamed, "You bastard! You lousy bastard!" She didn't try to hit me. She just glared at me and held her ground until two tight-lipped security guards approached, grasped her elbows, and ushered her back to her group, all standing, staring at this scene from a dozen feet away.
 After that incident, Hal pressed me to agree to hire a bodyguard. Each time, I declined. He reminded me that I was now instantly recognizable and that I was putting myself at extreme risk. "All it takes is one whacko to pull out a gun, you know," he said. "One whacko, who would love nothing more than to have his 15 minutes of fame by shooting you on a live, national TV show."
 I told him I acknowledged that possibility, but would take my

chances. He looked clearly exasperated.

What also exasperated Hal was the "rudderless course" (his phrase) we were on. While complimenting me on my ever-improving delivery, and my more poised and confident responses to questions, he frequently cited a "certain lack of content." He complained that the meaning of my story was being defined by the media and the public — precisely what he and Savage had feared — and that we had "totally lost control."

"Maybe that's the message you've been looking for, Hal," I said with a smile.

Now he looked genuinely puzzled.

"What are you talking about, Jeffrey?"

"Think about it. My whole story is about lost control, about circumstances taking over. This story — this story *about* my story — is also about lost control. I mean from the minute I got off the plane with Savage, it's taken on a life of its own. People have seen what they've wanted to see. And they've reacted accordingly. Think about that. Just think about that."

Hal couldn't seem to find a response. He and Sandy exchanged another of their meaningful glances. Then they made some polite professional-sounding banter and the meeting soon adjourned without resolving that most seminal of issues.

CHAPTER XXI

Dad enthusiastically accepted a hastily arranged invitation to visit Russia and Poland, to address august forums in a string of cities and, not coincidentally, to promote new translations of his books.

The prophet of the downfall of communism, he was gleeful at the prospect of this triumphal tour, this opportunity to validate his prophesy, to survey the results of the *new* Russian Revolution, the terrain of this new realm, this fledgling free society. And, of course, to garner the recognition — adulation? — he was due.

The week preceding his departure he was a whirlwind of activity. His movements quickened. His energy levels elevated. His color rose with his spirits, with the excitement of the impending journey.

Each day the phone began ringing before I was out of bed. And down in his study, he bounded from the phone to his PC keyboard on which he tapped away at eternally revised versions of his speeches, to a profusely dogeared, paperclipped copy of his book, his seminal tome, emblem of his life, centerpiece of his mission.

During our few meals together, he jabbered constantly, darting from one item to another.

"You know, Solzhenitsyn wants to see me... Haven't seen him in years... He'll be arriving in Moscow just before I do... Getting off that train... You know, that whistlestop from Vladivostok... a fine bit of theatre."

I looked up. I was going to interrupt, to interject the well-known fact that Solzhenitsyn's return was a disappointing event, perhaps a bitterly disillusioning experience for the protagonist. The fierce survivor and historian of the Gulags was viewed more as a relic than a hero, a herald of the new revolution. He was too old and had stayed away too long. He was believed by many to be painfully out of touch.

I stopped myself. Dad knew all that. And it didn't make any difference anyway. He was flying high and his enthusiasm was irrepressible.

He told me about scheduled meetings with Yeltsin, with Walesa, with their advisors and others, a parade of people with long, strange, consonant-laden names I never heard of. He told me about some of the groups he would be addressing— some literary, some academic, some political. And he told me other details and thoughts and anecdotes as they occurred to him, as they bubbled to the surface.

"The Russian desk at State called me today... Wanted to talk about *their* agenda... Janice, you know, my agent, called and said the Polish translation is selling like hotcakes... or blini, or whatever they call them there."

I nodded each time. I wanted to respond to his enthusiasm, to help him sustain it. But I was badly torn. I also wanted to get him off the race track, even for five minutes, to get back to Danny. ***Stop it! Enough Boris! Enough Lech! Enough of those hordes of Vlads and Pavels and Mishas halfway around the world!! Fuck 'em all!... and fuck even you!... What about Danny?... What about your slow-dying son lying in a godforsaken bed a couple of miles down the road? What about his so-called "infidelities"? What about all those questions that keep me up at night, that weigh so heavily on me during those countless hours I sit or walk with Danny?***

He did get off his main track early one evening. Not to talk about Danny. But to talk about me. He had picked up some media calls on the message machine. He relayed them to me and proceeded briefly, very briefly, from there.

BLURRED IMAGES

"How's it going?" he asked.

"OK."

"Just OK?"

"Yeah, just OK."

I wasn't helping him and he wasn't prepared to press it. His mind was definitely elsewhere. He had done his duty, then moved on.

At the end of the week, in the bright late-afternoon light, Dad stood between two hefty valises and a bulging, beaten-up leather briefcase, shook my hand, firmly pressed one shoulder, and grinned. Then he followed a chunky black cab driver down the steps and the walk, to the waiting taxi with the open rear door. Once seated, and the door closed, he turned to me, standing on the porch, and jauntily shot one thumb up, like a coach or a commander. I did the same. Then he was off, to an evening flight, for his four-week odyssey. I continued to stand there on the porch. Alone again.

CHAPTER XXII

A familiar yet somehow strange face stared back at me in the bathroom. Regular shape, a bit of jowl forming, ears slightly oversized, sticking out from the dark wet hair plastered down from the shower. The brown eyes clear from ample sleep (the permanent bags below notwithstanding), looking thoughtful, inquiring, a bit vulnerable.

I contemplated my image for several minutes. I didn't intend to; I just found myself doing it. Right after that long-ago surgery that gave me a brand-new face, I had stared at myself at every opportunity—in bathrooms, of course, and motel rooms, in car windows, and store windows. I stared in amazement and shock and dismay and sometimes fear. Who was this? Who was I? Was I still me? It passed. Eventually. My new face was my only face. The only face my new world knew. Nobody questioned it. Least of all me.

Now I was alone in the house and that face suddenly, surprisingly, interested me once again. I held its gaze awhile longer. I rotated it slightly to the left, to the right. Gave it a sidewise once-over. A critical appraisal.

The phone broke my concentration. It rang once, twice, three times, and then a fourth. I stopped and listened to each ring, until the voice message system kicked in. Then I filled the basin with hot water, soaked a washcloth and wet my face. I submerged the shaving brush, lifted it out, repeated the process till the brush was dripping. Then I squeezed some shaving cream from the Palmolive tube and applied it to the tip of the brush. I lifted the brush and swirled it across my

BLURRED IMAGES

cheeks, over my lip, under my chin, on my neck. For a moment, I studied yet another face, a third one, a soft Santa-like visage, eyes peering out over a pure-white snowy beard. Then I lifted the razor and started it out on its familiar route. It knew the way. As I slipped into auto drive, my mind wandered again. And again, my calm distraction was broken by the ringing of the phone. Was it ringing more than usual? Or was I imagining that? Were the peals about Dad's trip, tardy stragglers? Or were they **Dad**? Probably not. It wasn't like him; when he was on a mission, nothing deterred him. Unless there was some emergency.

I resumed my shaving, finished the job, washed off the slick residue around my ears and in them, on my neck, my chest. I dried my face and surveyed the results. The phone rang again. I waited for the second ring and then dashed down the hall to my room. At the third ring, I grabbed the phone receiver.

"Hello?" I asked, slightly breathless.

No answer.

"Hello?"

"You Jeffrey Stevenson?" a gruff male voice asked.

"Yes," I responded tentatively.

"Murdering fuck!" the voice bellowed.

"What?"

"You heard me... **Murdering fuck!**"

Then the phone clicked off. And after a long moment, the dial tone clicked on. I placed the receiver down. Then I suddenly picked it up and listened. A rapidly intermittent tone. Messages. I entered our mailbox number and password, going through the voice prompts. Five messages. All for me. One from the last caller. Same content. Another. Different voice, similar tone and content. A third from a Chicago talk show. A fourth from the Kidney Society soliciting a contribution. A fifth from a left-wing campus organization, probably a speaking invitation.

I erased each one after it was barely begun. I hit the "3" button, instantaneously killed the message, and moved on. When the system was purged, I put down the receiver again and looked down at it with satisfaction and relief. Then a thought occurred to me. One that both disturbed and soothed. Dad had been listening to and deleting dozens, scores — maybe *hundreds*(!) — of messages like this. I thought they had tapered off dramatically, down to a mere few a day. Nothing to worry about now. Or get excited about. Maybe they had dropped off a bit. It was only natural— after my initial re-emergence, the press conference, the first wave of interviews, the torrent of coverage. I mean how long could this thing sustain itself? Hal and Sandy said they had accomplished their mission in terms of "saturation" (although not, they reminded me constantly, of "message delivery"). They said with assurance that the story was "playing itself out," and I believed them. I assumed the media and the public had moved on to new issues, new controversies. Hal and Sandy could move on to their more typical, no doubt more motivated, kind of client. And I could also move on— to the reasons I came out, came back, in the first place. But now I learned we were all wrong. And I also learned something else— that Dad had been protecting me and never said a word. So now what? Cerberus was off duty. Away. And I was home alone. In the castle. The solitary, lightly armed sentry guarding the gates.

* * * * *

The mail was already there, waiting for me, more than could fit through the slot. I gingerly picked it up, inside and outside the door. I placed the stack carefully in the mail basket on the small antique table in the hallway. Without sorting or sifting. I just put it there and walked away.

* * * * *

I sat on a hard, rail-backed walnut chair in my sunbathed room

BLURRED IMAGES

and played the cello. I was working on the third Bach suite and it was coming along well. I was determined to play all of them, my choices for the senior project, the thesis, the recital that never happened. This was better. I was doing it for me and me alone. I was bringing the requisite maturity (ha! ha!) to this exquisite music. The phone wasn't ringing because I had taken it off the hook. Let the assholes talk to machines, digitized voices, and themselves. I was playing Bach.

* * * * *

I sat in the kitchen, having breakfast — my Cheerios with banana slices, and strong, black coffee — and absently flipping through the *Post*. I stopped at page 5 and stared. There was Dad, in long overcoat and furry Russian hat, shaking hands with Solzhenitsyn at the foot of granite steps leading up to pillars and an august hall. Surrounded by a small, admiring crowd of people, mostly middle-aged and older. Framed by oversized bronze statuary bearing instruments of war and of agriculture, striking poses respectively heroic and industrious. Dad looked tall and trim and imposing, even beside that formidable figure, that wispy-bearded icon whose very face often told the story.

* * * * *

I listened to messages. One after the other, sometimes a dozen, two dozen at a time. The phone was now always off the hook, so the messages piled up. Most were ugly, vitriolic. Some of these were bluntly threatening. Their repetition dulled them, rendered them tedious like bad pornography. I was often more amazed than afraid. Sometimes I was plain bored. Sometimes even amused. These were sick, unhappy losers with nothing better to do, I told myself. Caricatures. Cowards. And the other calls, the media calls, the interview and speaking invitations, kept coming. At a slower rate, but still coming. And some were more serious, less sensational, than the first wave. Talk show producers and assistant producers, earnest young men and women who wanted to ask probing, quasi-historic questions comparing decades, probing the psyche of a long-lost man, seeking links to others, my more famous contemporaries who actively sought fame. I erased all these messages and responded to none.

Then there was Hal, a touch of irony in his voice (after all, it was Hal who had said with certainty that the story had "played itself out"). *'The Today Show'* still wanted me, he said. Now that the initial feeding frenzy was over and many of the sharks were off exploring other waters, the show's producer apparently told Hal, Bryant Gumbel wanted to have a more "personal" chat with me, an intimate tête-a-tête before a studio audience of several hundred and a home-viewing audience of umpteen million. To my own surprise, I was intrigued and flattered. I jotted down the information and stuck the note in my shirt pocket, vowing to return Hal's call later.

One of those typical double clicks with no message. The giveaway. Somebody who changed his or her mind or chickened out at the last minute or who wielded silence as a meaner weapon than words (you can only imagine the worst thoughts, the worst threatened deeds). Then immediately a vaguely familiar female voice. A clear, appealing, professional-sounding voice used to the phone. But at the same time, tentative, hesitant. Maybe for real. Maybe to disarm. But who? Maybe somebody ambivalent about making the call.

The mystery was quickly solved. "Hello... I hope that's you, Jeff, who's hearing this. It's Sylvia. I want — **need** — to see you. Please call me when you can, as soon as you can. Here's my office number: two-oh-two, five-five-two, seventy-eight hundred, extension one-five-three. And my home number, three-oh-one, eight-seven-five, forty-two, twenty-two... Talk to you soon, I hope. Thanks..." Click.

* * * * *

On the third day, I went through the mail, now a veritable

BLURRED IMAGES

foothill. Bills. Grocery store flyers. Charitable solicitations. Credit card solicitations. Dividend statements. Bank statements. Publishers Clearinghouse. L.L.Bean. Victoria's Secret (*Victoria's Secret?!?*). The obligatory *Yankee Magazine*, plus a multitude of other periodicals, clear across the political spectrum. A postcard from Switzerland to Dad from somebody I never heard of. I put them all in a cardboard wine box, as Dad had asked me.

Then there was *my* mail. Letters in envelopes — some wrinkled and smudged — with crude penmanship and no return address; I dumped them unopened in the trash. Business-like letters to me from media and organizations and the like, in crisp, attractive envelopes with sharp logos, some embossed, and word-processed, customized addressing. I didn't toss them. But I didn't open them immediately either; I neatly encircled them with a rubber band and put them upstairs on my dresser top for perusal whenever, when I felt like it, or perhaps to pass on to Hal.

Almost lost in the stack was a postcard with a pretty picture of what turned out to be Bainbridge Island, out in Puget Sound, and a brief message on the other side in tight but wobbly handwriting: "I just knew you had a very interesting story, Mr. Bill Porter of Dubuque. Good luck with the next chapter." It was signed, "Fondly, Eve Farrington."

* * * * *

Each morning I visited Danny. And in the late afternoon, I came back to the empty house. I popped open a beer, listened to messages, the usual routine. I read magazines, some of Dad's, at either extreme, some my own, the pointy-headed, intelligentsia, literati stuff and the fun, popular stuff; I genuinely enjoyed *People*, relished the pictures, and read (nearly) every word. I didn't read any books; I wasn't prepared to make the commitment. I nuked some doggy-bagged Thai food and ate it in front of the TV. I watched a lot of TV, rationalizing

ARTHUR DIMOND

that it kept me company and got me back in touch with the mainstream culture. News and sitcoms. Soaps and talks. Sports and potboilers. I often enjoyed the ads more than the programs. After the 11 o'clock news and a little Letterman or Leno or whoever, I poured a healthy glassful of Scotch over a rock or two, and settled in for a late-night date with my cello. J. S. Bach, Chivas, and me. The night was dark. The house was silent except for the rich, soulful sounds I created in my room. And I was at peace for a rare and lovely time.

* * * * *

I jogged, the night music encoring over and over, lingering in my ears. I moved *pianissimo*, *moderato*, in one-two time, up and down quiet, pre-dawn streets, in and out of the mellow glow of well-spaced streetlights.

CHAPTER XXIII

On the late news one night, I saw a story about a cop-killing. Sitting in the living room, paying more attention to the cheese omelet I had just made than to the TV, I heard the anchor's opening lines and jerked to attention. Now, all but ignoring my late supper, I stared at the screen, at the images of the dead policeman, crumpled on the sidewalk, along the shopping street in Northwest D.C. where he had chased two young men who had just held up a dry cleaner. I continued to stare, now at images of the cop's home in Montgomery County, Maryland, at fleeting glimpses of his wife — his widow — and young kids entering and emerging from cars, their station wagon, and once or twice, a squad car. I sat in rapt attention as the dead cop's supervisor, his fellow patrolmen, some neighborhood people, pedestrians, merchants, provided expressions of remembrance and respect, of affection and grief. He was a "good cop," a "good guy." He "knew the people," he "knew the neighborhood." And on and on it went, trite but true and affecting, and me sitting there, utterly immersed, concentrating on every word and visual.

There would be a funeral in two days, attended by an army of cops, plus politicians and community residents and civic leaders, and of course, the cop's family members and friends. Without really thinking, without making any conscious decisions, I noted the funeral details on the back of an envelope lying on the coffee table. Then I turned off the TV with the remote-control device and dropped my head on the top of the couch back and closed my eyes and debated

183

ARTHUR DIMOND

what to do.

I decided to go. Why? I didn't know for sure. Why now? Ditto. Hundreds, maybe thousands of policemen had been killed in the line of duty over these many years. What was special about this? I didn't know. I still don't know. I was simply drawn and I couldn't resist.

On the funeral morning, hazy and tinged with the first hint of summer humidity, I left extra early to allow for traffic, missed turns, and other potential delays. I drove slowly, out Connecticut Avenue to the Beltway, around the broad highway to Silver Spring and then for ten or fifteen minutes to the cemetery. I had decided to forego the funeral Mass and the procession to the cemetery — too many risks and logistical complexities — and come directly here.

I parked in a small lot just inside the cemetery gates, and entered the small fieldstone building that housed the offices. A fleshy-faced man with a prominent mole next to one corner of his mouth gave me a questioning look when I stated my mission. Then he produced a little cemetery map and marked the location of the dead cop's gravesite with an X. I felt his eyes following me as I walked the few feet to the screen door.

Leaving my car in the lot, I walked down tranquil cemetery roads, overhung by the boughs of large, venerable trees, and lined with well-groomed, stone-punctuated lawns. I vaguely scanned the names carved into headstones nearest the road. Shortly after making the sole turn in my route, I found the Collins family plot. A pick-up truck was parked at the curb and two men, one barechested, the other in a soiled T-shirt, stood in the grave, up to their waists, silently, diligently, digging. Shoveling and tossing. Shoveling and tossing. Forming a neat, growing mound of rich dark soil next to the rectangular hole. Soil that would soon cover for the ages the casket of the fallen Officer Collins.

I walked up a short hill on the other side of the road, sat down under a stately shade tree, and waited. Watching the two men slowly descend into their deepening hole and their dirt hillock growing

BLURRED IMAGES

proportionately taller. Several times, when the men took a brief break, when they stood up, wiped their brows with the backs of hands and large handkerchiefs, took successive long slugs from a thermos, and leaned on upright shovel handles, they looked across the road at me and commented to each other and then went back to work. I didn't nod at them or wave or acknowledge them in any particular way. I just gazed at them, two toiling figures on a still, pristine vista. Eventually they finished their job. They climbed up a short wooden ladder, gathered up their tools, leaving one shovel next to the hole and loading the rest of the equipment onto the back of the pick-up. They gave me one final, suspicious look before clambering into the cab and driving off slowly. And then I was alone.

I'm not sure how long I sat there and waited. Maybe an hour. Maybe an hour-and-a-half. It was very quiet, very peaceful, sitting there among the birds, the stones, and the dead.

The first abrupt sound was that of a helicopter approaching. Then a second. Their blades cutting noisily through the still morning air, creating an incredible din. Then, moments later, rumbles and the slow roll of drums and what sounded like a human keening, a low, haunting prelude to something bigger. And then first sight of the sources of those sounds, coming over a slight rise in the cemetery road. A lone kilt-clad bagpiper leading a half-dozen uniformed drummers, followed first by fifteen or twenty D. C. Police choppers, two abreast, moving very slowly down the road, then by a very long motorcade— the shiny black hearse, the limos, then the dozens of police cruisers, and finally the scores of cars and vans and other vehicles of all colors and descriptions. Their headlights on, their motors emitting a low concerted hum.

The bagpiper and drummers briefly marched in place, then off the road and onto the manicured lawn to the gravesite, to the very edge of the ominous hole. The drummers stopped abruptly and rested their sticks while the bagpiper continued to play, the solitary plaintive tones he produced sending quick chills up my back.

ARTHUR DIMOND

    The motorcycles passed the site and stopped slightly beyond it, leaving ample space for the hearse and limos. Four black-suited men emerged from the hearse, moved to the rear door, and carefully slid out the lacquered, dark-wood, gold-trimmed casket, then solemnly carried it over the grass to the plot, and slowly lowered it to the bottom of the pit with the aid of broad leather straps.

    Then the mourners emerged from the vehicles. First the family, the black-clad, black-veiled widow, partially supported by a man, perhaps a brother, the children, a teenaged boy and two younger ones, an older woman. Then the scores of policemen from the squad cars, and hundreds of other mourners, in uniform and not, right up that long line.

    They moved in silence down the road and onto the grass, across the short distance to the gravesite, forming a large, tight human cortex around that deep, dark hole.

    With the helicopters now gone, the vehicles at rest, the bagpipe silent, all I could hear were soft bird sounds and muffled sobs. I didn't move. I sat under my tree and watched as a priest spoke from the head of the grave; he was a short man and I could just make out the top of his black square clerical cap over the heads of the many mourners. I couldn't hear what the priest was saying. It didn't matter. Then the shovel was presented to the widow. At first she didn't take it. Maybe she didn't notice, lost in thought, in grief. Maybe she didn't understand. It was gently offered again. This time she did take it and immediately bent down, becoming invisible behind the others.

    That first shovelful of dirt and pebbles crashed onto the bare hardwood surface of the coffin with the sound of an avalanche. My body lurched involuntarily, and the crowd stirred, slightly, almost imperceptibly, with the unspoken realization that a human being, alive and vibrant just days ago, was now under the soil, his final home, never to be seen again. After the eulogies, the drumrolls, the ceremonies, this is it. This is good-bye, Officer Collins, as we relegate your body to the ground.

BLURRED IMAGES

I sat and watched, tears filling my eyes, as the widow raised her head and stared down at what she had done, as the shovel was removed from her hands and passed to the older son, as the next heap of soil crashed down. I continued to sit as this grim ritual unfolded, as the sounds of sobs mounted, as I found myself increasingly absorbed, apart yet at one with this crowd.

Then suddenly, two uniformed cops were striding resolutely up the hill, arms pumping, faces grimacing, eyes directed straight at me as they approached. High-booted motorcycle cops who had been serving as sentries along the road, they were now standing in front of me, blocking my view.

"Get up!" one of them barked at me.

My heart was now beating furiously.

"Are you who we think you are?"

In a second, it all became clear to me. Why I was here. Why they were here. What could happen.

I nodded.

They exchanged quick scathing looks.

"What the fuck do you think you're doing here— you of all fucking people?"

Again. It's happening again. Another accidental, ill-starred, ill-timed encounter. Once again facing furious vengeful cops, out here in the open, in a beautiful green place.

"I don't know... I knew about this. I wanted to come. I... *needed* to come."

Again they exchanged looks, this time clearly of disbelief. Then the first cop turned back to me, his face red with fury.

"Listen to me, you scumbag. Your being here is an insult, a fucking insult to everybody here. All us cops. A great cop's family. Everybody! If we weren't here, right here with that funeral happening right now, you know what we'd do?"

I didn't answer.

"We'd beat the living shit out of you," he said. "We'd beat

the shit out of you so bad the next funeral you'd be going to would be yours."

I still didn't say anything. I couldn't. I just stared back mutely, my heart racing, my body feeling limp and very damp.

"Now get the fuck out of here before we change our minds!"

I stood for a moment, looking over their shoulders, beyond, to the gravesite, to the hundreds there oblivious to this drama playing itself out on this idyllic shady rise.

"Get!" the cop barked now, his hands, arms, poised threateningly.

So I turned and walked down the hill, to the road, and back toward the cemetery gate.

CHAPTER XXIV

Danny was having a good day. Relatively speaking. He had some theories: A several-day respite since his last chemo session. Painkillers giving him comfort. A good night's rest.
He was sitting up in bed reading a book. The first time I had seen him do that.
"You're looking good," I said.
"Compared to what?"
"Hey, take your compliments where you can."
"I know, I know... I'm sorry... But hey, what about you? You look like shit."
"Thanks a lot..."
"I mean it. Something happen?"
"Yeah."
"What?"
"I don't want to talk about it... not now anyway."
"OK, OK... whenever you feel like it."
I dropped into the vinyl chair, sighed deeply, and stretched my legs out. I sat there like that for a few minutes, silent, staring blankly. Danny stared quickly, questioningly, at me, then looked down at his book, reading, or pretending to.
"What're you reading?" I eventually asked, more to fill the void than out of real curiosity.
"Oh, that Clancy novel you gave me." He held it up, cover facing me.

"Oh, yeah, something deep," I said.

"Yeah, real deep."

He attempted a smile. With some effort, I returned it.

"You like it?"

"Oh, yeah, it's fine. Helps me pass the time. God knows, I've got plenty of that— at least for now," he said matter-of-factly, looking away.

"What do you mean by that?"

He turned and looked directly at me.

"Come on, Jeff, don't act dumb. You know what I mean."

"No, I don't, I really don't."

An irritated expression crossed his face but he didn't say anything.

"I mean, look at you. You look better than anytime in the last few weeks, since I've been back. I mean that's got to be good."

He looked even more irritated. I sputtered on.

"Hey, maybe I'm totally off the wall on this— but maybe this is some kind of turnaround. I mean..."

"Jeff!" he abruptly barked. "Don't be an asshole!..."

"What?" I exclaimed, stunned, almost tearful.

He softened. His voice dropped. He attempted a small smile.

"Hey, Jeff, sorry, guy. I'm really sorry. That was a bad choice of words. I didn't mean it."

"Well, what *did* you mean? I'm trying to be helpful... to be *hopeful*..."

"I know, I know."

"Then tell me."

"Tell you what this means? This 'turnaround'? It doesn't mean a damned thing. You've got to understand that. This is the nature of this fucking beast. And its nature is further fucked up by the shitty treatment these so-called doctors give... So it's up and down, a lot more down than up— but let me tell you, when it's up, it's *setting* you up. For the big fucking fall. And I'm a smart lawyer and I'm

BLURRED IMAGES

not going to let that happen."

"And me?"

"What do you mean?"

"I mean I'm just this poor shmuck, this non-lawyer, blue-skies jerk who wandered in from... wherever. Do you think I'm falling for it— that I want you to get better so badly that I grab at any straw, any grain of hope?"

He studied me for a minute. Thoughtfully. Tolerantly?

"I think you don't understand," he said softly.

"Understand what?"

"Understand that people don't get better from this... that I won't *ever* get better."

"Come on, people recover every day, go into remission, get out of these hospitals... go home."

Danny paused again before responding. He sighed deeply, audibly, then spoke rapidly and with real passion.

"Jeff, you don't understand. You really don't. I have **lymphoma**, a very *nasty* kind of lymphoma. People don't recover from this. Ever... I mean full cure, none of this remission bullshit, you know, when it comes back every few years and you've gotta get poisoned all over again to kill it— until it comes back yet again, and you're always a little worse off than before... And getting out of here? Going home? First of all, you've got to be nuts to even think it. And second of all, I don't even have a home to go to anymore. Remember? So what's the point?"

He stopped abruptly. And I stared at him for a long minute, as tears filled my eyes.

"Hey, Danny, whatever happens, you've got me. I'll be with you. That's why I came back. That's the only real reason."

He didn't respond so I kept talking.

"We'll catch up, we'll make up for all that lost time," I said. I was imploring him.

He nodded.

ARTHUR DIMOND

"Wouldn't that be worth getting through this for?"

Now he smiled benignly at me. He didn't say anything or even nod. He just smiled. Then he turned away from me and rested his head against the pillow and looked up at the far end of the ceiling where it met the facing wall. He closed his eyes and the smile disappeared and before long he was asleep, the open Clancy book, cover up, across his chest, a troubled expression cloaking his pallid face, that familiar hospital look restored.

CHAPTER XXV

As I crossed the hospital lobby, a vaguely familiar woman rose from a chair and walked directly towards me. A short, compact, dark-haired woman, dressed in designer jeans and a patterned sweater. A large burgundy leather bag slung over her shoulder. I instantly recalled the woman who breezed by me coming out of the elevator.

She blocked my path and I stopped, surprised and annoyed. She looked up at me, directly into my eyes. I forced myself to look back. Uneasily, with emerging recognition.

"Sylvia?" I asked hesitantly.

"Yes... Why didn't you return my calls?"

"I was going to..."

"It was three days ago... That was the first one."

"I'm sorry... I have a lot on my mind... I'm sure you..."

"Look, can we sit down someplace?" she abruptly asked.

"Sure," I murmured.

We made our way the short distance to the cafeteria. Familiar, sometimes dangerous, territory.

Once again, it was mid-afternoon, three-ish, between meals, and the large room was sparsely occupied. The usual assortment of lone souls sipping coffee, reading newspapers (or pretending to), staring blankly into space. No sign of the nutcase who assailed me.

We took a table near the entrance. She sat down. I didn't. Instead, I asked if she wanted anything. Coffee? Tea? Something cool? She shook her head. "No... thanks," she said. I said I was going to get some coffee. I didn't really want any. But I did need to create a buffer, to slow things down, to give myself a moment to think, collect myself. She smiled in a way that clearly indicated she knew. This was a lady who managed people, who honchoed projects, who ran meetings. She knew all the devices.

When I returned, she was ready, an invisible agenda before her. I gently placed the coffee mug on the lacquered, wood-veneer surface of the table. I sat down and pulled in the chair. And when I looked up into her inscrutable green eyes, she began to talk.

"Do you know why I wanted to see you... to talk to you?"

"Kind of."

A scornful look flashed on and off her face, immediately recalling her verbal response to that phrase in our recent conversation. "Kind of" was the kind of reply a woman like this obviously had no tolerance for; it simply wasn't in her vocabulary.

"Let me clarify things," she said.

I waited, telling myself not to be intimidated. To my surprise, she suddenly changed gears, lowered her voice, and softened her tone. She leaned forward. And in response, I leaned forward, too.

"You've probably heard everything by now from Daniel... and probably think I'm a world-class bitch, right? How could you miss?"

I didn't say anything. I just looked at her and waited.

"Well, first, to set the record straight, I'm not... I'm not your smile-button type, I can tell you that, even in better times. But you knew that back at Brailey," she said, referring to the prep school where we met all those years before. "Remember?"

I nodded, and smiled quickly.

"But I'm also not what you've probably heard..." she said, and paused.

I nodded again, almost imperceptibly, continued looking at her, and waited for her to resume. For the first time, to my surprise, she looked away. Just for a moment. Maybe a studied, calculated move.

BLURRED IMAGES

To relax, or disarm. Who knows? Then she turned back to me, but with a different look, a touch of hurt and vulnerability in the eyes. She crossed her elbows on the table and continued, in soft, measured tones.

"I wanted to meet with you because I know I'm being misrepresented— to put it mildly," she said with a quick-flashing smile. "That you're not getting the complete story, the *balanced* story."

She paused. To collect herself? For dramatic impact? Another studied device?

"Has anybody told you what Danny did? Any of the things? All of the things?"

Her voice was rising. She fixed me with a demanding stare.

"Did Danny have the honesty — the *balls* — to tell you?"

"Well, not really. I asked..."

"And?"

"Well, he hinted."

"Hinted?"

"You know— nothing specific. I can't push him, force him, when he's like this... You should see him."

"I have." And she didn't elaborate.

After a moment, she asked: "What about your father... the great man?"

"What *about* him?"

"Did you ask *him*?"

"Yes."

"And what did he say?"

"He said Danny had committed... infidelities."

"Infidelities? That's the word he used?"

"Yes."

And she laughed loudly.

"Did he tell you anything else? Anything *specific*?"

"No. He said I should ask Danny... And we've been through that."

ARTHUR DIMOND

"That's right," she said tartly. "We have."

She paused, lifted her elbows from the table, and clasped her hands together. She sat up straight.

"So it's up to me. And that's why we're here together."

She fixed her eyes on me and her voice grew taut and tough.

"Your brother screwed me... his family... so royally in so many ways. He had an affair, twelve, thirteen years ago, with his assistant... Our son was young, in nursery school, Sylvia! And Daniel was off— first late nights, you know, 'working hard'... 'big case,' all that trite bullshit, he couldn't even be original about it. Then overnights, then weekends and longer. It was easy because of the amount of travel he did anyway. So there he was, shacking up with this bimbo— great tits and nothing between the ears... and our boy at home asking, 'Where's Daddy? When's Daddy coming home?' And after awhile, he dumped her — he said — or she dumped him. Who knows? Who cares? And he was a real homebody for awhile. Almost too much of a good thing" (and she laughed loudly again)... "And then he took up with another assistant. Not as good-looking but smarter — *shrewder* — like a fox. Or a ferret. More experienced, a little mean, with a definite agenda. Now it was less of a lark and more of a long-term proposition— a bit of 'Fatal Attraction,' if you know what I mean. A bit of 'fuck-Sylvia' in it. And that's when I think he started crossing the line... *legally*."

She paused. I looked questioningly at her and she turned away again. I looked down at her hands, now clasped tightly together on the tabletop. I looked up at her face and she was facing me again, her lips pursed, her eyes moist, anger and hurt seeping out. I cupped my coffee mug with both hands and lifted it to my mouth. And when I placed the mug down, I looked up again and her expression hadn't changed.

"I know this probably comes as a great shock to you, Jeff, but your darling brother is not only a cheat and a liar, but a thief as well."

Before those words had a chance to sink in, more words poured

BLURRED IMAGES

out. Her indictment.

"He needed money— to support his habits, his lifestyle. Don't you love that word?" (And she laughed in that now-familiar short burst.) "... His whoring around, his trips to Barbados, supporting another apartment... Gifts?... God knows what else."

I must have arched an eyebrow or silently asked a question or raised a delicate issue.

"Drugs?" she asked. "Are you thinking drugs?"

I nodded.

"I don't know. His behavior was so strange, so erratic. I often thought, he's got to be doing drugs. But I don't know, I don't really know... The point is he needed money. He was desperate for money to support all this shit..."

"And that's where — *why* — he crossed the line?"

"What do you think?" And she crossed her arms and looked across at me with an odd smile of satisfaction. And then she said, "He stole from his clients— escrow funds, trust funds, whatever he could get his hands on."

I stared at her, momentarily speechless. Then I asked: "How do you know all this?"

"He was under investigation. I was questioned, by the D. A.'s office, once by the FBI— there were apparently securities involved in some of the trust stuff. And neighbors were being questioned... Imagine hearing that kind of thing on the phone when you're preparing dinner, on the street, at *Waldbaum's*—imagine! And files he kept in the house were being subpoenaed. Then there were the strange phone calls at strange hours... late-night appointments, and a tension— a definite, a *new* kind of tension... It was incredible."

She sat back, watching me, seemingly assessing the impact of her words. Then she said, with a satisfied, contemptuous little smile: "He was a real classic, a real man of the 80's, a fucking *prototype*. Rape and plunder and all that. So pure it's almost a cliche. It *is* a cliche..."

She smiled an odd smile and seemed to muse and drift into her own private thoughts. After a few long minutes of that, she abruptly focused on me again.

"Are you shocked... at all this?"

I *was* shocked. But strangely, very strangely, ***relieved***. Some real words were out in the open. Finally.

"Hey, I can understand," she said. "I was taken in, too. We've been married over 25 years, together for a year or so more... He was so... pleasant, so charming, likable..."

She paused and looked over me, over the top of my head, remotely out at something. Her eyes softened for a moment and then hardened and sharpened again.

"And you... you..."

I stared at her, waiting for her to form her words, her thoughts, not knowing what to expect.

"You disappear— for 25 years. You missed it all... At least I saw the *evolution*. You, Jeffrey, first you see him as a hot-shit young guy right out of college, right? And then you get in your little time machine and next thing you see him as a... the way he is now."

I felt my palms growing moist and rubbed them on my jeans, my forehead dampening, forming a visible sheen of oil and perspiration. She suppressed a small smile. Did she notice? Of course she did. She was hitting home with her captive. She stared at me again and leaned forward.

"Jeffrey, he really is an incredible shit! You know, your father's word is pretty good. Infidelities" (and she rolled out the word, syllable by syllable). "It's just a bit too elegant..."

She paused for a moment, seemed to soften, then harden again, then continued. "You should see the effect of... these infidelities... on our son," she said. And now her eyes and mouth formed into the starkest expression of anger yet. She paused again and collected her thoughts, herself.

"He's a basket case. Chronically angry— at everything... at

BLURRED IMAGES

every*body*, especially *him*."
  The words came out in a steady, measured cadence.
  "He hates his father. He hasn't come to visit him here. Not once. He said he hopes he dies. He said that about his own father, and he wasn't being dramatic. He was being very straightforward. And he meant it."
  "And you?"
  "Me?"
  "I mean... do you get along?"
  "Me and Michael... our son?"
  I nodded.
  She reflected for a moment.
  "On one level," she said.
  I looked at her questioningly.
  "I mean we're not in open combat or anything like that, but..."
  I waited.
  "But there's really no relationship. Not really. I see him in the morning... you know, running around the kitchen. But he doesn't say anything. He just grunts things. And we have dinner together... sometimes... And it's the same thing. He wolfs down his food and leaves the table as soon as he's finished— if we're even *at* the table. A lot of the time it's in front of the TV... the news and some junk... And he just stares at the tube and doesn't say a word. Not *one* word."
  We sat in silence for a few minutes. She looking down at her small hands, resting a foot apart from each other on the table. Me slowly rotating my now-empty coffee mug.
  "What about school?"
  She looked up, an expression of exaggerated — feigned? — amazement covering her face.
  "School?" she asked.
  "Yeah... I mean how's he doing?"
  She seemed to almost laugh. But didn't. Then her expression changed, grew serious.

ARTHUR DIMOND

"That's a whole other story. Do you want the short version, or the long one?"

"Whichever you want to tell me."

"OK. I'll tell you the short one. He's out more than he's in. He's been suspended for bad grades— I mean *abysmal* grades — for truancy, for behavioral problems..."

I waited. My standard mode.

She stared at her hands and took a deep breath.

"They say he's 'anti-social.' He sits in the backs of classrooms and slouches low in his seat and doesn't say a word, never participates. When called on, every so often, he doesn't respond, or he mumbles something, or..."

Another pause.

"Or he has an outburst. He shrieks. He actually *shrieks* in a classroom... at a teacher... in front of a whole class. He stands up and shrieks..."

"Like what?"

This time *she* looked at *me* questioningly.

"I mean what does he shriek?" I asked. "What does he *say*?"

She looked at me for a brief moment, then said: "Try 'Fuck off! Get out of my fucking face, faggot!'... That's a direct quote. That's what he's currently suspended for. And the teacher really is gay, which made it even worse, a *lot* worse."

I looked at her looking at her hands, now clasped, fingers playing with each other. Kneading each other. Worrying each other. I looked closely at her downcast face, noticing tears welling up in her eyes for the first time.

"The boy is a mess, a total mess.. School? Well, it speaks for itself. He's got no friends anymore. Not one. They've all left him, they can't put up with him, their parents don't want him around. He won't talk to me. He won't go for help. And..."

Again I waited.

"And I'm sure he's abusing himself... You know, alcohol— I

BLURRED IMAGES

check our bottles, I know he's drinking it, and I'm sure he's doing it outside the house, too... Drugs? I don't know, but it sure sounds likely... And he looks like hell. Like absolute hell. He's so skinny, and pale, and hopeless-looking. I really think he *is* hopeless. That's a word I never would have applied to him when he was younger. And I think something really terrible is going to happen."

And now she was crying, tears flowing down her cheeks, her eye shadow running. I pulled some napkins from the dispenser and stuck them out, under her face so she could see them. And she took them and blew her nose and dried her tears, and dabbed at the dark streaks on her cheeks. And I didn't know what else to do. I wanted to move around the table and put my arm around her and comfort her. But I couldn't bring myself to do it; it just didn't seem right. We were both out of character. So what do you do? You wait. While I did, for a very long four or five minutes, she regained some measure of composure. She neatly folded the wet, smudged napkins and placed them at the edge of the table. She clasped her hands in front of her. No kneading. No worrying. She looked across the table again. Her eyes still red and swollen. But under control. Remarkably under control.

"I'm sorry," she said.

"Sorry?"

"For that... display."

"Don't be. You're entitled... You've got a lot to deal with."

She nodded and after a moment, said: "Maybe you understand things better now, why I've done what I've done."

I nodded.

"Daniel has done a lot of damage. A lot... I'll be OK... I hope... I'm sure... But Michael? He's ruined, destroyed... He was the sweetest little boy. Mama's little helper..." (and she laughed, so softly this time) "... Bright, playful, energetic. And look at him now. Totally lost. Probably gone forever... And I blame Daniel. I absolutely, unequivocally blame Daniel."

It was too late in the conversation, too inappropriate a moment, to get clinical. To pursue a discussion about other contributing factors, about *her* role in all this, about just bad luck. In other words, to press her on whether she really believed that Danny bore *sole* responsibility for all this destruction. I resisted, but — again — she sensed something.

"It's not a perfect world. Believe me, I know that. Things happen. No matter what we do. But Danny, your charming brother, made things less perfect — a *lot* less perfect — than they might have been."

I absorbed that in silence. And she studied me across the table. She looked almost sympathetic.

"I know you were looking for something when you came back," she said softly. "It's *why* you came back, right?"

I nodded. Solemnly.

"Well, I'm sorry you didn't find it. I really am. Things change — *people* change — in 25 years. That's a long, long time."

CHAPTER XXVI

Amidst the usual assortment of voice mail messages — the solicitations and invitations, the taunts and threats, often zapped before the end of the first sentence — was Seth's voice, his unmistakable (and prefabricated) Southwestern twang. "We got a gig in D. C. — Georgetown, to be exact — week after next. How 'bout dropping by? We're better than ever without you (ha ha)... I'll call with details when we blow in." Click.

They came. He called. I dropped by, a dark crowded smoky club on M Street wall-to-wall with kids. I squeezed through the crowd and pried my way into a clump of students, in backwards baseball caps, to reach the bar. I ordered a Rolling Rock and turned to the stage. There they were. But just the three of them. They were mid-stream in a delicate Coltrane number, *Naima*, I think, and it sounded good, real good. I slugged deeply from the green Rock bottle, relaxed, and enjoyed this new, more polished sound. I ordered a second beer. And when I turned back toward the stage, Seth spotted me. He was introducing the next number — Coleman's grueling *Kaleidoscope*, no chance of forgetting it — and when he saw me, he grinned and saluted. Barely breaking stride, he said: "We have an extra attraction, an extra *special* attraction for this number... That distinguished internationally acclaimed bassman, Barry Stanton, who just happens to be in the nation's capital... here in this room... and he's kindly agreed to join us on stage... for this number."

I did a double take. I was Jeffrey Stevenson. I had reclaimed my

ARTHUR DIMOND

real name only a short time ago, and this other name — this *identity* — I had carried during a number of my 25 years on the run — seemed so strange, so... alien.

My first reaction was to beg off, to find the exit, to escape. But Seth was looking right at me, with that imperative expression of his. And the crowd's eyes had turned to me. With curiosity. Some with a faint hint of recognition. I clearly had no choice. So I placed the beer on the bar and made my way down the path created by the crowd. To the stage, up the two or three stairs. And there I was. In Nikes, jeans, and a light cotton sweater. Under the bright lights. Already sweating profusely, not entirely from the heat. Underscored when Seth disdainfully wiped his hands on his handkerchief after shaking my hand in a stagey sort of way.

Hank and Jerry nodded at me and smiled tight smiles. Definitely not overjoyed to see me. I lifted up a bass, lying on its side, in a way I never would have left mine. I propped it up and got into position, holding the neck with my left hand, wrapping my right hand around the body. Seth looked at me, grinned, gave that familiar jerking motion with his head. And we were off.

Seth raised the sax to his lips, arched his back, hit the first notes, strongly, confidently, soon joined by the drums, my bass, providing a strong rhythmic underpinning. Into Jerry's lightning-fast solo, fingers flying across the keyboard, literally dancing on it, creating a compelling confluence of rhythm, melody, momentum. Then back to Seth, alternately whispering and wailing and extracting every ounce of value from the driving theme. I got my solo, and despite some early halting and faking, managed to carry it off surprisingly well, all things considered. And then Hank's crescendo-building drum solo. The close. The silence on the stage, sullied by the now-exposed conversation and laughter from the floor. Then the polite, gathering applause. The short, perfunctory bows, more like nods. Lights bright. Then dim. Then bright again. Then off.

We spoke during the break. Sitting on folding chairs in a

BLURRED IMAGES

cluttered, seedy dressing room, Seth and I joshed about his adroit little introduction, his success at putting me on the spot. Hank and Jerry were quiet. When they abruptly rose and left, mumbling something about a pit stop, Seth and I sat in silence for a minute or two.

"What's with those guys?" I abruptly asked.

"They're pissed at you. Really pissed."

"Jesus, I couldn't tell."

After a moment, Seth said, "They didn't want to do this... with you... It was my idea."

"So... I guess you won."

"I usually do... But you know that."

I nodded and smiled lamely.

"So, tell me... Exactly *why* are they so pissed?"

"Hey, Barry or Steve... or is it Jeff?... whatever you're calling yourself..."

"Oh, fuck!" I blurted, and started to rise.

"Hey, take it easy, I was just kidding."

"Well, let's get serious. Just lay it out and get it over with. And then I'll get out of here... I really don't need this shit."

"OK, let's get serious. Just think about things for a second. We were a group. We were together for... how many years?"

"Five, six... whatever."

"OK, we were together for five, six years... We traveled a coupl'a hundred thousand miles together... like ten, fifteen times around the fucking *Equator* ... in that frigging van...We broke bread... how many times?... you figure it out... We popped brews, shared joints, got drunk together, stoned together... well, at least *we* did, now that I think of it... We always knew you were a little weird... OK?... You know, with your Mozart and your earphones and your sticking to yourself and your mysterious phone calls and..."

"Yeah?"

"Let's just say... in so many words... the way you were."

"But you put up with me."

"Hey, you were a terrific bassman... Let's say we did it for art." He grinned. It took me a moment, but I grinned back. Quickly.

"Then one day you disappear and next thing we know you're on Dan Rather... and it turns out you're some fugitive... some **murderer**... a cop-killer and a ... a fucking pinko to boot..."

He paused and just gazed at me for a minute.

"Well, that was some surprise for us... Some fucking surprise... I mean who the fuck is this guy anyway... This guy we've been with all this time? That's what we were thinking... And no matter *who* the fuck he is, how can he just leave — suddenly — with no word, no explanation, no good-bye... no fucking *nothing*."

Stunned, I stared at him for a minute before speaking.

"Seth, can't you understand — knowing what you know now — that I couldn't do that? I mean I was in limbo, in no-man's land for a couple of weeks... I couldn't say anything to anybody or it would've blown the whole thing... everything!"

"Hey, Barry — I mean, Jeff, whatever, — you know what the bottom line is. First you disappear. Then we learn you're a killer — a *cop* killer, for chrissake — that was really incredible for us, really incredible..."

"Seth, it wasn't like that... it wasn't like that at all... It was a huge accident... It destroyed my life... You didn't know me— we didn't meet till a lot of years after it happened. But it's not... It was nothing like what you imagine... Haven't you read the stories, heard..."

"Hey, Fred... or Larry..." he interrupted.

"It's *Jeff*! for crissakes. *Jeff!* How 'bout it, now? The joke's getting kind of thin."

Seth paused and gazed at me, a small smile at the corners of his mouth.

"OK, Jeff, OK... but hey, and this is what I started saying... I'm not interested in all the in's and out's. It's too big for me and I don't even want to get into it... Truth be told, I don't give a shit. The real bottom line... the real reason the other guys are having a little trouble

BLURRED IMAGES

with the auld lang syne bullshit is this very simple little fact: You said you were somebody you weren't. You disappeared without so much as a fare de well. And you turn up the way you did. And the rest is history... In other words, you betrayed us... you *fucked* us!"

"That's how you guys see it?"

"Yep, that's exactly how we see it."

"So the only reason you lured me over here tonight was to get that off your chest?"

"Yeah, that's about right."

"This whole charade... Having some fun with me out there?... Getting me up on stage with you?"

"Yep... I guess that's the long and the short of it."

I stared at him for a minute.

"Well, fuck you, Seth. You're the same asshole you always were."

"Hey, wait a minute."

"Hey, I'm not even waiting a *second*... I'm out of here."

I then rose, bulled my way between Hank and Jerry just as they returned, and left through the back door, out into a dank, narrow alley.

CHAPTER XXVII

I was playing the cello early one morning. The theme of the famous Elgar concerto. Another vicarious thrill. Pretending I was du Pre. I was in my room, lit only by the first rays of the sun filtering through trees, through the light cotton curtain, into the side window. Barefoot and in my pajamas, I sat on that straight, ladder-backed chair, working my way carefully, lovingly, through that wonderful passage.

The ringing of the phone cut through my mood, my reverie, like a fire alarm through a still church. I looked at the clock. Six-fifteen. Not too early for cranks or hate-mongers. Never too early. I waited for the ringing to stop, for the voice mail system to kick in, to intercept and disarm the likely nuisance. Then I resumed, starting at the beginning of the movement, recreating the mood.

Ten or fifteen minutes later, the phone rang again. Insistently. With a start, I realized it could be the hospital. I carefully laid down the cello, then jumped onto and over the bed, face forward, to grab the receiver.

I just missed it. Nothing but dial tone. And when I called up the mailbox for messages, nothing. A click. Then that bright female voice announcing there were no new messages.

Now alert and anxious, I sat near the phone. My nemesis had become, if not my friend, then my helpmate, my facilitator. There was a certain mysterious urgency to those calls. Something saying I should wait to connect. But now the phone — the cruel bastard — was having

BLURRED IMAGES

fun with me, toying with me. It rang and I grabbed it on the first ring. The Special Olympics. I grabbed another call. Wrong number. And a third. The beginnings of a vaguely threatening speech. A lingering growl. I cut it off and waited, now nervously flipping through the pages of a magazine.

At 7:30 or so, I took another call, again on the first ring. An official-sounding male voice, a pleasant even baritone, was on the other end, across a scratchy line.

"Mr. Stevenson? Mr. Jeffrey Stevenson?"

"Yes?" I answered cautiously, anxiously. "Who is this? What's this about?"

"I'm Fred Henley, an attache at the U. S. Embassy in Moscow."

"Moscow? ... My father..."

After a momentary pause, he said: "Something happened to your father... He got ill."

"Ill? What do you mean?"

"He had a heart attack..."

"What?" I asked, my voice rising.

"A heart attack... fortunately a mild one..."

"Mild?" I asked, wondering how a heart attack could be "mild," guessing that's when you survived.

"Where is he?"

"He's resting... Here in the embassy... It's safer than a Russian hospital."

"I guess," I said lamely, then asked, "Has a doctor seen him?"

"Yes, the embassy doctor... And he brought in a Russian cardiologist."

"And?"

"And what?"

"What's next? What do we do? What do *you* do?"

"He'll stay here for at least another few days. Resting. Being observed... Then as soon as the doctors think he's up to it, they want him to go home... We'll put him on a government plane... take

209

good care of him... And have him see his doctor, maybe check into a hospital back home."

"I see..."

"We'll keep you posted... And here's a number if you have to reach us."

I found a pencil in the night table drawer and jotted down the number on an empty envelope.

"I'm sorry about all this, Mr. Stevenson... about giving you this news."

"I know... Thank you."

"We'll do everything we can to help him."

"I know... Thanks... Thanks."

* * * * *

I jogged. At a bit faster pace than usual. And a bit later than usual, but still before the heaviest morning traffic.

On the way back, I stopped and bought a *Times*. I started leafing through it, walking down the sidewalk. Then continued while waiting for the coffee to perk. Finally, I found a small piece in "International News":

US HISTORIAN STRICKEN IN MOSCOW

MOSCOW, June 5 — Professor Simon Stevenson, a noted American historian, suffered a heart attack last night at a dinner event here hosted by the Russian Foreign Ministry.

Prof. Stevenson, a recognized expert on the former Soviet Union, was stricken in the course of what has been described as a heated debate with several members of President Boris Yeltsin's Cabinet.

He is now resting at the U. S. Embassy infirmary where he has been treated by U. S. and Russian physicians. Details of his

BLURRED IMAGES

condition have not been disclosed. The incident occurred during the third week of a month-long tour by Prof. Stevenson of post-Communist Russia and Poland.

* * * * *

I took the paper to the hospital. I sat in Danny's musty room, on the tan vinyl chair next to his bed, holding the paper, now rolled into a thick, tight tube. And watched Danny lying on his back, under the covers, his eyes closed, lips pursed, tolerating the side effects of his most recent chemotherapy session. Sleeping? Pretending? Rehearsing for the final act, the last bow? It didn't take much to imagine. And I sat there, tightly gripping that rolled-up newspaper like a poised truncheon. Gazing at my brother. Painfully aware of the tenuousness of it all. My family, its remaining members, barely hanging on. And me, desperate soul, hanging on to them.

* * * * *

Dad's plane arrived at Andrews Air Force Base within minutes of when the attache — a different one — said it would. The government "727" jockeyed slowly, even majestically, across the tarmac towards the terminal. I followed its progress through the terminal windows and then moved to the entry door.

The doors were opened slowly and a few minutes later, Dad emerged, in a wheelchair, being pushed by a beefy young man in a white uniform, some kind of medical insignia patch on his upper sleeve and cap.

Dad was pale — very pale — and thin. Not gaunt or haggard. Just thinner than I ever recalled. And his full snow-white mustache, though a bit sparser, were perfectly trimmed and shaped.

When he saw me, he broke into a tight grin which momentarily brought a tinge of pink to his cheeks. And he attempted to raise his right hand off the wheelchair arm, in salute, but got it only as high as shoulder level.

The attendant stopped. I nodded to him and I bent down low enough to shake Dad's hand, slightly extended, and to simultaneously, gently, grasp his upper arm. Oh, his hand was so soft and cool, the grip so weak. And that upper arm so thin, the skin, even under a couple of layers of tweed and cotton, so loose and malleable. I looked into his blue eyes. So clear. And smiling. Yet tinged with something else, something unfamiliar. Anxiety? Fear? I stood up and continued to smile down.

"Welcome home, Dad," I said.

"Thank you, son... Good to be here," he said softly.

"A close call, huh?"

"You could say that," he said. And then a moment later, "You don't ever want to be sick in Russia."

"I wasn't planning on it."

He chuckled, mildly, and with effort.

"It's a bloody Third World country..."

"No more 'Evil Empire'?" I asked with an ironic smile.

"You don't know the half of it," he said, without smiling, almost grimly. "I had revelations... *stark* revelations!... But more later... later..." And he went silent, as the attendant slowly rolled the wheelchair down the corridor and I walked beside, to the curb, to the waiting ambulance.

The attendant — now joined by a colleague — carefully, and with seemingly minimal effort, hoisted Dad from the wheelchair, placed him gently onto a portable bed, its back semi-upright, and rolled the bed onto an elevator platform and then into the vehicle. I entered through the side passenger door and sat down next to Dad, now breathing deeply, heavily, from his own exertions.

The two attendants got into the driver and passenger seats and in a moment or two, we were off.

BLURRED IMAGES

* * * * *

Now I was walking with Dad. Arm in arm, his weight bearing down on me, on that small crook of elbow, we walked slowly, very slowly, on gravel paths through artfully landscaped grounds. We passed other couples like us. An old person and a younger person, arms hooked, walking slowly, speaking softly, looking straight ahead.

Dad was dressed nattily and very casually by his standards. Gray slacks (sharply creased), blue V-neck sweater, tattersall-checked shirt.

"You look good, Dad," I said, and meant it.

"Thank you, Jeffrey," he said, partially turning to me.

"You're welcome," I said, and smiled.

He smiled back. But just with his lips — his eyes were flat, deadly serious — and then quickly faced forward again. After a minute, I asked, "How you feeling?"

"Not as good as I look," he replied.

"Really?"

"Yes... really."

I looked at him, wordlessly asking for elaboration. He ignored the question until I put it in words.

"I'm tired," he answered. "Bone tired... And frustrated... Angry! Angrier than I recall ever feeling."

"About... this?" I asked, vaguely alluding to our surroundings, to why he was here.

"About everything."

I absorbed that for a moment and then, inexplicably, pressed on.

"Was getting sick on the trip — having to come home — the worst part?" I asked.

"I was *glad* to come home," he said without hesitation. "I *hated* it there."

ARTHUR DIMOND

"What?!?"

I stopped and turned to him, staring. I was flabbergasted.

When he didn't reply, I exclaimed, "But why? This was the big moment, what you were waiting for..."

"Yes, and hoping for all those years... And never in my wildest dreams believing it would happen..."

"And it happened... finally... And you had a chance to see it... That's incredible... really incredible..."

"Yes, it was," he said, and softened with recollection of the first glimmerings, the first tremors, finally the news, the hard, concrete, irrefutable news that the Soviet Union, its satellites, its power, were no more.

"And then I went... to see for myself..."

"And...?"

"I was disappointed... No, that word doesn't even come close to describing it... I was *mortified*!"

I looked at him and waited. We were still standing, involuntarily stopped, on the gravel path. We were facing each other. His hands were at his sides. He was looking toward me, but not at me. His eyes were directed past me, peering at something in the distance.

"They're *animals*!" he suddenly blurted. "Aimless, purposeless, barbaric... animals... They threw off the yoke of Communism... that cruel, crude, stupid burden.. and didn't have anything to replace it with... Except crime and corruption and violence and chaos... economic chaos... political chaos... social chaos... The way people treat each other... Like animals... *Worse* than animals."

Now he was agitated, his arms moving jerkily about, making exclamation points in the air. Other couples, attendants, made wide circles around us on the path, warily watching Dad, us.

"OK, Dad, take it easy, please take it easy," I said.

"I can't take it easy," he said. "This wasn't the way it was supposed to happen."

"But, Dad, you said it yourself, it wasn't *supposed* to happen...

BLURRED IMAGES

at all."

"Yes, that's true, that's true."

For a moment he grew quiet and seemingly calm, pensive. And then he exploded again.

"And Solzhenitsyn! *Solzhenitsyn!*"

He stopped. He hung on that name. The name so imbued with meaning, with passion. With words unspoken. I waited, but nothing came. Dad just stood there, his face stiffened with indignation.

"What *about* him?" I finally asked. "You met him. What happened? I saw the *Times* picture but that was it."

"The meeting was a joke... *He's* a joke... A silly, pathetic joke."

Once again I was truly flabbergasted.

"Dad... I can't believe you're saying that..."

"*I* can't believe I'm saying it..."

"What did you used to call him?"

"*Call* him?... I don't remember calling him *anything*... I mean I read all his work... *The Gulag Archipelago*... twice... an Olympic feat" (and he chuckled softly and paused)... "And I wrote about those works... And lectured about them... and him... and..."

"Dad, I know all that... But what did you *call* him? What was that phrase... Very lofty... Very religious-sounding..."

"Oh, you mean 'The Prophet of Redemption'?" he asked.

"Right... The Prophet of Redemption."

And we let that phrase sink in during a protracted silence. Not an uncomfortable silence by any means. Just long.

Then Dad abruptly said, "Let's walk."

So we walked, down the path, past those slow-motion strollers and those frail still-life figures on benches.

"So what happened?" I finally asked.

"What happened with *what*?"

"With Solzhenitsyn... With the Prophet of Redemption."

"He didn't change... The great man wrote his great works and took up residence in bucolic Vermont. Away from it all... in all ways... Away from the turmoil back home. Away from the chaos. Away from the *culture*, that nurturing, so-insular Russian culture."

I walked and waited. Dad was on a roll again. Astride the lecture hall platform. Passing on wisdom in a fusillade of potent information pellets. Authoritatively — didactically? — delivered. In Dad's lecture hall, there was no legitimate dissent, no alternate opinion. Occasionally a devil's advocate— and that was invariably him.

"The poor man put himself in a time capsule. He came out nearly a generation later when the world had changed dramatically... *radically*... But he hadn't, with his Vermont's eye view of the world... And he waited too long. He should have gone back when Gorbachev was in power, when Perestroika... Oh, Perestroika!" (and he laughed) "... Then... **Then**... he could still lay claim to the prophet's mantle. The prophet to Gorbachev's savior... But afterwards, during the second, the third wave of change... the coups, the unrest, near civil war... Gorbachev's disgrace, his tragic disgrace... Forget it! **Forget it!**... It was a joke, a bloody joke!"

And now he laughed, rather snorted, contemptuously.

"Was it really that bad?" I piped in. "I mean... He's a great man. He did so much. He told so much. He got recognized... I mean he won a Nobel Prize, didn't he?"

"He did. But..."

"But what?"

"But that's past. And his time has passed... And you know, he doesn't know it. He still doesn't know it. And that's the saddest part of all... It's pathetic... bloody pathetic... That train ride? That heralded trans-Russia train ride. That slow ride home across Siberia, to civilized — so-called civilized — Russia" (and he snorted again) "... All that 'Mother Russia' stuff. Great public relations... if the message had meaning... or the spokesperson had credibility... relevance..."

Just when his voice was rising to a climax, it dropped. He visibly softened. He stopped, and his eyes grew distant again.

BLURRED IMAGES

"And as he droned on like that for weeks and weeks and thousands of miles, the dark side of Mother Russia was showing more and more of her face. You know, Zhirinovsky and his jingoists and fascists, out there, working furiously to create their own vision... And here's yet another sad part, the *ultimate* sad part... "

I waited, for a long suspenseful moment.

"In the end, *their* vision will win out... It's in the Russian nature... And that vision, not Solzhenitsyn's, is the future... Another form of tyranny... with all the same cruelty and suffering of past tyrannies... just under a different banner."

We now were stopped stock-still again. And his face now looked truly hopeless, even tragic.

"Solzhenitsyn's history. A footnote. A *big* footnote. But a footnote nonetheless."

He paused, softening again.

"You know that picture in the *Times* — Solzhenitsyn and I shaking hands in front of some ministry building."

I nodded.

"Well, it was *he* who requested that so-called meeting, that encounter... that... what do you call it... 'photo op'... because he needed every boost, every spark, he could get. At one of his little train stops a week or so earlier, I re-introduced myself, and he knew who I was immediately. Said he was very familiar with my work, said he loved my 'Prophet of Redemption' moniker... I was flattered, of course... And then he asked how long I would be in Russia and whether I could join him in Moscow... And I agreed. But I sensed something... That he was grasping at straws. That he was not being hailed as he had expected, not even close. That he felt foolish, ridiculous at times... So I felt sorry for him. Imagine that, sorry for Solzhenitsyn, the great man, the Nobel Laureate, during his supposedly triumphal return to a country he probably felt he symbolized... *defined*... So I agreed to see him — publicly — in Moscow. Mind you, I felt slightly used— but I did it for Mother Russia, who has suffered so much, and for an old prophet who has also suffered. I felt it was the least I could do."

At that point, he stopped talking. He turned 90 degrees and restarted our stroll. After a minute, he suddenly sat down on an empty bench. His breath was short and labored, his color drained. He suddenly looked old, very old.

"Dad, you OK?"

"No, I'm not OK."

"Should I get help?"

"No. Absolutely not... Please. I just feel tired, very tired."

So we sat there. Him staring forward across the path at a small, elegant flower planting. Me looking frequently, warily, at Dad by my side. I put my arm around his shoulders. Lightly. And, to my surprise, he let it remain there. He didn't mention Russia again that day, or much at all in the days that followed.

CHAPTER XXVIII

Sylvia was waiting for me just inside the hospital lobby. Wearing a flowery sundress exposing surprisingly small round shoulders and the hint of full breasts. Sitting cross-legged, seemingly patiently, greeting me with a tentative little smile. All in all, a more inviting feminine *persona* than I could have imagined.

I hesitated for a moment, then walked over to her. She rose and extended her hand. An odd sort of greeting. But when we shook hands, she held her grasp a moment longer than expected, than appropriate. Then she quickly squeezed my hand and released it. I kept my eyes on her face.

"I was very sorry to hear about your father."

"The 'great man'?" I said, reminding her of her own reference.

"Oh please, don't be sarcastic."

I didn't respond.

"We had an interesting relationship," she said.

"Had?"

"Well, you know... under the circumstances... But I am sorry, genuinely sorry, about his illness. I hope he's OK, really..."

"I know," I muttered.

"Please pass that on to him," she said.

"Yeah, sure, thanks," I said. Then: "Why don't you just write him a note?"

"I don't know. It somehow doesn't seem appropriate..."

"Yeah, under the circumstances."

ARTHUR DIMOND

We stood silently, uncomfortably, for a moment.

"Well, I've gotta go, Danny's expecting me," I abruptly said, starting to turn away.

She grabbed my elbow, startling me, stopping me in mid-stride. "Jeffrey?"

I turned and stared at her, feeling my irritation rising.

"What?... What do you *want* from me?"

She looked at me for a moment without saying anything. Then she said, "Can we sit down and talk?"

"Sylvia, Danny's waiting for me," I said tautly, emphasizing each syllable.

For a moment, she looked angry, like she was on the verge of verbalizing her anger. Then she visibly softened and said: "Just for a short while... a *very* short while... Please."

I thought for a moment, then nodded. We walked through the automatic lobby doors and out to the parking lot, past rows of cars, to hers, a red Saab convertible. She opened the doors with a sonar key device that made a short high-pitched sound, and we got in.

"Where're we going?" I asked.

"Nowhere. Let's just talk here."

"OK," I said.

For a few moments, she didn't say anything. She nestled into the corner, between tan leather seat and cushioned door, and gazed at me till I began to feel uncomfortable, more so than I had been feeling already. Finally, fortunately, she broke the silence.

"Jeff, do you remember when I said the other day how people change over time— over a time as long as 25 years?"

"Sure."

"Well, I didn't just mean Daniel... I meant everybody... Me, you, everybody."

"I know..."

"Do you remember me from back then?"

"Of course I do... From school, from field hockey..."

BLURRED IMAGES

"Right, my Scottish teammate, my prepubescent Scottish teammate in his cute little kilt... and my usurper."
"You remember that?"
"I remember everything."
"And you still hold it against me?"
"Of course I do... That was a threshhold event for me," she said and grinned.
Then her grin turned to a small smile, at first sweet, then quickly bittersweet.
"I remember the wedding... I remember dancing with you, Jeff. It was the closest, physically, I had been with you... to you..."
I nodded.
"You know what I was thinking when we were dancing?"
"No."
"I was thinking what a cute new brother I had. I was thinking how nice it would be to get to know each other better, much better, over time... I was thinking how lucky I was."
She went suddenly quiet. So we just sat there like that for a few minutes, gazing out the windshield at the field of cars glistening in the sun.
"You know," she eventually said, "when we first heard the news... about you... I was probably in greater shock than anybody. I'll bet you didn't know that..."
I just looked at her, across the narrow space in the front of her car. She looked back, studying my face for a reaction, exuding something I couldn't quite identify. Sympathy? Tenderness? Something more intimate?
"I'll bet you didn't know that I was your strongest defender. After the initial shock, your father put on a stiff upper lip, you know... at least in public, at family get-togethers... And your mother... she had her own version of that... although I know her private moments were different... very different."
I nodded.

"And your brother... Daniel... typical lawyer, objective, analytical" (and she laughed that snorting laugh of hers for the first time in this conversation). "Said he needed to know all the facts... when he had all the facts, he'd be able to figure things out... I mean, give me a break! He lived under the same roof with you for 18 years, he *knew* you, or should have... Anyway, he never did get all the facts because you went *incommunicado*... And that's how things stayed with them for most of the time during those first few years. Status quo."

"And you?" I asked. "How did you defend me?"

"Well, I had a simple position. I said I didn't think you were capable of doing what they said you did... committing first degree murder... If you were in your right mind, if you weren't provoked, driven to it."

"And what did you base this on? I mean, you hardly knew me."

"I knew you... better than you thought."

And now she smiled, openly, spontaneously. And when she did, she blushed and turned away.

"What did you know? I mean what *could* you know?"

She turned back toward me, and looked closely, staring right into my eyes.

"A lot. More than you might think... Way back then in school, you seemed like a sensitive kid, not like those rambunctuous boys — or girls — on the team. And later I knew about your music. I also knew about how your family felt about you, even Daniel, especially Daniel."

And now I felt a hand on my shoulder, then on my cheek, rising to the nape of my neck, the back of my head, her fingers enmeshed in my hair, stroking gently, steadily, with just the slightest pressure.

I looked at her questioningly but I didn't verbalize the question. What was she doing? What was I doing— here in this car, out in this field of cars, a mere few hundred yards from my dying brother? with my brother's wife? I mean, this is outrageous; am I totally out of my

BLURRED IMAGES

mind? But I let her continue stroking the back of my head, so softly, so intimately. I didn't stop her. That touch, that warm, soft touch, so unfamiliar, was such a comfort after so long. So I let her do what she was doing and I let her talk, uninterrupted, while she did it.

"I felt from the beginning that you were different, really different, from your brother, your father... The Stevenson men" (and she laughed again)... "You were the sensitive one, the cultured one... The one who would be the famous musician one day. Creating beauty every day. A lovely picture, huh?"

I nodded, and said nothing as she continued her monologue, the pressure of her fingers reflecting the emotional substance and rhythms of her words.

"I tried to picture you out there. Wherever. On the run. Probably scared, lonely. And I would think, what shitty luck. What a shitty bit of irony. That the Stevenson male least likely to be in a situation like that, least likely to *survive* in a situation like that, was the one who was in it... And Jeff, I felt for you, I *really* felt for you."

And now I turned and looked directly at her and her eyes were filled with tears. And instinctively I reached out to her and stroked her cheek, wiping away tears, and tentatively shifted position, moved closer to her, and enfolded her in my arms. And we remained like that in a tight embrace, across that narrow chasm between the seats, our breathing quick and loud and thick with tears.

A near-by car door suddenly opened with a terrible metallic squeak and then slammed shut, startling us, pulling us apart, shattering the serenity of these many moments. I looked at my watch.

"Sylvia, I've gotta go."
"Oh, please, stay awhile longer."
"I can't... Danny's waiting. I told him I'd be there by 1..."
Her face, so soft all this time, suddenly turned red and harsh.
"Oh, screw Danny... He can wait..."
"No, he can't... And I won't make him... I mean, think about it, it's not fair."

"*Fair?*" she asked incredulously. "After everything I told you — about him? about you? — how can you talk about *fair?*"

"Sylvia, you have to understand... why I'm back... how I feel about my brother."

She studied me for a moment and as she did, her face again grew thoughtful, tender.

"What about how I feel about *this* brother?... how you may feel about *me*?"

"Sylvia, look, this is all new to me... a total surprise, to put it mildly... I mean, I had no idea you felt this way ..."

"I didn't know, really know, until now..."

"But now that you do... think about it. I mean, *really* think about it..."

She didn't reply. She just kept looking at me, silently imploring.

I opened the car door and as I got out, she placed her hand on mine and said gently, but with a hint of insistence, "Jeffrey, you think about it, too. We've suffered, you and I... We're kindred spirits, I really believe that... We've been lonely. Hurt. Scared... Think about that... Think about what we deserve."

I listened and nodded and gave her hand a little squeeze. Then, with some effort, I lifted myself from the car seat, closed the door, and walked briskly back to the hospital entrance.

CHAPTER XXIX

I spent a weekday afternoon nearly alone in the dark cocoon of a movie theatre. I drove out to a mega-mall deep in Montgomery County. I had no idea what I wanted to see, but I knew there was one of those ten-theatre complexes at the mall, and that would give me more than enough choices. I wasn't particular. My object was escape, pure and simple. Refuge from the dreary, asceptic, fluorescent-white atmosphere of the hospital. The dour, pasty complexions. The timelessness. The long wait for nothing to happen. Or something. But nothing good.

I parked the car in a vast lot, packed to the guardrails, and walked across the lot, past the shiny, late-model cars and jeeps and upscale sports utility vehicles.

I entered the movie megaplex, relatively empty except for several clumps of retiree types, and strode the few yards to the ticket window. A dark, smooth-complected young man in a grape-colored uniform with gold epaulets and piping and a single thin gold hoop in his left ear greeted me pleasantly.

"Which show, sir?"

I looked at him, equally pleasantly.

"What do you recommend?"

He seemed mildly surprised. That was a question waiters or bookstore clerks heard. But movie ticket-sellers?

"It's been awhile," I explained.

He nodded and picked up the beat.

ARTHUR DIMOND

"Well, what are you in the mood for?"

"Something different."

"How about *The Piano*?"

"Sure," I said immediately. To the apparent surprise and satisfaction of the young guy, I bought the ticket without further discussion.

I stopped at the refreshment counter and picked up a large box of popcorn and an orange soda. Then, thusly laden, I made my way to another pleasant, uniformed young man waiting at an opening in the velvet rope. He took my ticket, tore it in half, gave me the stub, and said with a sincere smile, "Enjoy the show."

I walked down a dim corridor until I found the right theatre, marked by a miniature marquis that announced: 'THE PIANO.'

I took a seat toward the rear of the theatre. There was only a handful of people scattered about. Solos and couples. Older people, older than me. Sitting patiently, quietly, while waiting for the film to begin. Obviously finding it a relaxing place to collect oneself, regain one's bearings. As I did.

I sat and methodically lifted small handfuls of the moistened kernels to my mouth, and slowly chewed them, washing them down with sips through a colorful straw of the orange soda.

The lights then dimmed. And the theatre soon went dark. An animated message came on the screen urging us to be considerate to our fellow viewers, to be quiet, not to smoke, and to responsibly dispose of our trash. Then the previews of films either coming to the megaplex or already there. Finally, with a blaring of trumpets, a huge message marched onto the screen: 'AND NOW... OUR FEATURE PRESENTATION.'

It began with the crashing of waves on a gray turbulent sea. The haunting strains of a timeless, placeless score— first orchestral, then piano. The image of a tiny woman, a young girl, and a huge crate on a fragile boat in the midst of this turbulence. The image filled — dominated — the screen, the room.

BLURRED IMAGES

I sat back in my seat and relaxed. My fingers still moving down and into the popcorn box, but more slowly, absently. I succumbed to the film, soon experiencing utter peace.

Time sped by. My mind, my consciousness, migrated effortlessly to that remote outpost at a far corner of the Pacific. To that surrealistic, indelible tableau— woman, girl, and of course, piano, on that desolate, storm-swept beach. To the dense, hilly forests and that lonely, sodden compound. To the eerie interplay between newcomers, oldcomers, and natives. Between the mute, mail-order bride and the bluff, sometimes cruel master— and the desperately searching semi-savage at the third point in the triangle. The most intriguing character in the tale.

Eventually, the characters' passions played out, the drama was over, the lights were up. Elderly, latter-day Marylanders revealed themselves, stretching, quietly chatting. Empty popcorn box nestled between my thighs. A rude awakening overall.

I debated seeing a second film but decided against it; guilt was encroaching. I moved slowly up the aisle, out into the brighter lobby lights, and through a metal side door, to the lot, the car, the road, and home.

* * * * *

A woman was waiting on the porch. Sitting stiffly on one of the wicker chairs. Plain, thickly set, with a long face and an austere look. Black hair with generous streaks of silver-grey. A pleated skirt and a tan raincoat. Glasses that curved up, cat-style, at the corners.

I stopped at the top step and looked at her, curious, anxious. She didn't get up. She just sat there and looked directly at me.

"Are you Jeffrey Stevenson?"

"Yes."

"You look different... a bit different... than the TV and newspaper pictures."

She was staring at me, studying me closely, intensely.

ARTHUR DIMOND

"Who are you?" I asked, more anxious than my voice betrayed.

"I'm Sally Dougherty... Raymond... **Patrolman** Raymond Dougherty's daughter."

I felt the color drain from my face. My sweat glands open. My heartbeat quicken. I forced myself to keep looking at her.

"When you first came back... out... scot free... I imagined coming here, sitting here, and holding a gun... and shooting you dead."

I had pictured a similar scene. I was surprised, genuinely surprised, it hadn't happened. All that hate. Hate mail. Hate calls. The blatant fury of that man in the cafeteria, those people outside the TV studios, those motorcycle cops at the funeral. All it took was one writer, one caller, one verbal assailant, going that one extra step. Doing what he — or she — felt, thought, threatened, imagined.

"But you didn't," I said softly. "Why not?"

"I don't know... Maybe it's not in me to do that... Maybe I don't have the courage."

I kept looking at her, but didn't — couldn't — say anything for a minute or more.

"So why are you here? Why did you come here?"

"To look you in the eye... and tell you what you did to our family..."

"I know what I did, and..."

"No, you don't. Not entirely. You only know what you did to Raymond... to my father..."

Her voice suddenly caught. And she looked down at her tightly clasped hands. Then she took a quick deep breath and looked up, directly at me.

I stood there mutely. I hadn't made a move toward her, toward a chair. I just stood there and waited.

"Now I'm going to tell you what you did... *everything* you did when you swung that bat of yours... when you..."

I waited a few moments more while she collected herself. Then she spoke clearly and evenly.

BLURRED IMAGES

"My mother had to go back to work... The insurance and the death benefits weren't enough... There were four of us... My mother worked herself nearly to death... Waitressing... two jobs... I was the oldest so I was responsible for the other kids... I was eleven when it happened... *Eleven!*... and I had to be responsible for three little kids... after school... dinner... bed time... sick time... I didn't have a childhood after that... I lost..."

Her eyes were now moist — with sadness? anger? She took a deep breath and resumed.

"That's how it went, for years... It was too much, really too much for me. My two brothers got out of hand... in trouble... too much drinking, the wrong friends, the usual... One's in jail now... Imagine, Ray Dougherty's boy in jail!..."

And again she got emotional, teary. She looked away, then down at the floor.

I didn't say anything for a moment and then asked, "Do you blame me for all this? I mean I'm sorry... So sorry."

Now she jerked her head up and fixed me with a fierce stare.

"Sorry?!... *Sorry?!*... How can you blither that word? That stupid, stupid word. What does sorry *mean*? You killed my father... my father and the father of three other little kids... and the husband of a simple woman who never knew what hit her..."

I silently absorbed that information, conjuring up the picture of Officer Collins' family, the children, the widow walking haltingly across the cemetery grass that recent day, hanging on the arm of a young man. Then slowly, apprehensively, I asked: "Where is your mother?... *How* is your mother?"

For a moment she stared at me, then looked away, out over the porch railing to the street and beyond.

"She's in a nursing home... a Catholic nursing home that takes care of her for practically nothing... She's the youngest person there... fifty-eight... Imagine that, fifty-eight and in a nursing home... And she's been there for five years... Worked to the bone... Heart problems...

Hasn't smiled for years."

I was about to say "I'm sorry," and stopped myself before the words left my mouth.

"So, Mr. Stevenson, Mr. Jeffrey Stevenson... let me answer your question... I *do* blame you... And my family... what's left of it... blames you, too... If Chris wasn't in jail, he would probably come and shoot you... He would've done it by now..."

She sat there, breathing heavily, but keeping her eyes fixed on me.

"Do you know that it was all an accident... a terrible accident?" I eventually asked.

"What difference does that make?" she shot back.

"What difference? All the difference in the world... I didn't **mean** to kill your father... I wasn't even supposed to *be* there that afternoon... I was on my way to play softball... **Softball**... That's why I had the bat... that goddamned bat... But there wasn't any game that day... Because of the rally... I got caught up in the rally... I got chased... Your father was one of the officers chasing me... I was scared... **Terrified!**... I was never political... I was never in trouble... I was a good kid... Boringly good... And in one moment I became a murderer... It was an incredible, stupid accident... It ruined my life, too."

"But you *have* a life. You're *alive!*" she fired back. "And you're free."

"Only in one sense."

She practically laughed.

"That's the only sense that means anything to me... or to my family," she said. "You're standing here. Alive and free as a bird on the porch of your pretty house in this cushy little neighborhood."

She was staring at me again, that fierce, laser-like stare. This time I stared back.

"What do you want from me?" I finally, wearily, asked.

"Nothing."

"You have to want something... I mean you came here... all the

BLURRED IMAGES

way from Massachusetts."

"From Maine now."

"Even further... So why did you come? What do you want?"

"I already got it... I told you what I wanted to tell you... To your face... You can't do anything or say anything to change what happened... And I don't want your 'sorry's'... They make me sick."

"So that's it?"

"Yeah, that's it."

And she quickly rose, picked up her pocket book, walked across the porch, toward me and past me without looking in my face again or saying anything, not a single word. I watched her stride purposefully down the path, cross the street to a station wagon, and get in. She started it up, pulled away from the curb and down the street slowly, without ever looking at me. I followed her progress, speechless, numb from the encounter, absently thinking about her brother and when he might get out of jail and whether he might pay me a different kind of visit.

CHAPTER XXX

I picked Dad up at the hospital late in the morning on a bright pleasant day. An attendant wheeled him to the curb at the main entrance under the canopy, gently but firmly helped him up and into the car, and placed his small blue valise in the trunk, pushing aside the two half-empty windshield washer containers, tool kit, empty wine carton, and a few pieces of paraphernalia.

I went around to the driver's side, got in, dropped into gear, and pulled away slowly, down the short drive. When we got to the avenue, and stopped momentarily, I turned to Dad. His face, pale and waxy, was bathed in sunshine, and he was looking up at the light, a small benign smile on his face.

I smiled at him. He seemed to sense it.

"Good to be out," he said. "Sprung."

"Feel OK?" I asked.

"I suppose... all things considered."

I turned right toward home. After we had driven a few blocks down the broad avenue, Dad abruptly said, "Let's see Danny."

I was surprised. Genuinely surprised. And instantly anxious. He had visited Danny in the hospital only once. And I gathered — from Danny, not from Dad, who didn't say anything about it — that it hadn't gone well.

"You sure?" I asked. "I mean... right now? You just got sprung yourself."

"Yes, I'm sure...Now."

BLURRED IMAGES

I glanced at him quickly. He didn't say anything else. He just sat there calmly, his hands clasped on his lap, eyes directed straight ahead. I turned the radio on to fill the void. I switched to a few stations. All talk or news or ads. Typical late-morning, noontime fare.

"Yack, yack, yack," Dad said, seemingly more amused than annoyed.

I nodded, smiled, and flipped off the radio.

We then rode the remaining ten or fifteen minutes in silence. An oddly intimate silence. Not the remote uncomfortable kind.

At Danny's hospital, I went directly to the main entrance. Leaving the engine running, I got out, went around, opened Dad's door, and helped him out. I lightly grasped his elbow and guided him to and through the wide automatic doors, into the bright familiar lobby, and to a seat amidst potted plants and magazines in a pleasant waiting area. Then out to park the car and back.

"You sure you're ready for this, Dad?" I asked.

He nodded.

"You haven't seen him for awhile. Quite awhile. He's changed... gone downhill... I didn't want to tell you while..."

"While I was sick, right?"

"Right."

"You didn't want to give the old guy a shock... maybe have a relapse, right...?" he asked, and laughed sharply like a bark.

"Well..."

"Well, don't worry about it... I'm tough." And he laughed again.

We were now standing in front of the elevator. When the door opened, we waited for several people, a nurse and a couple of apparent visitors, to exit. When we got in, Dad asked, "What floor?... I forget."

"Five," I said.

He pressed the button, the doors closed, and we ascended alone.

ARTHUR DIMOND

When the doors opened to the familiar sight of nursing station and white-lit corridor, I guided Dad leftward, slowly making our way to Danny's room. When we got there, the door was nearly closed. I gestured for Dad to wait while I gently pushed the door further open and looked in. At first, I couldn't quite make out Danny— the room was so dim, with the lights off and curtains drawn closed, and his emaciated form so still under the covers. I had seen him like this many times yet it still alarmed me. Slowly, quietly, I moved closer to the bed and relaxed when I saw his chest rising and falling, almost imperceptibly, with his faint breathing.

Dad whispered urgently, audibly, from the door.

"What is it?"

"Nothing, Dad, it's OK... Come in."

He pushed the door further open and stepped in, quietly moving toward me. When he reached me, he stood stock still, our shoulders practically touching, and gazed over at Danny. I glanced at Dad, his face somber, thoughtful. Instinctively, I put an arm around his slender waist; he let it stay there. And that's how we stood for what seemed a long while. Every so often, I glanced at Dad again, looking for a tear, or a clenched-jaw suppression of tears, some sign of emotion, shock, distress. I detected nothing.

Eventually a nurse came in. Walking in that brisk, professional way, she rounded the foot of the bed, with a quick hello to us. She looked closely at Danny's pale, inscrutable face, checked the IV bag and its entry point in his arm, that perforated, purple-splotched arm. Then with a quick good-bye, she left.

Something in her movement, the stirring of air, the light touch on his arm, aroused Danny. He opened his eyes, looked first at the ceiling, that well-navigated terrain, and then at us. He mustered a small smile, turned slightly quizzical when he saw Dad at my side.

"Hi, Danny," Dad said.

"Hi, Dad," Danny replied, his voice dry and grainy. "You're out?"

BLURRED IMAGES

"Yes."

"We *just* got him out," I offered. "He wanted to come right over here."

Danny glanced at Dad, who nodded assent.

"How are you?" Dad asked.

"I've been better," Danny said, without smiling.

Dad didn't say anything for a minute. Then he asked, "They treating you OK here? Do you have everything you need?"

Danny nodded.

None of us said anything for a few moments. Then, to my surprise, Danny broke the silence.

"Dad, why did you come here?" he asked, looking directly at the old man.

"Why? Because you're my son... You're..."

"Dad!" Danny interrupted, and then went silent, and then started up again: "I was your son last month, before you went to Russia... and six months ago when I was diagnosed and..."

"Oh, come on, Danny," I said, trying to calm things down, slow them down, feeling they were quickly getting out of hand.

"It's OK, Jeff," Dad said. "Let him talk... He's right, you know."

Danny looked thoughtfully at both of us. Dad had moved slightly away from me, releasing my arm from his waist. He stood closer to the bed and waited. Danny seemed to be collecting himself, gathering his words and the strength to deliver them. Finally he spoke, softly yet clearly and firmly.

"Dad, I've been your son forever. And my life's been falling apart for the last couple of years... and you abandoned me... *abandoned* me... And *now*... look at me *now*... My life's almost over... I'm *dying*..."

I glanced at Dad. For the first time he flinched, visibly shuddered at the raw, dread power of that word. And I struggled to suppress my own physical response, to maintain some control.

ARTHUR DIMOND

"I'm dying... I've been dying for **months**...I've been in this shithole all this time and this is the second time... the second *fucking* time..."

"Don't use profanity with me!" Dad bellowed. Danny stopped and stared in disbelief at our father. He laughed and coughed on his laugh. Then he collected himself, diluting, swallowing, his own phlegm. I instinctively moved toward him to help him up, to make it easier. But he waved me away and swallowed several times with some effort, concentrating very hard. Then he took a breath, as deep as he seemed capable of, and raised and turned his head, ever so slightly, and continued staring directly at Dad.

"This is a joke, a real joke!" he said. "And you don't get it, Dad, you just don't get it... I really am dying... I'll be dead... *dead*!... very soon... And you're getting upset over a little 'profanity'... If you're so proper... so *fucking* proper and upstanding, Dad... how come you abandoned me... how come you came now... made the grand sacrifice... Are you trying to clear your precious conscience before..."

"*Enough!*" Dad suddenly roared, the old righteous, patriarchal fury surging to the surface, cutting through his frail frame, through the shroudlike atmosphere of the room.

Danny stopped and stared at our father. We all hung on the ringing, lingering presence of that command. We fell uncomfortably silent, waiting, wondering where to go next. Then Dad turned to me and spoke, softly and calmly.

"Jeff, would you please excuse us... just for a short while? ... I want to talk to Danny... alone."

For a moment, I was stunned, hurt. This was no time for secrets, for confidences. I balked.

"Please, Jeff... We need to talk... I need to talk... to Danny... alone."

For a moment, I didn't move. I looked at Danny, now quiet and resigned and staring up at the ceiling. So I turned toward the door and the corridor.

BLURRED IMAGES

"I'll see you in the lobby... in awhile."

I left the room and quickly strode toward the elevators, my throat aching, a wellspring of tears rising to my cheeks, my eyes. I entered a soon-arriving elevator and when the doors opened up, I strode straight across and through the lobby, to the automatic doors, and out into the little park where I found the bench across from the pond, and sat still and stolid and eventually dry-eyed, staring at that "Statue of Hope," utterly oblivious to its irony.

Eventually I rose and walked back to the lobby. Dad was sitting on a chair near the entrance. He looked at me with reddened eyes and a grim expression. Then he got up and walked toward me and we left the hospital. I didn't offer to come around and pick him up at the curb — and he didn't ask — and we moved slowly, wordlessly, toward the parking lot. Once in the car, he stared straight ahead. At one point when I glanced at him, he was still in that pose, a single nerve now visibly pulsating in his jaw.

CHAPTER XXXI

I called Danny's doctor the next morning and was told he was on rounds; I left a message. I called later in the afternoon and was told he was lecturing. I called the following morning and was told he was with a patient. I came back from several errands to find a terse voice mail message: "This is Dr. Ambling. Sorry I missed your call. Please try between 5:30 and 6 this evening." I tried him between 5:30 and 6, and the line was constantly busy. And so it went until we finally connected the following afternoon.

"Dr. Ambling..."

"Yes?" he responded with a tone of professional boredom.

"This is Jeff Stevenson..."

"Oh, yes, Daniel's brother... Sorry it's been so difficult connecting."

I didn't respond.

"What can I do for you, Mr. Stevenson?" he asked.

"I need to know about Danny... Every time I see him he's further downhill... The other day..."

"He seemed worse?"

"Yes, definitely worse... He looked terrible."

"Part of that might be the result of the chemotherapy."

"What about it?"

"We've adjusted the dosage... We've upped it."

"I didn't know that."

"I'm sorry. It's difficult to inform relatives of every step in the

BLURRED IMAGES

treatment of patients... I'm sure..."

"Yes, I understand," I said, interrupting him, anticipating his next words. "But what does this mean?"

"It means we need to treat Daniel's illness more aggressively."

"'Aggressively'?" My heart was beginning to beat quickly.

"Yes, higher dosages of the medication... the previous dosage level was inadequate."

Now I was gripping the phone, staring at it, my heart galloping, my breathing quick and shallow.

"Where's this heading, doctor?... Is any of this going to work?"

"You mean, *cure* him?... or extend his life?"

"I mean cure him and... *give* him a life... This is a living... a *barely* living... hell for him."

He paused momentarily, then said, "No." Simply. Finally. Then he said, "I'm sorry."

How many times had he said that? In just that way? Softly, somberly, sympathetically. Yet with no real warmth. No further explanation or elaboration. At this point, it was self-evident, a done deal. Danny had known it for weeks, months. His doctor had no doubt known it even longer. I needed to be told. Unequivocally. I needed to be hit over the head with it. And now calmer, clearer-eyed, I asked: "How long do we have here? How much time does Danny have?"

"Several weeks... A month if he's lucky... I'm sorry."

* * * * *

This time *I* needed to speak to *her*. I tried her at her office and got her voice mail message, clear, crisp — the professional Sylvia — advising that she was on a business trip, due to return the next morning, that her assistant was available at extension such and such, and so on. I left a message, saying it was urgent, though my voice would have told her that anyway. I left a similiar message on her home machine.

ARTHUR DIMOND

I tiptoed upstairs and looked in on my father. He was on his back, under a light blanket, sleeping deeply, snoring loudly. Then I descended to the kitchen, grabbed a beer from the fridge and took it and the cordless phone out to the porch and waited. For hours I sat on one of the wicker chairs. For awhile I leafed aimlessly through the day's newspaper and random magazines. Now and then I got up to stretch, to get another beer, to take a leak, to quickly cruise the downstairs rooms. Most of the time, I sat and stared out at the darkening street, at the business commuters coming home from the bus stop, briefcases dangling or swinging, at the dogwalkers, at the occasional joggers and couples strolling in the summer night after dinner. And then it was just dark and quiet and still.

At one point I must have dozed off. When the phone rang, I awoke with a lurch, fumbling with the cordless phone till I found the "Talk" button.

"Jeffrey?"

Her unmistakable voice.

"Yes."

"It's me."

"I know."

A momentary pause.

"I just got in and got your message. What's the matter?"

She sounded breathless.

I told her about my conversation with Ambling. In increasingly tremulous tones, my voice starting to break. A long pause at the other end.

"Sylvia... You still there?"

"Yes... I'm here."

Another pause.

"Meet me," she abruptly said.

"Now?" I asked. "What time is it?"

"About 11."

"Oh, Jesus... I don't know if I can leave my father..."

BLURRED IMAGES

A long breathy pause this time.

"Look, I'm in my car, heading in from National... I'll pick you up in 15 minutes. We'll go near-by, have you back in no time."

"OK," I said tentatively.

"See you soon... Be on the porch, OK?"

"That's where I am."

"Good."

The headlights flashed as she pulled up, and I went down the steps to meet her, locking the front door on the way.

When I dropped onto that comfortable, contoured leather seat, she turned to me, leaned into me, and kissed my cheek sweetly and softly, an innocent gesture which she seemed to imbue with a particular intimacy.

"You're really hurting," she said. "I'm very sorry. I really am."

Then she slowly drove down the street.

"Where're we going?"

"Let's go out to the Marriott."

I gave her a questioning look, which she seemed to sense even as her eyes remained focused straight ahead on the road.

"The bar," she said with a vaguely mischievous smile. "They have a nice bar. And it's open late."

We were there in about ten minutes. She pulled into a space in the outdoor lot, turned off the engine, and sat for a moment—gathering herself? trying to anticipate, plan, what would follow? Then she turned to me with a small smile, squeezed my hand the same way as before, and unlocked the doors. We walked without touching or talking across the still lot to the canopied entrance, through the bright-lit lobby to the dim, nearly-empty bar, to a comfortable booth against an interior wall. As I started sitting down, across from her, she said, "Come over here, next to me." I hesitated momentarily, then did as she said.

The waiter, a thankfully dour sort, came over and took our orders. And then we were alone again, an inch apart on the tufted booth bench.

"You know, Jeff, as I said the other day, we have a bond." And as she said that, she took my hand in both of hers and put it on her lap and stroked it gently. I didn't resist.

"We're tied by the two most intimate relationships Daniel every had," she continued. "Your love and loyalty for him. And the love and loyalty I had for him for so many years... Until he did all the things he did... and things... *everything!* ... started falling apart. And now I hate him. Fiercely. Relentlessly. And you still love him."

She smiled in an odd, ironic sort of way, and continued to stroke my hand, looking at me with such warmth, such caring. The drinks arrived, the waiter wordlessly departed, and she continued.

"But I'm sure you're thinking, that would seem to be pretty flimsy grounds for a bond. You'd think it would have the *opposite* effect. I mean, that's the direction — the *logical* direction — we were heading in. Right?"

I nodded.

"But I think you know, there's something here. There's something good, very good, coming out of such a history, such a terrible history."

And now I felt the heat of her thigh against mine as she continued to caress my hand oh so gently and firmly at the same time. As she continued to talk in such soft but certain tones. And despite myself, despite my chronic gloom and the grim reason we were sitting in that booth together at that hour, I was feeling surprisingly, shamelessly, aroused.

"Remember in the car at the hospital when I told you that we both have suffered? We've been hurt and lonely and sometimes scared, really scared? Remember that?"

I nodded.

"Well, we were dealing with different problems. But the end result, the end feeling, was the same. And it's lasted so long... And that's a big part of the bond I think we have..."

BLURRED IMAGES

And then she smiled that little, often enigmatic smile again, and said, "But this isn't a misery loves company kind of thing, I mean it's nothing mawkish or maudlin or whatever... I mean, Jeffrey" (and now the warmth of her leg and her hands felt like they were permeating me, her face was closer, her breath light on my cheek)... "Jeffrey, I feel a bond that is something else... kind of what might have happened if Danny hadn't shown up for that game and stayed for the summer... and you were a few years older" (and we both smiled now).

I was feeling overwhelmed by the sweet steady flow of words, the warm enveloping physical presence of Sylvia. And now I was struggling mightily to control how my body was responding.

"Jeff, I feel something happening now, really happening... and I don't want to stop it..."

"Sylvia, please" I said, and she ignored me.

"*Sylvia!*" I now said sharply, and pulled away.

She didn't move. She just sat there staring at me, the same look of hurt and anger as the last time in the car in the hospital lot, only more intense.

"Sylvia, this is crazy. Crazy! I can't do this. I can't listen to this. I came to talk about Danny... For chrissakes, he's dying! *Dying!* You're coming on like this and my brother... your husband..."

"*Ex*-husband!" she barked, now a foot away and visibly upset.

"Danny... Danny is dying... He'll be dead in a month... And I came to talk, to commiserate..."

"I don't want to talk about Danny... I'm talked out about the son of a bitch... You and I are talking about two very different people anyway... two *totally* different people... I want to talk about you... me..." she said softly, through lips quivering ever so slightly.

Now I reached out to her and took her hand and held it across the tabletop.

"Sylvia," I said as gently as I could. "I understand, I really understand now, how you feel, why you feel the way you do... Believe me, I understand. But you have to understand that right now I can only think about my brother — the Danny I know — and the strong feelings, the very strong feelings I have for him ... and my father, too... I love them both... I just don't have room... emotional room... for anything else... any*body* else... and..."

"And..."

"Sylvia, even if I had the room, I couldn't do this... I couldn't hurt them... I mean, for God's sake, please, let's get back to reality... Think about what all this means... These relationships... I mean, you're my sister-in-law, the wife, ex-wife, whatever, of my brother... and he is dying... He is dying and no matter what he did or what you think..."

At that point, I began to break down. I couldn't speak any more. And she just sat there, seemingly making an effort to compose herself, maybe to think of what she wanted to say and how to say it.

"Look, Jeffrey," she said, now softly, soothingly again. "We're two people whose lives have been turned inside out — that have been badly damaged, *devastated* — by terrible events, things we never ever would have expected. What we're dealing with here, right now, is one surprise that could be a wonderful thing... Hey, Jeffrey, I've been thinking about you for two whole days, on two plane trips, on a long night in a depressing hotel room in God's country... thinking things that would probably, definitely, embarrass you. When I called before... from the car... I was prepared to take you up to a room in this Marriott tonight and seduce you... I even called ahead to make a reservation... Really."

"Not tonight, Sylvia," I said, barely audibly, after a moment. "Sorry."

"Maybe some other time," she said, and smiled, apparently trying to make a small joke, to ease us out gracefully.

I nodded and smiled back.

"I hope so," she said, "and I hope you won't *feel* like you were seduced."

She smiled again, maybe drawing some encouragement, intended

BLURRED IMAGES

or not, from something in this exchange.

"I have to go home... check on my father, you know."

"I know," she said, and we got up and made our way out. As we walked through the lobby, she took my hand and I let her hold it all the way to the car.

* * * * *

The next morning I visited Danny. As on many previous visits, he was lying motionlessly on his back, in the dim, musty room. Only the subtle rise and fall of his blanket reassured me that he was alive. And as usual, the faint sounds of my arrival, my gentle footfalls, the stirring of the air, disturbed his sleep or a dreamy, sleep-like state. He opened his eyes and slowly turned his head, displaying a small, enigmatic smile. I made an effort to smile back.

"How you feeling?" I asked.

"You know," he murmured.

"Yeah, I guess I do."

He nodded at the easy chair and I dropped into it. We silently gazed at each other for a few moments before Danny turned away and stared up at the ceiling with which he was now on such intimate terms.

"You and Dad had quite a conversation the other day, I gather."

Danny quickly turned to me, suddenly attentive and alert.

"He told you?"

"No, he didn't tell me anything."

"So?..."

"It was obvious."

Danny considered that for a moment, uttered a "Hmmmm," then faced the ceiling again.

"Danny," I eventually said, "I need to talk to you."

"You *always* talk to me," he said with the hint of a smile.

"I need to talk to you about something specific."

The combination of the words and the firm, serious tone captured his attention and he turned to me again. Slowly, questioningly.

"What?" he asked.

"What you've done," I replied. "I asked you awhile ago and you put me off. You said you quote fucked up unquote, and that was it. Dad speaks in large generalities. And Sylvia..."

"She crucifies me... She tells you everything... absolutely fucking everything! Right?"

"Right."

"So what do you need me for?"

"To tell me if it's true, if she's right... These are incredible — *terrible!* — things she's talking about. I mean..."

"You mean did I do those things she told you about?... Well, I don't want to go through the whole fucking litany all over again— what a lying, stealing, cheating, philandering prick I am... what a shitty father I am... in minute fucking detail. But are you asking me if, broadly speaking, in a word, yes or no, it's true?"

"Yes, Danny, that's what I'm asking. I'm sorry to put you through this, I really am. But you've got to tell me. Is it true? I need to know."

I stared directly into his deep-sunken eyes. And he stared right back.

"Yes," he said, softly but clearly.

I continued to stare.

"And what she told me about your son, about Michael— is that true, too?"

"You mean about how I'm solely and exclusively responsible for what's happened to him? How I'm the cause of his prematurity, his colic, his early learning disability, his chronic anger, the concussion he got from a bike accident? et cetera et cetera et cetera."

"Oh, come on, don't get sarcastic. I'm just trying..."

"You're just trying to get the truth about your big brother, right?"

BLURRED IMAGES

"Right."

"Before I die."

"Oh, shut the fuck up!" I blurted. "I'm not going to listen to that shit... Just talk to me. Help me understand."

My outburst temporarily stunned him. He stared at me for a long moment, and I wasn't sure he would continue. But then he did.

"Well, the truth is that I haven't been an angel, or anything close to one. But Sylvia can't blame me for *everything*. Some things are my fault. Definitely. Other things are her fault or nobody's fault or fate or whatever. They just *happened*."

Through this exchange, Danny had gotten more and more agitated. And with the agitation, he had raised his head from his pillow and made an effort to turn and support himself on his elbow. But now he seemed spent, totally exhausted from the exertion, and he dropped back onto the bed. He lay on his back again, staring up at the ceiling, and breathing quickly and shallowly.

"Danny, I'm sorry."

"Sorry for what?" he murmured through tight, quivering lips between breaths.

"Sorry to put you through all that. Just sorry."

"Don't be sorry. It needed to be said."

I didn't reply.

"I should have told you before. I should have told you what Sylvia told you, *before* she told you."

I remained mute. Anything I said would have sounded trivial or stupid.

"I'm sorry I disappointed you... and Dad... and Michael... and everybody."

Then his eyes closed and they stayed that way until I rose and quietly left the room ten or fifteen minutes later.

* * * * *

ARTHUR DIMOND

I jogged through my father's neighborhood. Up and down those green blocks with the comfortable brick and frame houses set back from the street. I lost myself in the tranquility of the streets and the rhythmic motion of my legs, the repetitive thuds of my Nikes on the pavement.

I sat in my room on that straight, ladder-backed chair and played all six of the cello suites. Better than I had ever played them.

I knocked lightly on my father's door. He seemed to be recovering, day by day. But now he was trying to deal with a cold.

"Come in," he said.

He was sitting up in bed, clad in blue pajamas, wearing rimless trifocals, reading *The New York Times*.

"Hi, Jeff," he said, pleasantly with a gentle little smile. A refreshing change.

"Hi, Dad, how you feeling?"

"Getting there... I hope... If it's not one thing, it's another."

I nodded, and sat down on the arm chair, near the bed.

"Say, Jeff, was that you or the Casals CD?"

"Very funny," I responded.

"I'm serious."

"OK... Casals."

He chuckled.

"Nice of you to ask," I said.

"Nice of you to play... Like a private recital. It sounded beautiful."

"Thank you."

He eased back into the pillows and dropped the newspaper across his lap.

"You ever think of what might have happened...if all that hadn't happened?"

"You mean with my life?"

"Yes."

"All the time," I said without hesitation.

BLURRED IMAGES

He nodded and gazed at me.

"You think, if it didn't happen, you'd be playing that instrument for more than one old man lying in bed?"

"Maybe... or maybe I'd be an accountant... or a bus driver... or some homeless guy on the street."

"Come on, seriously."

"I *am* being serious. Things happen, things we can't see coming, that we have no control over. I mean..."

"I understand," he said. And that's all he said. I sank back into the easy chair and surveyed the room. The impressive watercolor landscapes and seascapes my mother had painted. Some Ansel Adams Yosemite photos. A wallful of pictures of my father with an array of notables including prime ministers, a Nobel laureate historian, and a couple of U. S. presidents. On the dresser were framed photos of Danny, my mother, my father, myself, individual and together in different groupings, at various stages of our lives.

I felt Dad silently following my visual survey. When my gaze returned to him, he seemed calm and thoughtful.

"There's a lifetime in here," he said.

"*Several* lifetimes," I responded.

He nodded, and looked at the facing wall, the one with my mother's paintings.

"Dad," I eventually said.

"Yes?" he responded, dimly, from a distance.

"I spoke to Danny's doctor."

He turned to me.

"And... what did he say?"

"He said... the worst."

"I know," he murmured.

"Did you call him, too?"

"No... I didn't have to... I just knew."

He continued to stare at the far wall, at those watercolor scenes softly radiating the early-morning light. His mouth was trembling, his eyes visibly working hard to suppress his emotions. And then they gave up and the tears flowed and small tormented sounds forced their way up and out, ever louder, ever more painful to witness.

*****

As I drifted on a raft in an impenetrably dark, fog-enshrouded lagoon, a bell rang. At first I was startled. Then I became irritated with the intrusion. I opened my eyes and scanned the immediate area. I was on my bed, not the raft. And in my room, not that eerie but tranquil, somehow comforting lagoon. And the bell belonged to the phone, that insistent, infuriating companion.

Just as I grabbed it, Dad picked it up in his room.

"Yes?" Dad asked, his voice low and gravelly.

"This is Dr. Ernst. I'm a resident at Baskin Park Hospital ... Who am I speaking to?"

"Professor Stevenson... Daniel Stevenson's father."

"I'm on, too, Dad... This is Jeffrey Stevenson, Daniel's brother... What is it? What's happened?"

I was now fully alert.

"I'm afraid I have bad news for you..."

I heard Dad's phone click.

"You still there?" he asked.

"Yes," I said, now remotely. "Just me. Jeffrey."

"Your brother — Daniel — died a half-hour ago..."

The news was inevitable. But so soon? So conclusive? That was it. The abruptness. The finality. A life all over. I was stunned, speechless, sitting stiffly on the edge of the bed, gripping the phone, holding it close to my ear.

"You still there, Mr. Stevenson?"

"Yes... Yes... I don't understand, though... I just spoke to his doctor..."

"Ambling?"

BLURRED IMAGES

"Yes... I just spoke to him... the other day. He said it was bad, getting worse, but he gave Danny three, maybe four weeks... What happened?... What *could* have happened?"

"He must have just given out. He was very sick. Sometimes things happen much faster than we can predict. It just happens... There's nothing anybody can do... I'm sorry."

* * * * *

I softly descended to Dad's room. The door was open. The lights were off, but in the moonlight shining through the window, I could clearly see Dad lying on his back, staring up at the ceiling, his eyes dry.

"You OK?" I asked.

He nodded, an almost imperceptible little gesture.

"How could it happen so soon?" I asked.

"It wasn't so soon..."

I stared at him, silent, puzzled.

"It was late, weeks later than he wanted. It was hopeless... He was doomed."

"He knew that? I mean he said it all the time... but was he really convinced? Was he that sure?"

"Yes."

And the full reality suddenly engulfed me.

"He did this?"

"Yes..."

"He told you that," I said with a sudden certainty. "That day... that conversation."

"No... not exactly."

"Well?"

"I knew... I just knew."

Tears were now welling up. Those familiar tears on their well-worn path. Tears of grief and of anger. I thought I would have none left at this point.

"I never even had a chance to say good-bye. I mean our last conversation..." And my voice dropped off with the memory of that exchange.

He looked directly at me. No vague stare. But rather, in that stark white moonlight, clearly a look of deeper feeling, greater poignance, than I could remember ever seeing in my father's face.

"Jeff, you said so much. And you had a good-bye— an *extended* good-bye. You know, you're the reason he stayed as long as he did. His life was a shambles— a *disaster*. Even before this... He was miserable. One way or another, he wanted it all to end. When you came back... Well, that gave him a reason to stay alive... it *forced* him to stay alive."

I looked at my father as he spoke and tried to absorb what he was saying in soft, measured, empathetic tones.

"You knew all this... like you knew how far gone he was?"

He nodded.

"But you barely *saw* him."

He nodded again. Then, after a moment, he said: "I didn't have to." And after another moment: "I didn't *want* to... I *couldn't!* I *absolutely couldn't!*... It was so painful... What happened to him... What he *allowed* to happen... *made* to happen... The promise... The *promise* of that boy... that man... Squandered... then lost... *lost!*"

Now he was staring at me. I stared back, sharing the significance of this moment with him, then growing uneasy as those old, pale-blue eyes shifted focus, grew vacant and remote.

Who is he talking about, thinking about? *Which* lost son? *Which* squandered life?

My eyes tentatively questioned, tried to initiate a silent dialogue. But nothing came back. Then he closed his eyes and drifted away. And I watched him as his breathing, ever shallow, grew regular and rhythmical.

I stayed in the room for awhile and calmly observed my father

BLURRED IMAGES

asleep amidst the images of a lifetime. I leaned against the wall. And crossed my arms and hugged myself for comfort and for warmth. Because suddenly I felt very cold and very alone.

EPILOGUE

ONE YEAR LATER

I sat on the stage, bow poised over the strings of the cello, and gazed out at the hundreds of young, mostly black, faces, in this northeast Washington, D. C. high school auditorium. Many of the faces looked bored. Others looked animated, alive with wisecracks and horseplay. Others still looked dull and sullen.

This was my seventh or eighth monthly appearance in this high school. Intermingled with similar appearances at an elementary school, a junior high school, and a special needs school, this represented my community service commitment under the terms of my agreement with the Government.

The first time I appeared at this high school, I was terrified to the point of catatonia; this was an entirely different kind of gig than I was used to from all those years on the road. I could barely move the bow, let alone produce the words, the very brief words, to introduce the piece I would play. And when I finally began to play, the jeers and whistles and derisive laughs rose in such volume and duration, I could barely hear the notes. Flying objects — balls, paper planes, pens, even books — distracted me. I glanced desperately in the direction of the principal, a stern-faced, bow-tied, old-school-type black man named Mr. Kimball, who soon rescued me by walking briskly to center stage, standing at the mike, effectively eclipsing me and giving me momentary solace, and lecturing the rowdy assemblage on proper

BLURRED IMAGES

behavior, on courtesy towards guests of the school. He stared silently at the students, then slowly panned the auditorium with his eyes. Eventually, he turned back towards me, and in a stage whisper, apologized for the students' behavior and asked me to resume. I did, but in moments was interrupted yet again by the same cacaphony of sounds and blur of hurled projectiles. This time the principal re-emerged at the mike with a yet harsher tone and threats of removal from the auditorium and worse. And so it went through the most painful 45 minutes of my recent life; until the bell finally, mercifully, rang.

Now I was back in the very same auditorium before the very same audience (minus, perhaps, some students suspended by Mr. Kimball). And we had settled into a kind of peaceful, *tenuously* peaceful, co-existence. My face, my cello, and my kind of music were now familiar to this group. And it seemed that we each accepted the other, that we each agreed to tolerate, if not embrace, each other for this relatively short period of time just once a month. The principal's appearances at the mike were now relatively rare. Even more promising was my belief that I had actually made some conversions or activated some latent affinity for a breed of music so alien from the rap and reggae and hip-hop that dominated — no, *defined* — their lives. I could pick out faces that seemed connected to me, to the sounds I was producing, to this strange new, largely European world I was attempting to share.

At each appearance, I tried to do something different, to form different ensembles, to diversify the music, to create some relevance. This time I sat on the stage, at the center of a small semi-circle. On my right was a senior at this school, a handsome young black violist named Aaron Jackson, who was going to Juillard the next year on a full scholarship. On my left was my nephew, Michael, sitting stiffly, his violin raised to his shoulder, nervously waiting to begin the Ravel trio.

When Danny died, I finally met Michael. Despite his mother's pleas, Michael refused to go to the funeral. He furiously told Sylvia, she related to me, that he couldn't bring himself to listen to "the kind of holy bullshit" people spouted at funerals about the deceased. He said people conveniently forget, or try to forget, how the newly dead led their lives. What they did. What damage they wreaked. She told me this was the gist of what he told her. But the *way* he told her was chilling, he was so full of uncontrollable rage. The expletive-laced diatribe kept fueling itself until Michael ran out of words, and the words were replaced by convulsive sobs, and he went upstairs to his room and slammed the door shut behind him. She said she tried earnestly to persuade him to go — for her, not for him — and he just glared at her and said he just couldn't do it; if she made him go, who knows what he might do or say? So she let him have his way.

I saw him after the funeral back at Sylvia's house. As people milled about the house, speaking in muted tones, stopping at the dining room buffet to pour a glass of wine and fix a ham sandwich, I sought out Michael and eventually found him out in the backyard sitting on a chaise lounge, expressionless, staring in the direction of the neighboring house, possibly following the progress of two squirrels chasing each other up and around the trunk of a large maple tree. As I sat down in the adjoining chair, I asked, "Can I join you?" He grunted something and I settled into the chair. We sat like that for several minutes. Eventually I said to him, "Michael, I'm sorry..."

"Save it," he said. "Spare me the bullshit."

"Michael, I don't mean what you think I mean..."

"What the hell *do* you mean then?"

"I mean I'm especially sorry about what you've gone through..."

"Oh, Jesus..."

I looked at his face, the face I was seeing for the first time (yet which looked so familiar, so uncannily resembling Danny's at that age), the face whose eyes were now narrowing, the mouth contorting,

BLURRED IMAGES

in rekindled anger.

"I want to talk," I said softly. "But now's not the time."

I got up, stood over Michael for a second, and resisted squeezing his shoulder.

"See you around."

"Yeah," he mumbled.

* * * * *

I discovered the violin in a corner of the attic one day a few weeks later when I was helping Sylvia go through Danny's belongings, his numerous suits, his golf clubs and tennis and squash racquets, all the bricabrac he could never bring himself to part with.

There it was, in its case, leaning against the side of an old bookcase. I opened the case slowly and carefully, to behold an instrument that appeared to be in good condition. I then closed the case and brought it over to Sylvia, crouched down on her knees, going through boxes at the other end of the attic. I asked her whose it was, and she said, "Michael's." No further explanation. When I pressed her, she said he had taken lessons when he was younger, as young as six or seven, but had given them up abruptly sometime in junior high. "He actually had some talent; it must run in the family. OK, you satisfied?" she said with a sardonic smile. Then she looked back down at the box of papers she was going through. Aware that I was still there, holding the case, waiting for more, she murmured, "He had to be happy to play. And he stopped being happy."

* * * * *

During the first month or so after Danny's funeral, I was over at Sylvia's several times a week. The ostensible reason was to help her organize Danny's extensive belongings and dispose of them appropriately, to Goodwill, to the trash barrel, and — in a few selected, sentimental cases — to me or my father. Sylvia didn't want any of it; she wanted it all out of her house.

After several hours of that work, we would often sit on her porch and drink iced tea or beer from bottles, and talk, or choose not to talk. We were each still suffering from the effects of Danny's death and legacy, and we respected each other's lengthy, often sudden silences.

Late afternoon would meld into evening and I would typically stay for a light dinner. But Michael's dark, sullen presence dominated the atmosphere to the point where even idle chit-chat was nearly impossible.

Once I brought up the subject of the violin, to break the ice, to draw Michael out through a subject directly relevant to him, and also because I was genuinely curious about what he did with it, whether there was any lingering interest. This could be the avenue to him, and for him to come out. A hopeful two-way conduit of opportunity.

When I first brought up the subject of the instrument, Michael looked at me questioningly, and then angrily.

"Would you like to try it out with me? *for* me?" I asked.

He grunted, "No!" and looked down at his plate.

Sylvia said, "You know, Michael, Uncle Jeff knows a thing or two about music."

"I know all about Uncle Jeff," Michael said sharply in his longest statement of the evening.

I looked across at Sylvia for further support. But she just looked at Michael with moist, offended eyes.

* * * * *

One evening, as I was saying good night to Sylvia, right after I kissed her on the cheek, she asked me to bring my cello over the next time I came.

"Sure," I said. Then, a moment later: "Is this for you or

BLURRED IMAGES

Michael?"

"For both of us," she said quickly.

So I complied. A few days later I arrived at Sylvia's with the instrument. When nobody came to the front door after several rings of the bell, I hoisted the cello and went around back. There was Sylvia, on hands and knees in the vegetable garden, weeding around young lettuce plants. It was a beautiful spring day and the sunshine glistened on her nearly black hair as she slowly, methodically, moved about, chopping at the soil with a three-pronged tool, then grasping each green interloper, gently tugging it out, and tossing it in a bucket.

She looked absorbed and relaxed, and I chose not to disturb her. I quietly walked back to the patio and sat down on one of the straight-backed metal-mesh chairs. As quietly as I could, I set down the case and removed the cello and set it up between my legs and began to play one of the Bach suites. And as the first sonorous notes emerged from the instrument and filled the yard, Sylvia looked up from her work, smiled sweetly, rose, and walked toward me. She looked prettier than ever, beautiful really, in those cut-off jeans and T shirt, and her olive skin glistening with a thin film of perspiration from her labors. I started to pause, to say something, but she gestured, almost like a conductor, for me to continue, and I did. She sat down a comfortable distance away and stretched out her legs and listened. Each time I looked up from my instrument and over at her, she was smiling peacefully. And when I eventually reached the end and rested the bow on my leg, she waited for a moment and then applauded loudly and enthusiastically.

"That was wonderful, Jeffrey, just wonderful."

"Thank you, Sylvia, thank you very much. I enjoyed playing it for you. You're a great audience."

After a moment, she asked: "Is that what you played for Danny?"

I nodded. "That and other things. He was also a great audience."

"I'm sure he was." She rolled her eyes ever so slightly, and looked like she was going to say something else, but stopped herself.

After another moment, she asked me to resume.

"Any preference?"

"Your choice."

"OK... It's a beautiful day... How about something pastoral?"

She smiled and nodded. So I began with the cello part of a Rachmaninoff trio and then played everything pastoral I knew for at least an hour. She listened with obvious pleasure, with absolute rapture at times, eyes closed, hugging herself tightly. At one point between pieces, I asked, "Where's Michael? I'd love for him to hear some of this." She said, "I asked him but he declined." "Should I ask him myself?" "You can... but you don't really have to. He's in the mezzanine section."

I looked at her questioningly. She smiled and tilted her eyes up to my right, to the second floor of the house. I followed her scan across the upstairs windows as surreptitiously as possible but couldn't locate him.

"What? I don't see him," I said.

"He was there a minute ago, in his room."

I got annoyed and must have looked it.

"He's got this thing about you."

"I gather, but he doesn't even know me."

"That's not the point."

"Well, what is?"

"The same point that I had, that I first had..."

"Yes?"

"That your allegiance — your first and only alligance — was to Danny, that you had no real understanding for what your brother had done to us, to him..."

"But *you* worked your way through that."

"Jeffrey!" she blurted.

"What?"

"Jeffrey, for Pete's sake, I'm an adult. Angry as I was — *am*!

BLURRED IMAGES

— I'm an adult and have the ability to work my way through things. I haven't — by a long shot — worked my way through all this, and maybe I never will. But at least I have the capacity... But Michael? He's still a *kid*! A very angry, unhappy, confused kid who doesn't have that capacity. He doesn't have the *equipment* to do it. You have to understand that."

Then she waved her hand, urging me to resume playing. And now I felt the special moment had passed, that my playing was a substitute for conversation, to fill the vacuum, and that I was playing under duress. Once, when I looked up, a hint of tension had returned to Sylvia's face, especially around her eyes. And when she spoke, a bit of that early edge had returned as well.

* * * * *

When I left a short while later, I was irritated. And I stayed that way for several days.

Then, early one evening, when I was sitting on my father's porch reading the newspaper, Sylvia arrived unannounced and sat down near me. She presented me with a bouquet of white roses from her garden and said, softly, sweetly, "I'm sorry."

I didn't say anything. I just gazed at her and waited.

"I took advantage of you, of that whole visit. I asked you to come over, to play for us, and you did. And it was great, it was wonderful, until I started laying all that shit on you. And that changed everything. So..."

"So... what?"

"So I'm sorry... I don't blame you for feeling the way you probably do."

"I'll get over it," I said. She looked so sweet and soft in her sundress, the same one she wore at the hospital that day, and with her earnest smile, that my irritation literally melted away.

She extended her hand across the narrow space between us and took my hand and held it gently.

"And Jeffrey?"

"Yes?"

"You should know something."

"What's that?"

"You did something very special that afternoon... something for Michael."

"Yes?"

"I think you actually touched something."

"You think?"

"I do. I hadn't seen him show an interest in anything for a while, a very long while..."

"That's good," I said. "That's really good." And I squeezed her hand firmly.

* * * * *

Dad now lived a genuinely reclusive life. It began the day of the funeral when he declined to go to Sylvia's house after the burial. He asked me to drive him home, which I did, and then he promptly got into bed and stayed there, in a semi-somnolent state, for nearly a week. I checked in on him a half-dozen times a day and brought him meals and tea in between. He drank the tea but ate very little. He refused to take phone calls, of which there were many, and indicated absolutely no interest in seeing the newspapers or watching TV (even the news) and certainly not in engaging in lengthy conversations with me.

His room took on a dark, sour smell. I suggested he take a shower. When he mumbled that he didn't feel like it, I offered to help him. And when I did, he snapped, "If you can't stand the smell, get out of the bedroom," and then guffawed briefly at his paraphrase.

I kept visiting him in his bedroom, but I didn't linger; the reek was indeed overpowering. Then one morning, on the fifth or sixth

BLURRED IMAGES

day, he abruptly, without any further prodding from me, got up from his bed, immersed himself in the bathroom for at least an hour, and emerged well-groomed, pink-faced, and exuding fresh, masculine aromas of shaving cream, aftershave, and deodorant. In short, a thinner version of his former self. He then dressed himself in one of his impeccable outfits.

We had breakfast together— I made his favorite omelet. We chatted idly, about everything but what was on both our minds. He subsequently excused himself to spend several hours at his desk going through a stack of condolence notes and other mail and sifting through phone messages I had left for him. Then he took up his post on the porch, and that was as far as he ventured into the outside world, the world beyond his house. Ironic for a man who used to promenade easily and regularly around that world.

*****

One evening, on one of those rare occasions when I stayed for awhile after dinner, Sylvia and I sat quietly on her porch, sipping iced coffee and gazing out at the dusky front yard. Michael was presumably up in his room.

Sylvia broke the silence with a surprising question.

"Jeffrey, do you ever think of that night I picked you up and took you to the Marriott?"

I turned and looked at her. She was smiling softly, without a trace of guile.

"Yes... a lot."

"And what do you think?"

"I think we did the right thing... I would do the same thing again. I would react the same way."

She didn't respond, and we both looked away, out at the yard again.

After a few minutes, I asked, "What about you?"

ARTHUR DIMOND

"What *about* me?"

"Do you think about that evening, too?"

"Yes... Like you, a lot."

"And?"

"When I think of it, I feel embarrassed," she said quickly.

I studied her, not saying anything, allowing her to continue at her own pace.

"Jeffrey, I was in such pain, you have to understand. I mean I'm still in pain and probably always will be. But this is a dull, deep kind of pain, you know what I mean? And that... that was a hot, a red-hot, kind. I felt such anger, such longing, desperation, all at the same time. I didn't really understand how I felt then. All I did was act and react and that's how I seemed to go day in and day out until Danny died. I don't even know how I got out of bed and functioned, performed in a demanding job. And then..."

"Yes?"

"And then he died and the boil burst. After that, everything cooled down, calmed down. And the pain became different, more manageable. I felt in control of my life again. I felt I understood my feelings..."

I didn't say anything. Again I waited. She turned toward me and suddenly smiled.

"Are you wondering whether I still feel the way I said I felt about you that night, that very strange night?"

"Yes."

"And?"

"And... nothing."

"Well, I said a lot of things that night... and I meant every one of them. But I'm comfortable — happy — with the way things are right now."

"Really?"

"For now, anyway," she answered, and smiled, this time with a bit of playful coquettishness.

BLURRED IMAGES

Then we both went quiet again, sitting now in darkness except for the faint light filtering out from the kitchen and, through the trees, from the streetlight.

I was hoping she would ask me how I was feeling. About Danny. About my loss, my lingering pain, the pain that I knew would never go away entirely. This would have been a perfect moment to ask me. And I was so anxious to be asked, to have an opportunity to talk about it. But she let the moment pass. Since Danny's funeral, she had uttered his name only in the context of their son or of such practical matters as his will, his life insurance, or of the inconvenience of disposing of a lifetime of material possessions. Everything else — including, maybe especially, my feelings about him — had seemingly become off bounds for discussion.

* * * * *

To my surprise, I went on a date, or at least something approximating one. With a pretty Chinese-American dance instructor named Sally Eng whom I met at the high school.

I was playing alone on the stage of the empty school auditorium one afternoon, decompressing from a few back-to-back student sessions. I was having the vicarious (and not too original) thrill of imagining that I was playing just a few miles away, at the Kennedy Center, in a very different kind of hall. My eyes must have been closed because when I finished my piece and paused for a moment, the void was quickly filled by applause. Two lonely hands clapping about ten or twelve rows back. And there was Sally, a big grin across her broad face, clapping, stopping only when I rose and took a bow.

"Encore, encore," she yelled.

I considered the demand for a moment and then sat down and accommodated her, but with a jazzy version of *Summertime*.

She laughed and applauded and then she rose and walked down the aisle directly toward me on the stage. She looked up at me, and introduced herself. When I introduced myself, she said, "I know who *you* are... Very pleased to meet you."

I didn't ask her how she knew, but I could guess. I kneeled down and simply shook her hand and smiled back at her. We stayed like that for a moment until she smiled and giggled nervously, then said, "Well, very nice to meet you, Jeffrey... And thank you. Thank you very much."

"For what?" I asked.

"For the music, of course."

She turned and started to walk up the center aisle. When she had gone up several rows, to my surprise, I called after her.

"Do you want to go out... and get a coffee or something?"

She turned around, looking surprised herself. Then she smiled pleasantly and said, "Sure, why not? I have to be somewhere around five, but sure..."

I asked her to give me a minute while I packed up. Then I hoisted up the cello in its case, and joined her. We left the auditorium, into the now-quiet main corridor and out a side door into the small, now sparsely occupied parking lot.

We drove a few dozen blocks, to 16th Street, where we found a corner coffee shop. Two black men who looked like construction workers were talking quietly over their coffees. And in one of the booths, an elderly woman was eating a sandwich alone, staring out the window as she slowly chewed.

Sally and I sat across from each other in the last booth. She smiled that broad smile across the table, directly at me.

"So, Jeffrey, do you usually ask women out two minutes after you meet them?"

"Well, I usually don't meet too many women."

"Oh, I see," she said with a smaller, more guarded smile.

"No, nothing like that," I quickly said.

"I didn't think so," she replied, and smiled broadly again.

I looked down at my hands, certain she was continuing to

BLURRED IMAGES

look right at me.

"I've led an unusual life for some time," I said.

"I gathered."

The counter waitress, a cheerful stocky Hispanic-looking lady, came over and took our orders. A moment later, I asked, "Why did you come to the auditorium before?"

"Well, I was in the hallway heading for the exit — it'd been a really long day — and I heard this music. And it was lovely. And, hey, I'm a dancer. I gravitate to music..."

"So you gravitated..."

"Right, I gravitated," she said, and we both laughed. Then we sat for a moment or two not saying anything. I was enjoying the flirtatious direction of the conversation — a real adventure for me — but was feeling uncomfortable with the silences.

"So what did you think?" I eventually asked. "Of the music, I mean."

"Are you fishing for compliments?" she asked with that big open smile and those sparkling black-pupiled eyes which seemed to be teasing me good-naturedly. "I already told you I thought it was wonderful. I mean I asked for more... That's what encore means, right?"

I smiled back, enjoying the playful repartee. Then her face turned serious, earnest really.

"It was wonderful. I mean I've heard your little recitals— your music appreciation sessions in the auditorium. But those can be crazy affairs, you know, with those kids going nuts, all that rowdy stuff..."

"Oh, I know, all right..."

"But anyway, your playing... It's what I'd expect of somebody with your background, your aspirations..."

"Sounds like you've been doing your research."

"I wouldn't call it research... All I had to do was read the papers, watch TV awhile ago... I mean, you were a media star."

"Sure, if you want to call it that."

"Well, anyway, that's how I first learned about you... and I must say all that coverage definitely caught my attention... I mean your story really stood out from all the other stuff that flies by everyday. And then..."

"Then?"

"Then I forgot about it until you showed up here..."

"And?"

"And nothing."

"So here we are," I said, and smiled.

"Yes, here we are."

We sat for a moment.

"So what'd you think when I showed up at school?"

"What did I think? I guess I thought this was a really interesting guy."

"And you gravitate to really interesting guys?"

She instantly recognized my attempt at humor and laughed.

"Yeah. I guess I do," she said, and this time, for the first time, she looked away, just for a moment.

"So what is this guy like in person? As interesting as you imagined?"

"I don't really know him. I can't really say... I mean I know a bit about his story— but I don't really know about *him*."

I studied her face for a moment.

"I'm curious, Sally, how old were you in 1968, when my story began, when that thing happened?"

That big smile re-appeared.

"Why don't you just ask me how old I am and do the math?"

"No, no, I'm serious. I'm trying to learn something... what your perspective was back then... if you had any concept of what was going on."

"Well, I'm a little older than I look. I guess I was eleven then."

"Were you aware of what was going on in Vietnam?... What

BLURRED IMAGES

was going on here?"
"Yes, but in a vague sort of way."
"What do you mean?"
"Well, I was brought up in LA. My parents were from Hong Kong. They were anti-Communist — fiercely anti-Communist — so they talked about what was happening over there just about every evening, at dinner. And we watched the TV news every night... Walter Cronkite."
"And were you aware of what was happening here? On college campuses— Kent State? In the streets?"
"I was... I mean how could you miss? It was all around us."
"Did you understand all that stuff?"
"In a vague sort of way, like I said," she replied, and we both smiled.
"Do you want to hear something amazing?"
She looked at me, her eyes opened wide with anticipation.
"Yes."
"I didn't know much more than you. I was just about as vague... And I was in college, for God's sake!"
Her face grew slightly skeptical. She clearly didn't know if I was putting her on.
"Really, Sally, crazy as it sounds, I was 21 years old, a college student, son of a famous historian — do you believe that? — and all I was really interested in was music... all this stuff swirling around and I was just blithely playing the cello... I knew more about Beethoven than I did about Ho Chi Minh."
Now, the skeptical look gone, she looked genuinely amazed and puzzled.
"Then how..."
"How did I come to do what I did?"
She nodded.
"That's what I was trying to explain when you first heard my story last year... when I became a 'media star,'" I said. "Did you see

that? Did that ever come across?"

Now she looked confused and frustrated. She had a question in her eyes but couldn't seem to express it in words.

"Who — what — did you think I was, based on what you saw... heard?"

She didn't answer.

"Did you think it was all black-and-white — that I was this angry protester who got violent, whose violence killed a guy, a cop?... Or did you think I was a victim— of circumstance, of the times, whatever?"

She shook her head. She either didn't know or couldn't answer. And I realized I had gotten excited, and she had gotten upset, maybe a bit scared.

"I'm sorry, Sally... I guess I got carried away."

"It's OK," she said. "You have a right to be. You've been through a lot."

"Well, I didn't mean to get into a speech, to get this heavy— especially on a first date. I guess I gave you a lot more than you asked for."

"It's OK, really."

"Thanks, you're very nice, Sally. Very nice."

"Thank you," she said softly, and glanced at her watch.

"You have to go... That appointment?"

"Yes, I do... in a minute."

"Could you take that minute to tell me about yourself? I mean I've been doing most of the talking..."

She sighed audibly.

"I mean it's only fair. Equal time and all that."

"OK, what do you want to know?"

"Well, do you lead an interesting life?"

"Well, some people might think so. I mean I'm a dancer and a dance instructor. I guess that's more interesting than what my sister does."

BLURRED IMAGES

"What's that?"
"She's a CPA."
"Oh."
"That's what people usually say when you tell them that."
"'Oh'?"
"Yeah, 'oh.'"
"But getting back to you... and your interesting life."
"Well, truth is, Jeffrey, it's not all that interesting."
"Despite what some people tell you."
"Yes, I guess so."
"So what's missing?"

She considered that for a moment, then swallowed her coffee and looked up at me with a smile I could only describe as wistful.

"Well, that's a long story," she said, and suddenly looking anxious and glancing at her watch, added: "And I'm afraid I really do have to go now."

We got up abruptly. I left some change on the table and we hurriedly walked out together. On the sidewalk, I offered to give her a lift. She declined, saying she could take the Metro.

"To be continued?" I asked.

She hesitated for a moment and then said, "Let me think about it, OK?"

"OK."

I extended my hand and she extended hers, tentatively. It felt small and warm and slightly moist. We shook hands and it seemed like a very odd way to say good-bye.

"Well, see you."

She quickly turned and walked briskly to the big "M" sign on the corner.

* * * * *

I stopped by Sylvia's one day on a whim, armed with some

pretense to finish her family room shelves. As I walked up the front walkway, I heard music wafting through the living room window. At first I thought it was a recording. Then I quickly realized these were the halting sounds of a novice, the wrong notes and repeated notes, the pauses, the faulty, inconsistent tempos. I tiptoed up the porch steps and looked through the porch window. There, in the far corner next to the French doors leading out to the backyard patio was Michael. He was sitting stiffly in front of a music stand, struggling through what sounded like some beginner Mozart piece. He would frequently lean forward to get a closer look at the music. Then he would resume his upright pose, violin positioned between jaw and shoulder, an expression of intense concentration on his pale face. I watched and listened for several more minutes. Then I tiptoed back across the porch and down the stairs. With Sylvia's car not in the driveway, and Sylvia presumably not at home, I got back in my car, as softly as possible closed the door, started the engine, and drove away feeling buoyant, certain that I had witnessed something important there.

* * * * *

I was right. Now, seven or eight months after I first saw Michael, alone in his living room, struggling with that instrument, he was sitting up here on a stage with me and another, very proficient musician. A *bona fide* member of an ensemble. Tense, yes. Inexperienced, certainly. But what potential, and what passion.

* * * * *

I hadn't said anything to Michael directly after that episode, that surreptitious observation; it would have caused an explosion and ruined everything. But I had told Sylvia, and her face lit up from within in a way I had never seen. Her cheeks flushed, her eyes glowed and instantly filled with tears. Then she spontaneously hugged me in

BLURRED IMAGES

a joyous, absolutely wonderful moment.

In subsequent weeks, I made some inquiries regarding teachers— for Michael, only a certain kind of teacher would do. I passed on my findings to Sylvia, who then followed up with calls and appointments.

Sylvia knew the right teacher during the first five minutes of her initial meeting with him. He was a faculty member at Georgetown University, who maintained a small private practice of non-university students, a calm, soft-spoken man in his late-thirties who expressed an immediate interest in Michael. He said his story reminded him of somebody he knew, a college student who, through music and other channels, including religion, had overcome some serious obstacles in his own life.

At that first meeting, Sylvia and the teacher, Henry Weiser, talked for over an hour, longer than either expected. And at the end of the session, they agreed to try to arrange a meeting with Michael.

Sylvia told me she didn't know what to expect. Michael was seeing a counselor at school, and a psychologist outside school (twice a week), and his behavior was much steadier, calmer — sometimes eerily calmer — than it had been. Not a single outburst at school. Only an occasional real protest at home. But no real interaction with other students, no real contact with former friends. And minimal communications with her. Dinners, when they ate together, were quiet affairs, with the sounds of utensils on plates, and food being chewed and beverages being drunk, punctuated only occasionally by a perfunctory exchange.

That changed dramatically the evening Sylvia broached the subject of violin lessons. She got an immediate response.

"Why?" he asked.

"Because I think you're telling me you want them— without actually coming out and telling me."

He looked at her oddly, but didn't say anything.

"I think I'm on to you," she said with a sudden grin. "You've been playing that violin at strategic times..."

"Like when?"

"Like none of your business... Let's say I know. I just know."

He smiled sheepishly, and she said, "That's a beautiful sight, Michael, that's the first real smile I've seen on that handsome face of yours for quite some time."

Then she told him about her research, about Henry Weiser. He looked suddenly suspicious. If he was pleased, he didn't show it.

"What do you think?" she asked him.

"I don't know."

"What don't you know?" she asked, her voice tightening slightly.

"I don't know whether I'm ready to take this on... I mean it sounds like a big deal."

"Michael, it *is* a big deal... I mean what if you have real talent? Wouldn't that be something?"

"Yeah, but what if I don't?"

She paused for a moment, then reponded calmly and firmly.

"You won't ever know unless you try," she said. "How's that for a motherly observation?"

He rolled his eyes.

"What do you think, Michael? Do you want to give it a try?"

He considered the question. Then he suddenly said, "Hold on, does Jeff have something to do with this?"

She quickly calculated the pros and cons of each possible answer, and decided to lie.

"No, nothing at all. It's all my idea; I didn't even consult him. I heard you one evening when I came home early, and I thought about it and it seemed like a great thing to do... And Michael, it *is* a great thing. You should do it."

He looked at her thoughtfully.

"What do you say?"

She was aware she was now imploring him. This had become

BLURRED IMAGES

extremely important to her.

He looked back at her and nodded.

"OK, Mom, let's do it."

When he said "let's" — when he communicated so clearly that it was not his solo, but rather their joint, project — she felt a catch in her throat and almost cried. Instead she stifled the cry and reached over the table and placed her hand on his and pressed it softly, lovingly.

"I'm very pleased, Michael. I think this will be wonderful for you."

And now, months later, in that sea of black faces, in the third row center, I saw the contrasting white faces of Sylvia and Henry, smiling broadly as they applauded, as they actually *led* the applause, prompting a growing wave of enthusiasm from the students— mixed, of course, with catcalls and the like. I gestured for Michael and Aaron to stand and take their bows, and when they did, Sylvia and Henry were on their feet applauding ever louder, and yelling, "Bravo! Bravo!" And then, to my surprise and pleasure, a number of the students in the front rows also stood up, and more and more towards the rear followed suit, and they all continued to applaud and ultimately echo and drown out Sylvia and Henry's "Bravo!"'s. For sure, most of the students remained in their seats, looking blank-faced and bored. But that didn't matter to me, and hopefully not to Michael, especially, or to Aaron. Something momentous and definitive had happened that morning.

ABOUT THE AUTHOR

Arthur Dimond

After starting out as a journalist, Arthur Dimond has spent the bulk of his 30-year professional career as a public relations executive and entrepreneur in Washington, D. C. and Boston.

Blurred Images reflects Dimond's extensive professional experience as well as his lifelong devotion to music; he is a serious amateur pianist who has played the instrument since the age of six.

Blurred Images is Dimond's first published novel.

A native of Brooklyn, New York, he lives in Newton Centre, Massachusetts with his wife and two children.

Printed in the United States
2822